Further Praise for *A State of Freedom*

'A writer who can envelop you in the worlds he creates, and whose piercing eye for detail can send you reeling. . . . [Mukherjee] seeds his tales with images of unexpected beauty . . . an extraordinary account of the tenacious will to survive.'

—Siobhan Murphy, *The Times*

'Dostoevsky-like in its juxtaposition of unbearable cruelty with an equally unbearable yearning for security and love. . . . [*A State of Freedom* is] a powerful, memorable treatment of a theme too often reduced to uninvolving didacticism.'   —Adam Lively, *Sunday Times*

'His best work yet. . . . This bleak and entirely justified vision of modern India is what binds together Mukherjee's stories and indeed his oeuvre.'   —Sonia Faleiro, *Financial Times*

'[Mukherjee] homes in on the restless, the disinherited, the socially trapped. . . . Mercilessly observant, he does not spare the reader but leavens scenes of savagery, squalor and despair with moments of rainbow vividness, all the more striking for the muddy, cacophonous backdrop from which they are brought forth. . . . In a significant and porous work, Mukherjee gives congruence and visibility to these fractured, hidden lives.'   —Catherine Taylor, *New Statesman*

'Neel Mukherjee's fiction about class is as good as Jane Austen's was 200 years ago. . . . He does what good novelists should, which is to hold up a mirror to society and remind people that what passes for normal is often barbaric. His quiet observation is effective—and damning.'   —*The Economist*

'Narrated with the precise realism that we have come to expect of Neel Mukherjee's novels . . . *A State of Freedom* resonates with intricate and disturbing echoes.'

—Tabish Khair, *Times Literary Supplement*

'A thing of wonder. . . . One of the most wonderful novels I've read for ages and ages.'

—Deborah Moggach, *Saturday Review*, BBC Radio 4

'[Mukherjee's] world is textured and complex. . . . Each story is intimate and universal, concrete and elusive. . . . *A State of Freedom* is ambitious, and it succeeds on all levels.'

—Eoin McNamee, *Irish Times*

'Mukherjee's characters are so well drawn and their plights so affecting that we . . . simply lose ourselves in masterful storytelling. . . . Electrifying prose.' —Malcolm Forbes, *The Herald*

A STATE OF FREEDOM

A STATE OF FREEDOM

a novel

Neel Mukherjee

W. W. NORTON & COMPANY
Independent Publishers Since 1923
NEW YORK | LONDON

This is a work of fiction. Names, characters, places, and incidents are the products
of the author's imagination or are used fictitiously. Any resemblance to actual events,
locales, or persons, living or dead, is entirely coincidental.

Christopher

After all, we make ourselves according to the ideas we have of our possibilities.

V. S. Naipaul, *A Bend in the River*

'Migrants? We are not migrants! We are ghosts, that's what we are, ghosts.'

Syrian refugee at the border of Austria,
August 2015

I

While trying to check the bill before settling – an old habit, inculcated by his father, of giving any bill the once-over to see that he had not been overcharged – he realised that he had lost the ability to perform the simple function of adding up the individual items and the tax that together made up the grand total. Standing at the reception desk, he tried again and again. Then he took out his wallet and tried to count the rupee and US dollar notes nestled inside; he failed. Something as fundamental to intelligence as counting was eluding him. In the peripheries of his vision he could see a small crowd gathering to look at him; discreetly, nonchalantly, they thought. The news had spread. It was then that he broke down and wept for his son.

He had hesitated about taking the boy to Fatehpur Sikri right after their lunchtime tour of the Taj Mahal; two major Mughal monuments in one afternoon could be considered excessive. But, he reasoned, it was less than an hour's drive and to fit the two sites into one day was the generally accepted practice. They could be back at their hotel in Agra by early evening and after an early night with the television and room service they could leave for Delhi, refreshed, the following morning. The reasoning prevailed.

When he mentioned part of this plan to the driver of his hired car, the young man, all longish hair and golden chain around his neck and golden wristlet and chunky watch, took it as a veiled order to go about the business in record time. He revelled in the opportunity to drive along the dusty, cratered slip road to Fatehpur Sikri at organ-jostling speed, punctuated by abrupt jerking into rest when impeded, and launching as suddenly into motion again. They passed a string of dingy roadside eateries, tea-shops, cigarette-and-snacks shacks. The bigger ones boasted signboards and names. There were the predictable 'Akbar', 'Shahjahan', 'Shahenshah', a 'Jodha Bai', even a 'Tansen', which was '100% VAGETARIAN'. There had been a speed-warning sign earlier: 'Batter late than never.' Not for the first time he wondered, in a country given over to a dizzying plenitude of signs, how unsettled their orthography was. A Coca-Cola hoarding adorned the top of one small shop, the brand name and shout line written in Hindi script.

'Coca-Cola,' the boy said, able to read that trademark universal wave even though he couldn't read the language.

'We can have one after we've done our tour,' he said, his mind occupied by trying to work out if another order to the driver to slow down to prevent the boy from being car-sick would be taken as wilfully contradictory; he worried about these things.

The boy seemed subdued; he didn't move from the bare identification of the familiar brand to wanting it. Ordinarily, he would have been compulsively spelling out and trying to read the names written in English on shopfronts and billboards. While he was grateful for his son's uncharacteristic placidity, he wondered if he hadn't imposed too much on a six-year-old, dragging him from one historical monument to another. He now read a kind of polite forbearance in the boy's quietness, a way of letting him know that this kind of tourism was wholly outside his sphere of interest but he was going to tolerate his father indulging in it. After a few questions at the Taj Mahal, which began as enthusiastic, then quickly burned out into perfunctory – 'Baba, what is a mau-so-le-um?', 'Is Moom-taz under this building?', 'Was she walking and moving and talking when Shajjy-han built this over her?' – they had stopped altogether. Was it wonder that had silenced him or boredom? He had tried to keep the child interested by spinning stories that he thought would catch the boy's imagination: 'Do you see how white the building is? Do you know that the emperor who had it built, Shahjahan, had banquets on the terrace on full-moon nights where everything was white? The moonlight, the clothes the courtiers and the guests wore, the flowers, the food – everything was white, to go with the white of the marble and the white light of the full moon.' The boy had nodded, seemingly absorbing the information, but had betrayed no further curiosity.

Now he wondered if his son had not found all this business of tombs and immortal grief and erecting memorials to the dead macabre, unsettling. His son was American, so he was not growing up, as his father had, with the gift of ghost stories, first heard sitting on the laps of servants and aunts in his childhood home in Calcutta, then, when he was a little older, read in children's books. As a result, he did not understand quite what went on inside the child's head when novelties, such as the notion of an order of things created by the imagination residing *under* the visible world and as vivid as the real one, were introduced to him. He made a mental note to stick to historical facts only when they reached Fatehpur Sikri.

Or could it have been the terrible accident they had narrowly avoided witnessing yesterday at the moment of their arrival at the hotel? A huge multi-storeyed building was going up across the road, directly opposite, and a construction worker had apparently fallen to his death even while their car was getting into the slip lane for the hotel entrance. As they waited in the queue of vehicles, people had come running from all directions to congregate at one particular spot, about twenty metres from where they sat in their cars. Something about the urgency of the swarming, and the indescribable sound that emanated from that swiftly engorging clot of people, a tense noise between buzzing and truculent murmuring, instantly transmitted the message that a disaster had occurred. Otherwise how else would the child have known to ask, 'Baba, people running, look. What's happening there?' And how else could the driver have answered, mercifully in Hindi, 'A man's just fallen from the top of that building under construction. A mazdoor. Instant death, bechara.'

He had refused to translate. He had tried to pull his son back from craning his neck, but as the queue of cars moved, and their vehicle moved forward, through a chance aperture in the hive of people around the death, he saw, for the briefest of flashes, a patch of dusty earth stained the colour of old scab from the blood it had thirstily drunk. Then the slit closed, the car started advancing inch by inch and the vision ended. He saw his son turning his head to continue to stare at the spot. But had the boy really seen the earth welt like that, or had he just imagined it? There was no way he could ask him to corroborate. Worries came stampeding in: had the child seen it? Was he going to be affected by it? How could he establish if he had, without planting the idea in the boy's head? All of last night his mind had been a pincushion to these sharp questions until he had fallen asleep.

They returned now, summoned by the boy's unnatural quietness. By the time they got out at Agra Gate, having shaved all of ten minutes from the journey, the boy was looking decidedly peaky, and he felt that his own lunch had risen in rebellion, to somewhere just behind his sternum. The driver grinned: there was just the right touch of the adversarial in the gleam of self-satisfaction.

More than twenty years of life in the academic communities of the East Coast of the USA had defanged him of the easy Indian ability to bark at people considered as servants, so he swallowed his irritation, even the intention to ask the driver to take it more gently on the journey back, in case he couldn't control the tone and it was interpreted as a peremptory order. Instead, he said in Hindi, 'We won't be more than an hour.'

The driver said, 'OK, sir,' nodding vigorously. 'I will be here.'

He checked the car to see if he had taken everything – a bottle of water, his wallet and passport, the guidebook, his small backpack, his phone, his son's little knapsack – then shut the car door and held out his hand. The boy's meek silence bothered him. Where was the usual firework display of chatter and fidgety energy, the constant soundtrack of his aliveness?

He knelt down to be on a level with the boy and asked tenderly, 'Are you tired? Do you want to go back to the hotel? We don't have to see this.'

The boy shook his head.

'Do you want a Parle's Orange Kream?' he asked, widening and rolling his eyes to simulate the representation of temptation in the advertisements.

The boy shook his head again.

Behind him, on a grass verge, a hoopoe was flitting across. He said, 'Look!' and turned the boy round.

The boy looked dutifully but didn't ask what it was.

'It's a hoopoe. You won't see this bird in New York.' He supplied the answer gratuitously.

The boy asked, 'Is this a moss-o-moll-lom?'

'No, sweetheart,' his father laughed, 'it's not a mausoleum. It's a palace. You know what a palace is, don't you? A very good and powerful king lived here. His name was Akbar. I told you about him last night, remember?'

'That was Shajjy-han, who built a big big marble stone on his wife and she died and he was very sad and cried all the time.'

Every time he spoke, the American accent made his father's insides go all squishy.

'No, this is different. Akbar was his grandfather. Come, we'll look at it. It's a different colour, see? All red and brown and orange, not the white that we saw earlier.'

They passed some ruined cloisters, then a triple-arched inner gateway, solidly restored and, slightly further from it, a big domed building that was awaiting restoration work. Touts, who had noticed a man and a small boy get out of the car, descended on them.

'Guide, sir, guide? Good English, sir. Full history, you won't find in book.' Not from one voice but from an entire choir.

Beggars with various forms of crippledness materialised. From the simplest pleading, with a hand repeatedly brought up to the lips to signify hunger, to hideous displays of amputated and bandaged limbs, even an inert, entirely limbless, alive torso laid out flat on a board with wheels – this extreme end of the spectrum of human agony filled him with horror, shame, pity, embarrassment, repulsion but, above all, a desire to protect his son from seeing them. How did all these other people drifting around him appear to be so sheathed in indifference and blindness? Or was the same churning going on inside them? Truth was, he felt, he was no longer a proper Indian; making a life in the plush West had made him skinless like a good, sheltered first-world liberal. He was now a tourist in his own country; no longer 'his own country', he corrected himself fastidiously. He suppressed the impulse to cover the boy's eyes with his hands and said impatiently, 'Sweetie, can we move a bit faster, please.' It came out as a command, the interrogative missing.

Men came up with accordions of postcards, maps, guidebooks, magazines, photos, toys, current bestsellers in pirated editions, snacks, rattles, drinks, confectionery, tinsel, dolls, plastic replicas of historical buildings, books, whistles and flutes … He kept shaking his head stoically, a tight half-smile on his lips, and ushered his boy along.

The child, distracted one moment by a tray of carved soapstone figures, then another instant by a flashing, crudely copied replica of an inflatable Superman toy, kept stalling to stare.

'Baba, Baba, look!'

'Yes, I know. Let's keep moving.' He was so relieved – and grateful – that the cheap toys had diverted the child's attention away from the suppuration and misery that he almost broke step to buy one of those baubles.

That small manifestation of interest was enough. The loose, dispersed assembly of touts and peddlers now tightened into a purposeful circle.

'Babu, my child is hungry, hasn't eaten for four days.' The shrivelled girl with matted hair in the woman's arms looked like the living dead; she had no energy or will to swipe at the flies clustering on a sore at the corner of her mouth.

'Here, look, babu, babu-sa'ab, look . . .' A button was pressed and a toy came to mechanical life, emitting tinny games-arcade sounds of shooting guns as it teetered forward.

A man came up uncomfortably close and, with the dexterity of a seasoned cardsharp, fanned open a deck of sepia prints of famous Indian historical buildings and temples. A picture of a naked woman appeared and disappeared so quickly that it could well have been the prestidigitator's illusion. He was shocked; didn't the man see that he had a small child with him? Or did he not care?

The surrounding gardens, well tended by Indian standards, shone in the white-gold light of the January afternoon, yet, looked at closely, all that riot of cannas and marigolds and manicured grass lawns could not really disguise their irredeemable municipal souls. There was the typical shoddiness – straggly borders; lines that could not keep straight; a certain patchiness to the planting, revealing the scalp of soil through the thinning hair of vegetation; the inevitable truculence of nature against the methodising human hand . . . and underpinning all this amateurish attempt at imposing order and beauty he could feel, no, almost *see*, what a battle it was to keep the earth, wet and dark now, from reverting to red dust in the obliterating heat of the Northern Plains in the summer. He bought tickets and entered the great courtyard of the Diwan-i-Am. The world transformed – in the burnished gold of the winter afternoon sun, the umber-red sand-stone used for the whole complex at Fatehpur Sikri seemed like carved fire, something the sun had magicked out of the red soil in their combined image and likeness.

He looked at his son, expecting to see a reflection of his own wonder on the child's face, but all he could discern in that mostly unreadable expression was ... was what? Boredom? Across another courtyard, all blazing copper in the light, lay the palace buildings. He backtracked to consult the map etched on to a stone block towards the entrance, but with no reference point to indicate 'You are here' he felt confused.

While retrieving the camera and the guidebook from his back-pack, he said to his son, 'Stay still for a moment, don't run off. We'll go to all those beautiful little palaces, do you see?' By the time he had slung the camera around his neck and opened the guidebook to the correct page, he could tell that the boy was itching to run across the courtyard. He tried to keep an eye on him while skim-reading the relevant page. Yes, he had found it – this must be the Mahal-i-Khas, the private palaces of Akbar. His head bobbed back and forth, like a foraging bird's, from page to surrounding environment. When he had established beyond any doubt that the two-and-a-half-storeyed building on the left, which had a touch of incompleteness to it, was Akbar's private apart-ments, he caught hold of his son's hand and made to enter the building.

But he had been spotted leafing through the travel-guide, his hesitation and momentary lostness read shrewdly. A man materialised behind him and began to speak as if he was in the middle of a talk he had been giving: 'The recesses in the ground floor that you will see were meant for his books and papers and documents ...'

He wheeled around. The sun caught his eyes and dazzled him. All he could make out was a dark, almost black, sharply pointed face, a human face on its way to becoming a fox's; or was it the other way round?

'If you go up to his sleeping chamber, the khwabgah, on the top floor,' the man continued, 'you will see fine stone latticework screens along the corridor leading to the women's quarters, the harem. These jaalis protected the women from the public gaze as they went back and forth from the khwabgah.'

The man spoke with practised fluency. If he was trying to advertise his skills as a guide to get hired, then there was nothing in his manner or his speech that betrayed this purposive bent. If anything, he seemed almost oblivious of his presence and his child's.

The sun had blinded him so he turned his head away, both to face his son, whom he was afraid to let out of his field of vision for any duration, and to signal to the man that he was not going to be needing his services. The buildings that lay in the slanted shade were an earthen matt pink. Elsewhere, the red sandstone that caught the sun burned a coppery-gold. When he turned around to see if he had shaken off the tout, there was no one to be seen.

In the rooms on the ground floor of the emperor's private quarters he was held by the flaky painted decorations depicting flowers and foliage; these faded ghosts still managed to carry a fraction of their original life-spirit. They had been touched up, restored, but with a brutal mugger's hand. From the vantage point of the courtyard, the interior had looked poky and pitch-dark and he had wondered about the smallness of the chambers and, correspondingly, the physical stature of those sixteenth-century people: did they have to huddle and stoop inside? Was it light enough to see things in there during the daytime? Why were there no doors and windows? What did they do for privacy? And then, the crowning question: did he know just too little about the architectural and domestic history of the Mughals?

Now that they were inside, the idea that the rooms were cramped somewhat diminished but the feeling that they were, or could be, dark remained. Was it something to do with his vision, or from having just come in from the brightness outside? He blinked several times. The interior seemed to shrink, expand and then shrink again, as if he were in the almost imperceptibly pulsating belly of a giant beast. In the pavilion at the top, where Akbar used to sleep, faded frescoes, nibbled away by time with a slow but tenacious voracity, covered the walls. But the fragments seemed to be under some kind of wash; a protective varnish, perhaps, but it had the effect of occluding them under a milky mist. A winged creature, holding an infant in front of a cave in a rockface, looked down at him from above a doorway. It looked as if it had been assembled from large flakes of once-coloured dandruff. His heart boiled against the cage of his chest.

'Baba, look, an angel!' the child said.

He closed his eyes, gripped his son's hand, turned his face away, then back again and opened his eyes. The angel continued to stare at him. There was intent in those eyes, and even the very first touch of a smile in those delicately upturned corners, as if Persian artists had brought forth a Chinese angel. He shut his eyes again; the face of the fox-guide, accompanied by shifting confetti-links of floaters, flickered across his retina.

Outside, the courtyard, large enough to be the central square in a city where the crowd congregates for the beginning of a revolution, held scattered groups of colourfully clothed visitors. The spiky phalanx of red cannas blazed in their plots. A square stone platform, bordered by jaalis, rose from the centre of a square rectangular pool, filled with stagnant water, virulent green with algae. Four raised narrow walkways, bisecting each side of the square, led to the platform. The musical rigour that the Mughals had brought to the quadrangular form struck him again; he riffled through his guidebook to read something illuminating about this pool, Anup Talao.

'Baba, can we go to the middle? There are lanes,' the boy said.

'I don't think we are allowed to,' he said, then tried to distract him by summarising the few lines on the feature: 'Look, it says here that musicians used to sit in the centre there, on that platform, and perform concerts for the emperor and his court.' After a few beats of silence, he added, 'Wasn't that interesting?', hearing his own need to keep the boy engaged fraying with exhaustion.

'Why aren't we allowed to?'

'Well,' he thought for a second or two, 'if people were allowed in, we would see a lot of tourists here walking in and out, posing on the platform, taking pictures . . . but there's none of that, do you see?'

It was better outside – the relative darkness inside had, oddly, unnerved him. But the pressure of tourism was relentless, bullying. Surely they hadn't come all this way to stand in the sun and look at pretty buildings from a distance, when they could be inside them, poring over the details, going into every room of every palace, absorbing what the guidebook had to say about each and then re-looking, armed with new knowledge?

In the strange and beautiful five-storeyed panch mahal, each ascending floor diminishing in size until there was only a small kiosk surmounted by a dome on top – eighty-four, fifty-six, twenty, twelve and four columns on each level, respectively, his guide told him – arches between columns took the place of walls and he had been glad of the light and the breeze that came in unimpeded.

Outside once again, he noticed the squares marked on the courtyard, with a raised stone seat at the centre of the regular cross formed by the squares, and pointed them out to his son. 'Do you see the squares in the four directions, making the four arms of a big plus-sign?' he asked, tapping a few with his feet and indicating the rest with his pointing hand, 'Here, and here, and this . . . do you see?'

The boy nodded.

'Show me the plus-sign then,' he asked.

The child danced around, stamping on each square, repeating his father's 'Here ... and here, and this one ...'

'Good,' he said. 'Do you know what they are for?'

'This square has X on it, and this one,' the boy said, jumping on each of them.

'Yes, so they do. Do you know what these squares are doing here?'

The boy shook his head and looked at him expectantly.

'This is a board game, like Ludo or chess. It's called pachisi. Instead of having a small board at the centre, which is surrounded by a circle of a few players, they had a big one marked out permanently in this courtyard.'

His son stared silently, as if digesting the information.

'But do you know why it's so big? I mean, so much bigger than a Ludo or a chess board?' He was hoping the child was not going to ask what Ludo was: why should the ubiquitous board game of the endless afternoons and evenings of his Calcutta childhood mean anything to an American boy? That worn question of his son's disconnection with his father's culture reared its head again, but weakly. He pushed it down, easily enough, and offered the answer to the question he had asked, by reading an excerpt from a nineteenth-century book quoted in his travel-guide: 'The game of *pachisi* was played by Akbar in a truly regal manner, the Court itself, divided into red and white squares, being the board, and an enormous stone raised on four feet, representing the central point. It was here that Akbar and his courtiers played this game; sixteen young slaves from the harem, wearing the players' colours, represented the pieces, and moved to the squares according to the throw of dice. It is said that the Emperor took such a fancy to playing the game on this grand scale that he had a court for *pachisi* constructed in all his palaces ...'

Again, that expression of wide-eyed nothingness on the boy's face. He explained the quotation slowly, in simple words, pointing to the squares and the stone seat, to spark some interest in the boy. The child's face lit up for an instant. He hopped from one square to another, then another, finally sat, cross-legged, on one of them and chirped, 'Am I a piece in this game?'

'You could be,' he laughed.

'What will happen when you throw the die? Will my head be chopped off? In one clean stroke?'

Before he could answer, a voice behind him intervened sharply, 'Get that child out of that square!'

He wheeled around. It was the man with the face of a fox. His eyes glittered. The moustache looked animal too.

'Don't you know it's bad luck to have children sit in these squares? Do you know what happened here? Don't you know the stories?'

He was sufficiently annoyed by the man's hectoring tone to protest: 'Show me a sign that says children are not allowed on this board. It's part of the courtyard, anyone can walk on it. And who are you, anyway?'

'Look around you – do you see any children?'

Almost involuntarily, he turned around: to his right, the extraordinary symmetry of the detached building of the Diwan-i-Khas; behind him, the jewel-box of the Turkish Sultana's house; and in the huge courtyard on which these structures stood, not a single child to be spotted. All those colourfully dressed tourists he had seen earlier seemed to have vanished. There were one or two to be seen standing in the shapely arches of buildings or colonnaded walkways, but there was no one in the courtyard and certainly no children. Incredulous, he turned a full circle to be sure he had let his gaze take in everything. No, no children. The man too was gone. There was a sudden, brief vacuum in his chest; then the sensation left.

'D-did you see the ... the man who was just here? Where did he go?' he asked his son.

The boy shook his head.

'But ... but you saw him speaking to me, didn't you?' He was nearly shouting.

'Speaking? What?' the boy asked.

Of course, the child wouldn't have understood a word; the man had been speaking in Hindi.

'B-but ... but ...' he began, then that futility was inside him again, making him feel weightless.

He extended his hand to his son and caught the warm little palm and fingers in his grip and wanted to hold on to them to moor himself and at the same to scrunch them, so fierce was the wave of love and terror that suddenly threatened to unbalance him. He took the boy and ran into the Turkish Sultana's house but was blind to the ways craftsmen had made every available surface blossom into teeming life with dense carvings of gardens, trees, leaves, flowers, geometric patterns, birds, animals, abstract designs. At another time he would have been rooted to the spot, marvelling, but now his senses were disengaged and distant and all he saw was the frozen work of artisans and their tools. In one of the lower panels, the heads of the birds of paradise sitting on trees had been destroyed. An animal, crouching below, had been defaced too, making it look much like the lower half of a human child, decapitated in the act of squatting; it brought to mind ritual sacrifice. A small thrill of repulsion went through him. The mutilated carvings had the nature of fantastical creatures from Bosch's sick imagination; left untouched, they would have been simply beautiful. Then the dimness started to play havoc with his perception. Shapes and colours got unmoored and recoalesced in different configurations. It was like discovering a camel smoking a pipe, formed in clouds in the sky, shift and morph into a crawling baby held in the cradling trunk of an elephant, except there was no movement here, no external change of shape to warrant one thing becoming another.

He forced himself to read a few lines from the relevant section of his guidebook but they remained locked too; signs without meanings. He asked his son, 'Do you like what you see? Can you tell me what these are?' He couldn't make the words come out animated.

The boy shook his head.

'All right, let's go look at something else.' No amount of beauty could counter the permanent twilight of the interiors.

The baize-table lawns and the begonia shrubs radiated light like a merciless weapon. A ripple passed through the blazing froth of bushes, as if the vegetation was shuddering at his presence. Almost dragging his son along, he ran towards a small, perfectly formed building, standing in the flag of shade that it flung on the pied stones of the courtyard. Mariam's House, the guidebook said. It was the colour of something that had been sluiced indelibly in blood in its distant past. Under the stone awning three-quarters of the way up, the ventilation slots – surely they were too small to be windows? – looked like blinded eyes, yet the house gave the effect of looking watchful. It struck him then, suddenly, a feeling that the walls and stones and cupolas and courtyards were all, as one organism, watching him and his son.

And something was: another angel, this time above a doorway. Barely discernible through the slow, colourless disappearing act that time and the well-intentioned but wrong kind of preservative varnish had together enforced on it, it still managed, through some inexplicable resurrection, to fix him with its eye. It was like looking into the face of ancient light transmitted back from the beginnings of time.

He took hold of his son's hand to return to the car, moving as fast as having a six-year-old physically attached to him would allow. The larger half of the site remained unvisited; he had had enough. The very air of the place seemed unsettled, as if it had slipped into some avenue where ordinary time and ordinary circumstance did not press against it. Then, with rising anxiety, he knew what was going to happen next, and it did. From the dark inside of a square building, the fox-man came out and stood under the domed canopy of a platform at one corner of the building. He could see the man so clearly, so close, that it was as if all the distance between them across the courtyard had been telescoped into nothing. Then the man retreated into the dark again. He had known the exact sequence of events beforehand, even known the bending of distance that would occur, known that the platform on which the man had stood was called the Astrologer's Seat even though he had not visited that section of the palace quadrangle. He felt himself pursued by the place as they ran out, retracing the route through which they had made their way into and through the palace complex.

While waiting for the car, he dared to look up: the sky was an immense canvas of orange and red, not from the setting sun, it seemed to him, but from the red sandstone that burned, without decaying, under it. Everything was ablaze.

On the road back, a huge, slow procession of shouting men, hundreds and hundreds of them, coming from the direction in which they were travelling, stalled all traffic. The car windows were rolled up instantly; the protestors were within touching distance. The vast, crawling snake seemed to be an election rally, although he could not tell – the posters were all in Urdu, a language he couldn't read, and he couldn't make out a single word amidst the shouting of slogans. They could have been in an utterly foreign country. The boy had his nose pressed to the window; he had never seen anything like this.

'We just have to wait until it passes, right?' he asked the driver. A pointless question. The driver shrugged.

Time in this country flowed in a different way from the rest of the world. It was the flow that had carried him a long time ago, when he was a boy, growing up in Calcutta, but now he could no longer step into it: he had become a tourist in his own country.

The rally seemed endless. Occasionally, it stopped altogether. After forty minutes of sitting inside the car, the driver said, 'They're moving.'

A brave taxi up ahead had decided to cut through a narrow lane on the left – a dust-and-straggling-dead-grass path, really – with the hope of rejoining the main road at a point further up where it would already have been traversed by the rally. Like mechanical sheep, cars started leaving the main route and entering this side-lane. Their driver was quick – he manoeuvred the car sideways with manic energy and was into the path before the rush to get in there created total gridlock. But he was still behind a few vehicles and the juddering stop-start stop-start stop-start movement down an unmetalled alley was the modern equivalent of running the gauntlet. Soon they came to a complete halt. The procession, well behind them, still seemed to be in full spate, but at least they were now not in the flow of something volatile and unpredictable.

He must have dozed off. The next thing he knew was a shadow blooming inside the car at the same time as he heard a timid pattering on the window next to the boy. A bear, standing on its hind legs, was looking in, its muzzle almost pressed to the glass. There was an irregular patch of mist that changed shape in rhythm to the animal's breathing. Its pelt was a dark slate-grey shag-cushion of dust and tiny insects and bits of straw and grass. Up close, the hairs looked coarse and thick, somewhat like the quills of a hedgehog. Behind him, a man extended his arm forward and tapped on the glass with his black fingernails. The child pushed back on the heels of his palms and moved backwards, trying to burrow into his father's lap, but couldn't turn his fascinated head away. The man outside looked eerily familiar – he had the sharp, pointy face of a rodent's and a moustache that seemed alive. Surely he must be dreaming? They were still in the country lane, and the terracotta late-afternoon light had turned to ashy dusk, but that ... that man at the car window ... He felt that the spinning of the earth carried him like dice in the slot of a roulette machine and delivered him to destinations that were endlessly repeatable, each ever so slightly different from the other, all more or less the same.

Encouraged by the unblinking gaze of father and son, the bear-wallah tapped on the glass again, and made a shallow bowl of his palm to beg. Those glittering, scaly eyes indicated a sickness that would finish him soon. Inside, he was too frozen even to shake his head in disapproval. At a signal from his keeper, the bear lifted its paw and replicated the human's begging gesture. The chain, attached to the animal and run through the space between two of its fingers, obliged clinkingly. He saw the head of a huge iron nail driven through the paw – or was it a callus? The claws at the end were open brackets of dirty gunmetal. The paw could easily smash the window, reach in and tear out the child's entrails. He tried to ask the driver to shoo the man away but no sound emerged from his throat. He tried again.

'Driver, ask them to move on,' he said in a kind of low rasp. He couldn't bring up his arm to mime 'Go away' to the beggar.

The driver lowered his window and barked, 'Ei, buzz off.'

The man paid no heed; the begging from both creatures continued. Presumably at another signal from the man, the bear nodded, then grinned. Where it met the teeth, the gum was a bright pink but further up the colour of cooked liver with a violet tinge. There were sticky threads of saliva gleaming whitely against all that dirty ivory and raw flesh. Then the animal started shaking, as if it was having a malarial fit. The boy screamed, once, twice.

He shouted, 'Driver, why isn't he going? Ask him again, now. Ask!'

The driver complied, his command issuing more forcefully this time. The traffic unclotted. As the car moved to life, the pinning gaze of those scaly eyes receding backwards seemed to have become a solid, unfrayable rope. Then motion and the gathering dark severed it.

The boy coughed all night and kept him awake. Occasionally, he cried out in his sleep loudly enough for him to turn on his bedside lamp, get out of his bed and go to his son's to see what was wrong, to soothe his nightmares away.

Towards the end of the night, the child woke up with what he could only call a howl and continued to cry with an abandonment that brought back to mind the inexplicable and seemingly endless runs of crying during infancy. He couldn't establish now if the boy was still lodged in his world of dreams during this fit or whether something in the real world, colic or feeling ill or an onset of some sickness, was making him scream like this. Questions had yielded nothing.

Should he ring for room service and ask for a doctor? Surely a hotel of this class would have access to one? The boy's forehead and neck were not hot.

'What is it? Tell me, what is it?' he asked over and over again, reaching the edge of anger on the other side of his helplessness.

Then, a tiny chink in this wall of repetition: 'I feel afraid,' the boy managed to articulate.

He bobbed afloat on a swell of relief. 'Afraid?' he asked. 'Afraid of what? There's nothing to be afraid of, I'm here with you. Here, I'll sleep in your bed, my arms around you. Everything will be all right.'

But the child wouldn't stop. He caught something in his son's gaze, a brief focusing of his eyes on something behind his shoulder, as if he had seen something behind his father, something that made him wail louder, before the focus dissolved.

He turned his head to look. There could be nothing outside the wall of windows – they were on the sixteenth floor of the hotel. The dark glass reflected back at him a dramatically lit-and-shadowed scene of his staring face, twisted around on the stalk of his neck; his son lying on the bed with his mouth open in a rictus of horror and pain; the white bed linen twisted and roped and peaked in the great turbulence that was being enacted upon it; the whole tableau shading off into the darkness that framed it. As his vision moved away from that sharp chiaroscuro foreground of the reflection, he could see, in the refracted light from the hotel grounds, the skeleton of the skyscraper on the other side of the road. On the very top few floors, he could make out the scaffolding – was it still the bamboo-and-coir-rope of his childhood or had they moved on to something more reliable and advanced nowadays? – and the billowing pieces of sackcloth or plastic or whatever it was that the workers had set up there. He wondered, not for the first time, what purpose those sheets served. A safety net, perhaps? They had certainly not prevented one of them from meeting a terrible end yesterday.

By the early hours, not far off from dawn, his son exhausted himself to sleep. He drifted off too, one arm around the boy. The light woke him; he had forgotten to draw the curtains in the night. Next to him, the child was dead.

II

When I think of her – not often, admittedly, before I decided to write this – the first image is always from an evening in July. The night before, it had rained like I had always imagined it must have done during prehistoric eras, the Pleistocene or the Triassic, say. It brought back my boyhood, lying awake, listening to the sound of relentless sheets of water coming down, imagining a low, red, early-era sky, and strange vegetation and fearful creatures and dangerous landscapes pelted by a downpour that must have been untempered, closer to a natural cataclysm than just simple, heavy rainfall. It even brought back the memory of Bible classes in school, of how all the fountains of the great deep woke up and the windows of heaven opened and it rained upon the face of the earth for forty days and forty nights.

There were dark rain-clouds covering most of the sky next morning but at least the rain had let up for a while. My parents' living room, on the first floor of a block of flats in Bombay, had an unimpeded view of the sea, which was no more than a few metres away, across the Band Stand in Bandra where, in British times, the band used to gather and play every afternoon. Now between the window and the sea was a road, forked at our end by a narrow, tri-angular sliver of green, at the vertex of which stood a pair of solid-looking, heavy metal statues, all chunky cuboids and rectangular masses and straight lines, some city council's idea of cubist primi-tivism. The pedestal on which the figures stood bore the legend *Time is/Too late for those who wait/Too swift for those who fear/Too long for those who grieve/Too short for those who rejoice/But for those who love/Time is eternity.*

As if in response, Band Stand, and the mile-long seafront prome-nade, dotted with concrete benches and sea-poison trees at regular intervals, had become the focal point for romancing couples in the afternoons and evenings.

The Arabian Sea, a placid pond for most of the year, became ruffled and turbulent in its bathetic, minor-mode way during the monsoon, and this morning it looked wild by its standards, with white breakers crashing, one after another, on to the black, rocky shore, which was now totally submerged, the sea having swollen and reached the brim of the sea wall. The horizon was an inky bank of clouds. Far away, I could make out the painted red hull of a fishing boat. It looked like a child's paper contraption that would soon unravel on the wild slate-grey surface which it rode, tossed almost rhythmically like a seesaw.

I had a meeting in Colaba at 10 a.m., which meant that I had to leave early in order to avoid the notorious morning traffic. These were the days before the Bandra-Worli Sea Link, so it could – and sometimes did – take two hours to travel a distance of twenty kilo-metres. In another couple of years the Sea Link would open, shocking everyone that something which had nominally been under construction for decades, with nothing except a few fist-like stubs rising from the surface of the sea across the Reclamation (as it was called) to show for it, could be finished so quickly. Who knew what kind of pressure the World Bank, which funded the majority of the project, had brought to bear on the stalled rusty machinery of corrupt politicians and bureaucrats and construction companies to get it moving again?

Last night's rain would mean flooded roads and waterlogging, so the prospect of a long, stop-start journey into town seemed almost inevitable. I left home just after eight. Amit, my father's driver, usually reported for duty slightly later in the day but he had been asked to come early that morning. By the time the car reached Mahim, the skies opened again. Despite the windscreen wipers semaphoring furiously back and forth, I could barely see anything in front and nothing very much at all through the streaking wall of water which was the passenger window. The whole world seemed to be deliquescing. After twenty minutes or so, the strafing abated somewhat although the rainfall continued; a seen-through-streams-of-liquid kind of visibility was restored; the world became that of an Impressionist painting. At the obligatory traffic standstill at Haji Ali, I saw that the long walkway on the sea leading to the offshore mosque was nearly obliterated to the sight by the spray, so that the mosque, wreathed in low mist, looked as if it were floating in the air, untethered from its umbilical cord connecting it to land. Normally the walkway, a gauntlet of seriously maimed, crippled and diseased people begging, would be a seething corridor of people, either making their way into or out of the mosque. I was too mesmerised by the fairytale dream-vision castle it had transformed into to pay much attention to the long-range view of plagued humanity seeking succour. Then the traffic lights changed, the boys selling pirated copies of bestsellers, self-help books and glossy magazines, out even in this weather, dispersed and the car left the scene of accidental enchantment.

It was that evening, around six o'clock, while Baba and I were debating whether to bring forward our routine pre-dinner drinking – a couple of whisky-and-sodas for each of us – by half an hour to six-thirty, that the doorbell rang.

'Who could it be?' Ma asked, almost to herself. 'It's too early for Renu ...' Renu was the cook.

I got up, went to the door and opened it. Renu was standing on the other side of the threshold. Or not exactly standing; she had one hand stretched out, holding on to the doorjamb to support herself, as she swayed on the balls of her feet. On her desiccated face her bloodshot eyes were swimming. Her hair, normally oiled and combed tightly on to her scalp and tied into a loose bun at the neck, was dry and frizzy, escaping in disobedient wisps all over.

'Are you all right?' I asked her, then turned my head to say to my mother, who was already halfway to the front door, 'It's cooking-aunty.' I could never bring myself to call Renu by her name and add a suffix such as 'di', older sister, or 'mashi', aunty, either of which would have been the expected or normal thing to do.

'I had no sleep last night,' Renu began. 'The police came in vans and asked us to get out of our rooms. The sea was rising because of the rain, they asked us to get out, they thought our jhopri was going to be swallowed under water.'

She could barely stand straight on her feet.

'Not a wink of sleep,' she said. 'They chased us out at ten, then asked us to go back in around midnight, then they came at two again and drove us out. I've had to work all day after a night of no sleep ... I can't keep my eyes open. So I was thinking, I know it's too early, but if I start now and cook something quickly, I ... I could ...'

Something about her unbending sense of duty pierced me. I said, 'Nothing doing. You go home right now, there's no need to cook tonight. You go get some sleep.'

Ma added her voice to this – 'Yes, Renu, don't worry about cooking this evening, you go back home.'

Renu hesitated. Even in this state of extreme exhaustion, she felt some compulsion to resist something so easily given – it wasn't right, it wasn't the normal order of things for families to intercept a servant's unarticulated request and accede to it. And yet I could see on her face relief, so much stronger than professionalism.

Before she could make another weak attempt – not because she was insincere but because she did not have the necessary energy – I forestalled her and repeated, 'Shush, not another word. We'll see you tomorrow morning. You need to sleep. Go.'

She was not a person much given to smiling, or expressing any kind of pleasant emotion, but the imprint of gratitude beneath that wrung-out face was unmistakable, a silver-gelatin film beginning to take on the lineaments of the photographic negative in its chemical bath.

I asked, 'Where did all of you go when you left your homes?'

'We sat on the road, here, right here,' she said, pointing in a vague westerly direction.

'You mean in Band Stand? Just outside our house?'

'Yes, there.'

'But it was pouring . . .'

She inclined her head sideways, a way of saying yes that stoically dealt with her plight.

I said, 'Listen, if it happens again, you come straight here and ring the bell. I'll tell the guards downstairs that you may come in the middle of the night and they're to let you in. You come and sleep here in the living room if you get thrown out of your home again.'

Ma said, 'Or the kitchen. You can sleep in the kitchen.'

I was tempted to turn slightly sideways to give Ma a look, but I controlled myself. It was an old, old battle between us and it had just let me know, gently, that it was still there, deferred and waiting, waiting to be roused from its sleep.

Instead, I carried on looking at cooking-aunty and said emphatically, 'There's much more space in the living room. Come and sleep here if you need to.' A bit too emphatically.

She gave a dismissive wave of her hand, a gesture that doubled as a goodbye, as she turned to take the stairs down – 'Achha, achha, we'll see, but there's no need, they say that it's not going to rain so much tonight.' That was the closest she was going to get to a smile.

I wanted to ask her so much more: the layout of her living quarters in the slum, how many people had been dragged out of bed and made to stand out in the driving rain all night as a way of preventing death by flooding, how close the slum was to the sea . . . but she was gone.

*

It was the year before this incident that I first met cooking-aunty, on my regular January visit to Bombay.

It became obvious soon enough that she did not like me. She was my parents' new cook and she'd been with them only a few months. A Bengali cook, they had wanted; stressing especially the cook's origins, when the previous one, a Maharashtrian woman from the fishing community, the Koli, proved to be too limited – and, no doubt, too foreign – for their sophisticated Bengali palates. My father was nearing sixty, my mother nearly fifty-eight; too late for them to experiment with regional Indian cuisines, especially in view of the fact that they were Bengalis, a people not known to think that anything other than their own culture – be it culinary, literary, linguistic, artistic or anything else – was worth engaging with.

On one of the fortnightly phone calls to my mother, she explained to me how difficult it was to get a good cook in Bombay but, after a month of looking, she thought she had found someone who met the requirements. 'She works for six homes but she's just lost one of them,' Ma said. 'She'll be looking to fill that gap. I hope I get lucky enough to bag her.'

'Six homes?' I asked. 'That's a lot. How does she fit them all in? She must work at least twelve hours a day, if not fourteen.'

The next time I rang my mother, Renu was working for them. This, as far as I can remember, was in July or August, so it would be five or six months before I was to meet her.

My design job in London was flexible. I worked for a progressive, thinking-outside-the-box class of trendy outfit, the kind of place that was being talked of as the future of both working and the workplace, in publications such as *Wallflower**, *i-D*, *Wired*, so it was possible for me to bunch together all my statutory leave in January and take off for the entire month to India.

30

Over the months preceding my visit, I had asked Ma a couple of times about their new cook and she had sounded cautiously pleased. I had never known Ma to be effusive about domestic staff, so I took it as a reasonably good sign when she had said – and I'm conflating several snatches of conversation here – 'She's all right. She's lived most of her working life outside Bengal, so she's either forgotten or doesn't know traditional Bengali cooking. I have to tell her what to do. I caught her putting onions and garlic in a light fish stew. And she puts hing in everything, can you believe it? I don't know where she picked up this kind of cooking. In non-Bengali households, clearly.'

And so it went; carping was a way of praise with my mother.

I need to say a little about my interest in food because it touches, if only glancingly, upon our story. I cooked for myself in London and entertained friends and work-people at home, of course, but my engagement with food ran deeper than the functional. I loved eating, I thought about cooking and recipes and different culinary cultures a lot of the time, and one of my current assignments, perhaps because this enthusiasm of mine was widely known, was to write and design a full-length book devoted entirely to regional Indian breakfasts, state by state. A young editor, at an imprint specialising in beautifully produced cookbooks, had spotted a blog on breakfasts across the world and mentioned it casually at a dinner with friends of friends. Someone in that serendipitous chain thought that I was some kind of authority on Indian food, and a project had been born – a lavish and substantial book, sitting on the intersection between food- and travel-writing. It was not an original or underexplored territory but we were enthusiastic and all agreed that what it lacked in novelty, it could make up for in content, visual feel and production values.

There was work that one did in a kind of professional, mandatory, bread-and-butter kind of way, and there was work that caught the tindery and flammable bits of one's passion and began a long, slow, steady combustion; this book was the latter. The research and sourcing of recipes were the easy bits. I was continually asking my mother to give me recipes from classical Bengali cuisine, particularly those that had been handed down generations within families, each family tweaking a given dish in ways that made a new, different thing of it. For example, my mother, in the days when she used to cook, or at least instruct the several persons, over time, who were employed to cook, had only two ways of making kalai dal (called 'biuli' in our family; most of the rest of India call it 'urid dal'): one in which the boiled lentils were spiced with fennel seeds and julienned ginger; the other where the lentils were toasted first, then boiled, and spiced with whole red chillies and hing spluttered in very hot oil. Both methods had been learned from her mother. But in my paternal grandparents' home, my mother once said to me, they cooked the same lentils in a completely different style: lots of finely chopped garlic, whole dried red chillies and that quintessentially Bengali spice, panchphoron – a mixture of equal amounts of fennel, cumin, fenugreek, nigella and mustard seeds – were sizzled briefly in smoking-hot mustard oil, then added to the toasted and boiled lentils. 'Some old Oriya cook's influence, no doubt,' Ma had dismissively added.

Now I thought I could pick up a couple of things from my parents' new cook's repertoire. It would add a certain spark to my annual visit.

Around noon on the day after I arrived in Bombay, I was sitting by the window in Baba and Ma's long, uncluttered living room, looking out to an imperturbable sea under a clear, sunny sky. It was low tide and the expanse of madly serrated and pitted black rock that was the beach here had emerged, glistening, the extremity of some enormous mythical undersea creature. The outcrop was dotted with men going about their morning ablutions: there were a couple bathing in the rock pools; quite a few of them washing their clothes, first stretching their sheets and towels and vests on the rocky surface and running a bar of soap along them vigorously, as if grating a carrot, then threshing the soaped clothes on the rough rocks to get the dirt out, and finally rinsing them ... creamy rings of suds had formed around some of these men. Slightly further out, towards the sea end of the rocks, there were three or four men, each standing at a spot they considered to be sufficiently apart from the rest, pissing into the sea. Two boys appeared along the promenade-wall, their arms hugging plastic bags full of flowers, presumably the clear-out from a temple or a shrine, and, hopscotching along the rocks right to the edge of the sea, flung everything they were carrying into the water. I could see the orange marigolds and dried leaves and other assorted vegetation and rubbish disperse in a wide garland, which lost its shape as the circumference became bigger and bigger.

Ma was doing her usual thing of ministering to me fussily: 'Do you want more tea?', 'Why aren't you eating the fruits? The papaya is very nice', 'Tell me when you want the upma heated up.' All she wanted to do was to serve me. On the first day, it felt comforting, as if I had regressed to childhood. By the third week, I would be thinking of the solitude of my mornings in London with such intense longing that I often barked at her to leave me alone. Sometimes her face would crumple and she would go quiet. At other times, she would strike back: 'Alone, alone,' she would mutter, 'this is what you've learned from living abroad, you've lost all understanding of family and affection and how to live in society and be less self-centred.'

On the dining table, under a sizeable fine-mesh cover, sat small bowls of chunks of papaya, red jewels of pomegranate arils, halved guavas; and a large bowl, covered with a saucer, of upma, coarse-grained semolina cooked with mustard seeds and curry leaves and onions. It had fried cashews thrown in sometimes, or peanuts, or a small handful of peas. It was a South Indian breakfast dish and my mother knew it was one of my favourites, so she had asked the cook to prepare some this morning. By the time I had got up, the cook had left.

The upma was delicious. I had no idea why, but it was one of those things that I never cooked for myself in London, although it was a very simple and quick affair. In a divided life that was lived in two countries, separately and in rigorous succession, maybe I had saved a few things to belong to each of them solely, without flowing between the two.

'This is lovely,' I said. 'I could eat this for breakfast every day.'

'You can hardly call it breakfast at this time of the day. Here, have some more,' Ma said, getting up to serve me.

The young woman who cleaned and did the washing up was going about her business as Ma and I chatted.

'Is she new?' I asked, indicating the cleaning woman, confident that she wouldn't understand Bengali.

'No, she's been with us for nearly a year,' Ma said, then addressed the woman in Hindi, 'Milly, this is my son. He lives abroad. He has come here for a month.'

My mother's Hindi was more than competent; unusual in a Bengali woman but, then, she had spent nearly twenty years in Bombay because my father's work had brought them here in the mid-1980s. It was assumed that after my father's retirement they would move back to Calcutta (Kolkata, now) but, to be fair to them, they had found Bombay – that was the name of the city then, and the name I still use – not an unsympathetic place, growing more and more over time to like its energy and urban, unprovincial personality.

The introduction was more an advertisement of my mother's pride in her son than a courtesy extended to a maidservant, and Milly probably read it correctly: she refused to look at me, smile or nod or do whatever it was she did in these situations and instead turned her face away, as if in a calculatedly opposite response, and carried on with the dusting.

'How friendly,' I said in English.

'Achha, enough,' Ma hastily added, indicating with a gesture for me to stop being so openly critical of Milly's attitude.

'But she won't understand what I'm saying,' I persisted out of sheer cussedness.

'Uff, stop now, will you?' There was real annoyance in my mother's voice. I was surprised, but I assumed that she was going to explain later, so I shut up. I dutifully lifted my feet while Milly swept the floor with the broom, then again when, on all fours, she swabbed it with a wet cloth dipped in water and wrung out, working it in wide arcs. The room filled with the odour of citronella oil.

When Milly went to the kitchen, my mother said in a breathless run of sotto voce, 'She's from Jharkhand, she's a Christian convert, she says she understands Bengali and English', then ran off to the kitchen to supervise Milly.

Jharkhand. It was one of India's newest states, carved out of the southern and eastern part of Bihar only three or four years ago, after decades of agitation and activism by tribal peoples and backward castes – they had that dreaded Indian distinction, the branding iron of an acronym: OBC, Other Backward Castes – for a separate state where their interests and welfare would not be counted as nothing. It was also one of India's most troubled states, with a strong Maoist presence and, consequently, brutal state-sponsored repression. It was the repository of vast mineral resources, and the state was not going to let a bunch of ragtag militants and expendable tribal peoples whining about their ancient land rights get in the way of those riches.

Perhaps Milly belonged to one of those tribes that had been displaced by mining companies grabbing their land? Perhaps her life did not hold much for her there: from Jharkhand to Bombay was a long distance for her to have come to work as a domestic help. (My mother's generation still called them servants. My politically correct tag had not a jot of correlation to their status: their position in the Indian social hierarchy or economy had never changed.)

I went to the kitchen to deposit my empty bowl and spoon for Milly to wash up and discovered her sitting cross-legged on the floor, in the corner between the fridge and the cupboard, almost hiding, a plate heaped with food on her lap, eating her lunch. In the couple of awkward seconds that I was there, wishing I had not walked in on her eating, all kinds of childhood strictures about not watching servants eat flooded back, along with a new kind of discomfort.

Milly did not look up. I fled.

After Milly had gone, Ma filled me in on her background over the course of the day as I pottered around aimlessly, doing nothing at all and enjoying the lazing. I even paid a kind of passive attention to Ma's intermittent chatter – chit-chat about her friends and neighbours, gossip about celebrities and Bombay film stars culled from glossy magazines. It turned out that even Ma had noticed that Milly did not talk to, or even look at, men, so my mother had assumed that the girl had an unpleasant history with them and had left it at that. What she had done instead was to engage the young woman in conversation during the hours that she came to work and, in the process, had pieced together a sort of surface narrative of her life.

It went something like this: Milly was married to a man from Jharkhand who worked as kitchen staff in a low-end restaurant in Bandra. They had a daughter, who was around three or four years old, and a son, who was just under one. Milly was pregnant when she began working for my parents, so Ma decided to give her a heavy meal every day. The good practice had continued, I was cheered to note, even though Milly, I assumed, had stopped breastfeeding.

'But where does she leave the children when she goes to work?' I asked.

'With her husband, of course,' Ma answered. 'He does the evening shift in the restaurant.'

'Does she come from far?'

'No, no, she lives just around the corner, in the slum along the
sea wall on that side,' she said, indicating with her hand the direction towards Taj Land's End, the luxury hotel which sat on the tip
of this centre-west finger of Bombay jutting out into the sea and
forming the top part of the curve of land nestling Mahim Bay.

'Is there a slum there?' I asked; I had no idea. 'But where? I
thought there was only the sea on the other side of the wall.'

'Have a look when you're out there for your morning walk,' she
said.

Around seven in the evening, Renu arrived to cook dinner. She was
short and dark and could have been any age between forty and
fifty-five. The way she wore her sari Bengali-style, with the aanchol thrown over on the front but her head uncovered, made her
look even more shapeless than she was. My mother introduced us.
Without looking at me, Renu nodded at Ma, almost imperceptibly,
and asked her, 'What shall I cook?' This, I gathered, was the order
of things – she would arrive and, while still standing just over the
threshold, ask my mother what she wanted for dinner, then she
would go into the kitchen and set about her business.

Ma, indicating me, said, 'While he's here, he's going to be in
charge of these things. I'm on holiday now. Mind you, he's a very
good cook. And he loves eating.' She tried to sound amusing, as if
encouraging Renu to step up her game for the visiting son, but in a
bantering, tongue-in-cheek kind of way.

Renu, looking impassive and unimpressed, gave no sign that she
had even registered this and instead asked Ma again, 'Tell me, quick
quick, what you want cooked. I have to go at seven-thirty, they turn
the tap off after half an hour, I can't stand here all day.' She made a
gesture, even gave a ghost of a forced smile, that lent her impatient

words the cast of a joke, too; the implied insubordination in her words would otherwise have been intolerable.

Ma repeated, 'He'll tell you.'

Renu continued to look resolutely at my mother.

Her voice was like a child's tin recorder made by an amateur, with every stop hitting the wrong frequency. It reminded me of nails scraping down a blackboard, or the pitch of a screech of metal on metal that seemingly existed merely to shred the uninsulated edge of nerve-endings. This voice was the most immediately conspicuous thing about her and unignorable.

I said, using the most formal and respectful version of 'you', 'Let's go into the kitchen and see what there is ...'

These things are difficult to give cast-iron evidence in support of, but I could sense that she hadn't taken to me. It was as if she had developed an invisible force field around her. She seemed to be surly – even impertinent – by nature, but my unease seemed disproportionate to the brusqueness of her manner. What was it that was really bothering me?

'Show me what's in the fridge,' I said, 'and we can decide after that. Achchha, this morning's upma was delicious, I've never had such good upma. You can make that again. What do you think are your best dishes? We can have one of those tonight.'

I jabbered on; even recalling it now is a touch neuralgic. Instead of answering the question, she emptied the contents of the vegetable crisper on to the floor and on the worktop, running through them one by one, 'Here. Green bananas. Spinach. Green papaya. Cauliflower. Cabbage. Brinjal. Carrots. Spring onions ...'

The language she spoke in, although identifiably Bengali, had flecks of hybridity marking it – she had earlier used the Hindi expression for 'quick quick', now she said 'palak' for 'spinach'.

'What about green-banana koftas?' I suggested.

'No,' she said peremptorily. 'If you want to eat koftas, you tell me the day before – it's a lot of work and it takes time.'

A deep-seated, almost hard-wired, cultural training injected out-rage into my system at the fact of a servant answering back. But no sooner had it manifested than the overriding educated-liberal reaction to the retrogressive nature of that first response pushed it down. I had managed to put my finger on what was bothering me. The knowledge was shaming. The whole cognition process had taken a fraction of a second.

'Yes, yes, of course koftas take a long time,' I wittered, 'that's true, very true. OK, then, what about brinjal bharta? And green papaya with prawns? Are there prawns in the freezer? Let's see what fish there is in the freezer.'

My mother, who must have been listening from the living room, called out, 'Yes, your father bought lots of fish last weekend from the fish market. The freezer is full.'

This was one of the Bengali rituals my parents had held on to: the man, too busy or elevated to be involved in the domestic drudg-ery of daily or even weekly grocery-shopping, made an exception for buying fish because fish held a special place in Bengali cuisine and only a man could discern the freshest and the best specimens. Baba went to the big indoor fish market in Khar every Saturday morning to stock up on weekly supplies.

Renu now took out shallow Tupperware boxes from the freezer, prised open the lids and rattled off the names of the fish each held, 'Rui. Pomfret' – she pronounced this as 'pom-plate' – 'Rawas. Bombil . . .'

Bombil. I stopped her there. It would be only a mild exaggeration to say that this fish, also known as Bombay duck, was one of my main reasons for visiting the city at least once every year. Laid out on the fisherwomen's concrete, the collected fish looked like congeal-ing grey snot with a pinkish tinge, just one step up from liquid in the solidification ladder. Shallow-fried after a light dredging in semolina, or stuffed with a hot coriander-and-chilli green chutney and then fried, it was, in the words of my friend Ankita, 'life-changing'. You realised that there seemed to be a purpose in the near-incapability of the flesh in holding its form – that very amorphous nature transformed into the signature buttery meltedness after cooking.

I asked her to fry some bombil. 'That should be enough, no?' I asked, trying to be democratic. 'Green papaya, aubergine, bombil fry.'

Renu gave a nod and began her preparations. She went about them as if powered by some restless wind. Half a dozen things were started simultaneously: the container of frozen Bombay duck was left in the sink, under running water, to thaw; pots and pans were taken out; the vegetables that were not needed for the evening meal were returned to the fridge; a chopping board and knife appeared ... she seemed to have ten hands.

Without looking at me, she asked, 'Rice or chapatis? And would you like a dal?'

I noticed that she too was using the most respectful form of 'you' in the conjugations of her verbs to talk to me; also, that her Bengali was slightly awry – if I had to translate her question literally, it would be, 'Will you take some dal?'

'Chapatis,' I answered. 'Dal ... yes ...' I hesitated.

'Jaldi jaldi, I'll be in trouble if they turn the tap off before I get to it,' she said again. This time the ameliorating gesture or smile was missing.

I curtly said, 'Whichever dal you think goes best with chapatis' and left the kitchen, making sure to draw shut the sliding door that divided it from the living room.

Keeping my voice down, I said, 'Well, a personality like good mustard oil – it goes straight up your nose', trying to make a joke of it.

My mother indicated to me in signs and whispers that we should speak about this only after Renu had left.

'But what is all this going-to-the-tap-on-time business?' I asked, my voice still low.

'She has to get her water from the municipal tap,' Ma said. 'The corporation water supply is limited to fixed hours, so she has to be there, at the tap, during those times, otherwise she'll be without water for an entire day.'

'But what water?' I was still baffled.

'Water for daily use – bathing, washing, cleaning ...'

'Doesn't she have water where she lives?'

'She lives in the slum over there' – again, that pointing towards the west – 'there's no running water in the slum.'

'You mean the same slum where Milly lives?'

Ma nodded. Then she added, 'Renu can't abide her.'

'Who, Milly?'

'Yes. I'll fill you in later.'

Half an hour later, Renu came out of the kitchen, made for the front door with the words, 'I'll be back soon' and left.

Ma said to me, 'In a couple of minutes you'll see her, if you stand at the window.'

Yes, there she was, I could discern, standing in a small queue, with two large buckets and what looked like an industrial-sized plastic container. The promenade was full of people – strollers, wooing lovers, children – and the road crawling with buses, motor-bikes, auto-rickshaws. The snack-vendors had come out in force, drawing good business from the evening crowd. All life, and all of life's motions and sounds and energies, seemed to be concentrated there. In the island of green, where the tap was situated, there were three old men on the red stone bench, three or four stray dogs, half a dozen children running around. The big trees around it blocked the orange sodium-vapour light and kept most of the area in the shadows. In the balmy sea breeze the trees stirred, making the dappled mass of orange light and black shade sway and move.

Baba returned from work and I went to the kitchen to fix us drinks. The kitchen looked like a chaotic, thick still-life that was not quite still. The pressure cooker, presumably with lentils inside, was on the hob emitting dying staccato whistles, the fire underneath it turned off. On a stainless-steel plate, the bombil were lying dusted in salt and turmeric. On another plate, the giant, flaky pat of a flame-charred aubergine rested. The work-top between the cooker and the sink was entirely covered with onion skins, vegetable peelings, wilted coriander stalks, garlic husks, sprinklings of flour, a careless scattering of green chillies, a disfigured finger of ginger. In a big steel mixing-bowl sat a lump of kneaded dough. In another small container there was rice soaking under a couple of inches of water. I could barely find space on a surface to rest our glasses and pour whisky and cubes of ice into each.

'The kitchen is a mess,' I said, handing Baba his drink.

'Don't worry, she'll clean it all up before she leaves,' Ma said.

'Tell me now about why she can't stand Milly.'

Ma began, 'Renu is a difficult person, as you saw. She's very lippy—'

Baba interrupted us. 'I can't believe the two of you are sitting gossiping about servants,' he said with mild distaste.

Ma turned to me and said, almost in a whisper, 'Later'; she always conceded to my father.

I was in no mood to start an argument with Baba; we had clashed before on the subject of masters and servants several times and it would be ploughing the same arid furrow now. While swallowing the words I could have used to challenge him, a memory from my boyhood came back with sudden, sharp-edged clarity.

It was the year before we left Calcutta for Bombay and it must have been either during the school summer break or on a Thursday or Sunday, since I was at home during the day. It was the height of summer, June or July, around one in the afternoon, when the sun was at its most killing. The temperature must have been touching forty degrees, if not slightly above that, because the tar on the roads had gone all soft and yielding. Baba sent out our live-in maid, a girl called Nisha, who couldn't have been more than eleven or twelve years old, to get some batteries from the general store in the main market, which was about a fifteen-minute brisk walk from our home. In just over half an hour Nisha returned but with the wrong batteries. Baba shouted at her and sent her out again immediately. Nisha, crestfallen, made the trip a second time. This time it took her slightly longer than half an hour.

'Wrong batteries, again,' Baba roared and flung the packet at the wall. Nisha cowered. Her face looked shrivelled. My mother appeared but she looked timid too.

'Do you have nothing in your head?' Baba raged at the girl. 'I told you to ask for the small red ones, not the big ones. Small, SMALL, do you get it?'

My heart was rattling in my ribcage.

Ma said, 'Why don't you write it down for her? She can show the chit to the shopkeeper.'

'But the shopkeeper can't read,' Baba said. He turned to Nisha and barked, 'Go now. Ask for the small red batteries. Small ones. Go, go!'

I could see her chin quivering but she fled. How could she, or any of her kind, have answered back? She was making the trip a third time in this temperature, which felt like it could turn a human into vapour within minutes, and she hadn't had the chance to sit down to rest a bit and cool off and have a drink before she was dispatched again. I ran to the front veranda to see her tiny figure; it was running instead of walking, getting smaller and smaller as it reached the end of our long residential back street and turned the corner. There wasn't a single human around in this heat, not even a stray dog or cat or the ubiquitous crows. The houses stood dreaming, utterly still, heavy with shadows on one side, flayed by burning light on the other. I was baffled by why she was running; wouldn't walking be cooler, safer?

When she returned, it was with the wrong batteries again. Baba took one look at them, gave out a sound between a snarl and a groan, scrunched up his face and bared his teeth, an expression halfway between feral and despairing. He tried to utter some words but they didn't emerge. Ma, who looked stricken, interposed herself physically between Baba and Nisha.

Nisha's mouth twisted and opened; she could no longer check her tears. There was no restraint to it – she sobbed and hiccuped as she cried. Her knees bent and I couldn't tell if she wanted to sit down and cry because it would be easier, or if she wanted to fall to my mother's or my father's feet and beg to be excused from being sent out again. I could hear my own blood pumping away furiously. Perhaps I had even begun to tremble. All I could think of was how the girl had had to run around without any food or water, for it must have been a long while since her breakfast and it was well past lunchtime. She was ripe for a heatstroke.

Then I noticed her feet. There were tiny black stone-chips, of the sort that were used to create the surface of roads, sticking to her soles in small clusters, and singly, here and there, an archipelago in an atlas. It all fell into place: she had taken off her slippers because they kept getting stuck to the road, made slightly gooey in this heat, impeding her journey to and back from the shop; but the road was too hot for her bare feet, so she had been obliged to run in order not to get blistered. The tar, beginning to melt, had had an adhesive effect on the area of contact between the skin of her soles and the stone-chips, some of which had come loose and got stuck to her feet.

A switch tripped: with all the cold fury that I could summon to my voice, I turned to my father and said, 'Aren't you ashamed to send this little girl out in this heat so many times? She has been running from pillar to post without so much as a sip of water … And you, a big, able, pampered man, standing here, giving orders to a slip of a thing …'

I rolled my fist into a tight ball and brought it up, as if to punch him. My mother screamed.

That was a turning point, and both my parents and I knew it. Something in the very air between us had been cleaved and it was going to make its presence felt every time the subject of domestic servants came up.

Later I found out that my parents had been baffled, more than anything else, by the side I had chosen to take: I had, inexplicably to them, crossed over to the wrong side of the 'us versus them' equation. Years later, in a similar situation, my father had taunted me, 'Turned out to be quite a Gandhi type, haven't you? All that expensive education I'm paying for is teaching you all kinds of fancy posturing.' It had made my blood boil then; it still had the power to bring it to a low simmer if I dwelt on it for any length.

Baba's comment on gossiping about servants animated that memory, but now was not the time to make the three of us acknowledge its presence, not one day into my month-long visit here, so I tinkled the ice against my glass as Baba went to change into his home clothes and Ma and I sat making inconsequential chit-chat. I was a world away from them, yet I could choose – and I did choose, for most of the time – to let this temporary suspension of my London life feel cosy and cocooning, as if I had escaped back to the age of irresponsibility.

Cooking-aunty returned and went straight into the kitchen. In an hour's time, she put the food, in covered bowls and serving dishes, on to the dining table, set out plates and cutlery, said, improbably, 'Bye' in English to no one in particular while standing at the front door, then was gone.

'She never says "Bye". What's got into her?' Baba said; Baba, who normally never paid attention to domestic staff, or engaged in any way with them apart from paying their salaries.

'Maybe she's thrilled to have a shaheb in the house and to cook for him,' Ma joked.

I went to the kitchen to pour us another drink. It was spotless.

The conversation meandered in a pleasant, aimless way, touching on mildly interesting things that were neither urgent nor terribly serious. It was all very agreeable, although I think both my mother and I were mindful of steering away from the topic of 'the minutiae of servants' lives', as my father would put it, certainly in his presence. But my curiosity had been piqued and I wanted to ask her to tell me a little bit more about Renu; she seemed so determinedly truculent, something so out of character for a cook that I wanted to will into being events and causes more profound than the simple explanation of personality.

Beyond my mother cryptically saying 'Jealousy' to my question of 'Why can't Renu stand Milly?', we didn't get much further on the topic. The food was simple and textbook-perfect. The grammatical error in spicing, as it were, that my mother found so offensive in cooking-aunty's food, and that she thought she was prone to, was nowhere to be tasted: the green papaya and prawns had been spiced with cumin and bay leaves, with garam masala and ghee added right at the end; the aubergines were a mushy tomatoey medley, with caramelised onions and ginger and sparkling with raw fresh coriander and green chillies. It was as if Renu was countering, successfully, an accusation that had been silently – and not so silently – levelled at her and under whose yoke she laboured in my parents' home.

'Everything is exactly as it should be,' I said to my mother. 'Why did you say she has no clue about the rules of traditional spicing?'

Ma grimaced and said, 'Yes, she hasn't messed this up, but you wait and watch. It all depends on her moods.' Then she repeated, 'It's because you are here.'

An idea was slowly taking on edges and shape in my head. I wanted to sound it out with my mother. She knew about my current project, the regional Indian cookbook. In a way, she had seeded this project in me: years ago, she had sent me one of a series that Penguin published – *The Calcutta Cookbook*. It was atrociously printed and organised, the index was a hot mess; clearly the people behind the book had no idea how to go about producing a cookbook. But that series – an Assam cookbook, a Goa cookbook, a Parsi cookbook, and so on – was an inspired idea, if woefully executed and commissioned, with some gems lurking here and there. *The Calcutta Cookbook*, for example, had any number of brilliant recipes, among them things I had always heard talked about, but had never eaten, such as a beetroot-and-egg dish, khagina, and a toasted moong dal with mango ginger. Amazingly, it featured the street food-stall favourite of the '80s, chow mein. Indians have always known that there is nothing called Indian food, only different, sometimes wildly and thrillingly different, regional cuisines. This is a fact that has been flattened out in the West. Wouldn't it be worthwhile, if only for the makers of my book, to produce something that amounted to a manageable guided tour around these regional cuisines?

So, prompted by that thought, I asked Ma, 'Do you think she'll be able to give us recipes from ... from her part of Bengal?' I had no idea where this was.

My mother snorted with open contempt. 'What do you want Medinipur recipes for? What special things do they have, anyway? Why not go for a selection of general Bengali food? I can give you those recipes.'

I knew her ego had been slightly dented – why should her son ask this upstart cook for authentic Bengali recipes when she herself could give me any number of them, and better ones? – but she was entirely justified in her point. It was enough to give readers an idea of the differences between the different Indian states without having to get into the micro-details of intra-state district divisions. It was a cookbook after all, maybe even a coffee-table item, not a history-and-sociology book.

Over the next few days I mulled over the idea, called various friends who were well placed to help me with the book or had friends in the states that I would be visiting for research. I lazed around at home, read, wasted time online, depleted my father's fine and seemingly inexhaustible collection of single malts and, above all, ate some food that Ankita would surely have called 'life-changing' or, literally translated from the Bengali, 'life-turning'.

Milly came in around noon and on one occasion, when my mother was out somewhere, I gave her lunch, arranging all the dishes on a plate and telling her what each was. They were all leftovers from the night before, or even two nights previously, and Renu had done a fine job. In my rusty Hindi, I struggled to find the correct words for spices or vegetables whose names I had only ever known in Bengali and English and had to ask Milly once or twice if I was right or wrong. It was painful to watch her seized up with shyness or inhibition or whatever it was, so I quickly exited the kitchen, resolving never again to talk her through the dishes in future.

One day, as Milly was eating her lunch in the kitchen, the doorbell rang. I opened the door; it was Renu, with a plastic bag of vegetables and greens. She had already done her morning schedule and wasn't due to come in again until the evening. Before I could say 'Come in', she launched into an explanation of her untimely appearance.

'Tonight's vegetables,' she said. 'No green bananas, coriander, curry leaves, chillies, pumpkin in the pheeej . . . so I thought I would get some because I was going that way' – indicating the vegetable market – 'and it would save you having to go out.'

She had taken off her slippers outside the threshold.

'I'll put them away, don't worry,' she said and ran into the kitchen. I heard the sound of the fridge door being opened, vegetable trays being brought out and pushed back in, the scrunching of plastic bags, but not a single word between Renu and Milly. Then Renu came out and left the flat in one swift movement like a puff of wind. She didn't look back at me sitting in the living room, didn't say 'Bye' or 'I'll be back in the evening', just pulled the door shut from the outside and left.

She came back at half-past six to cook dinner. I had got into the swing of things by now, so I was ready with the menu – cabbage thoran, a Tamil pumpkin dish with tamarind and mustard paste, chicken chettinad – and with the recipes for two of the dishes she had never cooked before, the pumpkin and the chicken. Surliness I had come to expect from her, but not the degree of borderline rudeness that was on show that evening. She didn't look at me once, spoke minimally (and when she did, it was with extreme curtness) and snapped at me, twice, when I paused in the reading out of the recipes because I could see that she was doing three different things at the same time – taking out the vegetables from the fridge, putting the cut-up chicken in the sink to wash, taking out the cooking pans and wok from a cupboard – and would perhaps have preferred me to read them to her when she had a minute to pay attention.

'Arrey, read, read, I don't have all the time in the world,' she said.

'I was waiting for you to listen. So many instructions at once, you may forget what goes in when—'

She cut me short with a very Bengali expression of contempt – 'Arrey, dhur' – then repeated, 'Read, read. I'll remember.'

I was taken aback. With any other person I would have asked for the reason behind the edgy tone, or taken mild offence, but the difference in our social and class standing prevented me from doing either. How on earth did echt-Indian people, who had no notion of taking lip from people they considered their inferiors, react to her? Or did she let herself go only at my parents' home because my mother didn't indulge in the hallowed Indian practice of shouting at servants, certainly not in my presence? I read out the two recipes, one after the other, decided against asking, 'Will you remember?' or adding, 'Do ask me again if you need reminding', and went to the living room.

I caught my mother's eyes, raised my eyebrows and said in English, under my voice, 'Bad temper today. Best avoided.'

Ma, also switching to English, asked, 'What happened?' She had clearly not heard the brief exchange; besides, there wasn't much to hear – it was mostly in the realm of tone and attitude and facial expression. 'Shall I say something to her?'

'No,' I said firmly. 'Absolutely not. She's just in one of her moods this evening.'

'We're getting a bit tired of her moods. Sometimes she can be completely out of order.'

The conversation could potentially lead to a minefield, the 'correct' way for servants to behave, so I hastily and energetically tried to steer both of us away from the subject. It worked or, rather, Ma thought better of it, and I was relieved that we had avoided unpleasantness. Or so I thought; because sitting down later that evening to eat the food Renu had cooked brought everything back with renewed vigour.

Every single dish she had cooked was wrong. She had committed the cardinal sin, in my mother's books: adding hing to the thoran. The pumpkin tasted of nothing, despite containing two of the most powerful ingredients in Indian cuisine, tamarind and fresh mustard paste. At first I couldn't put my finger on what the chicken was lacking – it wasn't bad; it just wasn't the dish it was supposed to be – then I realised that she had left out the aromatics, cardamom, cloves and cinnamon, that were supposed to be fried in hot oil right at the beginning. It was clear to me that she had not been able to retain – as who would? – the long list of ingredients for not one but two dishes, and the subsequent processes for each, slightly involved and complicated in the case of the chettinad chicken, that I had read out only once.

My father was indifferent, but my mother was incensed and jubilant at the same time: here was evidence for her point about Renu being a hit-and-miss cook who didn't really have a proper understanding of the fundamental grammar and syntax of cooking. I felt nervous that we were again going to embark on the business of servant-bashing; such excruciatingly uncomfortable territory. Ma complained at length and my discomfort grew, to the extent that I found myself feeling slightly protective of cooking-aunty and defending her.

'Hing is not an entirely unintuitive addition to thoran, don't you think?' I pleaded. 'If there are already mustard seeds, curry leaves and coconut, hing seems to be naturally a part of that.'

Ma remained unconvinced. Baba, to his credit, added, 'The chicken is actually lovely. I don't know what it's supposed to be like in its perfect incarnation but this is great.'

I wanted to lean over and give him a hug, which was a complete no-no in my family and would probably be seen as a frivolous Western affectation.

Ma made a face but didn't counter this. Instead, she said, 'This is what we have to put up with, these moods. At first I thought: you put up with the kicks of the cow that gives you milk; but recently things seem to have worsened.'

Something clicked inside my head. 'She saw Milly here today, when she came in to drop off the vegetables,' I said.

'Aha. That must have set her off,' Ma said.

'But I don't understand why,' I said, genuinely baffled. 'You say it's jealousy, but jealousy about what?' While feeling nervous about edging close to this fraught subject, I was inwardly preparing myself to stare my father out on this one; I was too curious to let it pass.

'I can't quite tell the reason,' Ma said. 'Maybe something happened we don't know about – they both live in the same slum, after all. Or it could be that Milly has a husband, two children ... I can see how that would eat into Renu.'

'Doesn't she have children?' I asked.

'I think she has a daughter but doesn't have much to do with her.'

'What do you mean you "think"? You either know or you don't.'

'I dimly remember her saying something to me a while ago. I don't remember her exact words but I got the impression that she was married off early, she had a daughter, the husband perhaps used to beat her, which is why she left. I don't remember if she abandoned the daughter too when she left.'

'This was in Medinipur?' I was fascinated.

'Yes. I don't know which village.'

'Do you think I could ask her?'

Ma looked panicked. 'No, no, no need to do that. No need to upset her further.'

Baba said, 'Here we go again' and got up from the table.

'Please, don't go asking things to her,' Ma said again. 'No need to raise her to our heads, she'll take even more liberties with her behaviour and think we're giving her some kind of licence. Best not to become informal with servants, one must always maintain a distance with them.'

Rocks ahoy, I thought, and willed myself not to react; she did not mean it to be a bait.

The next morning Renu was back and I decided not to engage her in conversation. Usually I would compliment her on the previous night's cooking – she never responded, but I felt that she was secretly pleased to be praised – but today I withheld any such comment. Instead, I went out to have my first look at the slum.

I crossed the road and walked down the three steps to the paved area that marked one end of the promenade. Where the paving ended, the black rocks and sea began. There was a narrow path along one end, clinging to the last of the tyre shops and tea-sellers and snack stores, on what I only now noticed was a raised wall against which the sea lapped. The path curved around behind what I saw from my parents' living-room window as shops, trees, a tiny playing field, all bordered by this wall, which obstructed the view of the path running along it. I was on it now. It was so narrow that if two people could walk abreast on it, the one nearer the sea would be in constant danger of falling in. The water was barely inches below the lip of the wall. The path was muddy, with footprint-shaped puddles here and there. Was it submerged during high tide? I had a view of the slum spread out in front of me, on my left. It looked like the back of a huge black beast in camouflage, huddling low, perhaps dormant, lying pressed against the sea at two ends, its surface feathered with plastic on the roofs, mostly black, with an occasional flash of blue. When the breeze lifted, it seemed the beast's feathers were being ruffled. I pressed myself flat against what I assumed were back walls of houses to allow people behind me to pass. I followed them, with some misgiving, self-conscious about how I clearly stood out as an outsider. To my great relief, people noticed me but not in any egregious way; they didn't stare, or make comments, or even look curious or interested.

I realised that this outer path ringed around the sea-side perimeter of the slum and that even narrower alleys led off it into the interior. I took one of them. There were rooms packed on either side. I felt that if I stretched out both my arms, wingspan-style, the tips of my fingers could just about touch their exterior. Room after room after room, then another alley, easily missed because of its narrowness and the density of the living quarters. In fact you had to look hard to distinguish any passage at all threading through the houses, since it was often a practice rather than a physical thing; people made their way through the narrowest of spaces along the front, sides, backs of houses; a path was whatever people decided to tread. There were people walking, sitting, standing, doing nothing in particular, moving in and out of rooms. The interiors were so dark that I could barely make out anything, maybe a corner of a pallet, or just an expanse of floor, a section of a plastic chair. A woman was fanning a burning oven outside her front door in an effort to get the wood to catch. A small group of children ran around aimlessly; maybe they were playing a game. There was a motorbike parked outside one of the houses. How did they ever get it in here? People were now looking at me. My discomfort escalated and it was not only because of the stares. Edicts from a middle-class upbringing on looking into other people's lives through their open doors and windows combined with a liberal sensitivity, acquired later in life, about treating the poor as anthropological fieldwork or a tourist attraction, to produce a mixture of dread, guilt and self-loathing. I turned tail.

The question that most occupied me afterwards was whether each of those rooms was the entire house and home of one family.

Of course, I didn't tell cooking-aunty that I had seen the slum where she lived. I felt mildly depressed for the rest of the morning and when she came out of the kitchen to ask what we were planning to have for dinner, I gave a straight answer – chicken stir-fried with basil and nam pla, dry green beans with pork mince, garlic, nam pla and chillies – instead of the 'Why, I thought you needed to be told, just once, and just before you started!', which I could have delivered with a big grin to normalise the situation, at least to myself. I asked her if she was familiar with nam pla – she called it 'nampa' – and she gave a surprising answer: 'Yes, I cook with it in that house all the time. They eat a lot of this kind of food.'

'What house?' I asked.

'Oh, one of the houses I cook for over there.' She lifted her hand above her head and pointed behind her in a vague gesture that also managed to be typically dismissive.

That evening, I took her through the process, brief and very simple, of cooking the two dishes. Half an hour later, she slid the kitchen door open, peered out and said, 'I can't find the nampa.'

'Have you looked carefully?' Ma asked. 'It's in that cupboard to the right of where the glasses are kept. You know it.'

'Yes, I put it there myself. It arrived two days ago, I remember. You showed it to me.'

'Do you remember what it looks like?'

'Oi to, a small bottle, black cap.'

'Are you sure it's not there? Let me have a look.'

Ma got up and went to the kitchen. She came out after a few minutes. 'I can't find it. I looked everywhere it could be.'

'It can't have gone running away,' I said. 'Let me have a look.'

In the kitchen, I opened every drawer, every cupboard, looked in the overcrowded fridge, taking out every prehistoric jar of mustard, olives, kasundi, oyster sauce, marmalade, pickle from the door. It seemed that the Law of the Fridge was universal across cultures and continents: things went there to die slowly and be forgotten. But no; no nam pla in the fridge, although an unopened bottle wouldn't have been put there in the first place. I asked the usual questions – who put away the shopping that day, was there a sort of unspoken rule about which things went where (of course there was) – and got predictable answers. I looked inside the cupboards below the worktop, the spaces where flour and potatoes and onions were stored, and in the space for the blender, spice-grinder and rolling pin, even in the cupboard for plastic bags and the drawers for Tupperware. Nothing.

All four of us were now caught up in the search. Even Baba gave suggestions – have you looked here, or there, or what about that spot … For half an hour we were entirely consumed by finding a bottle of fish sauce; absurd and bathetic.

We gave up. I was left alone in the kitchen with cooking-aunty. I could see that everything for cooking the dishes had been prepared – the chicken diced, the garlic and chillies finely chopped, the beans cut into short lengths, the pork mince defrosted. I was contemplating whether to take an auto, go to the shop next to

Mehboob Studios and get a new bottle, when Renu said, 'That person took it, I know.'

'Who?' I had no idea what she was talking about.

'Oi je, the one who comes to clean.' The words were accompanied by that indicating-dismissing gesture of her hands that I was beginning to get familiar with.

It took a few beats to sink in. 'Milly? But why on earth would she do that?' I was genuinely nonplussed.

'I'm telling you,' she insisted.

'But why?'

'Because she's like that.'

'Like what?' I was annoyed. I wasn't going to let this go.

'I'm telling you,' she repeated.

'And I'm asking you what use she would have with it? Do you know if she's going to use it to cook? Why take something like that?'

'No, not to cook. She took it just like that. She'll look at it, show it to people. She's like that, I'm telling you.'

I said, 'I don't think so', trying not to let my anger inflect my words, tone or expression in any way. 'This does not sound convincing to me.'

'I'm telling you—' she began again, but I cut her short.

'Use soya sauce instead,' I said curtly and left the kitchen.

In the living room my mother asked if we had found it. I said no, put a firm lid on what was bothering me and proceeded with the usual chit-chat and drinking. I didn't want to talk about it in front of my father at all, so I waited until we had finished eating and he had gone to bed, then asked Ma to come to my room.

'Listen,' I said, 'Renu thinks Milly stole the nam pla. I was a bit flabbergasted. I don't believe her at all but I can't work out what's going on.'

Ma was baffled too. 'She said that to you? Did you ask her why she thought so? I mean, what an odd thing to steal.'

'Or: what an odd thing to accuse someone of stealing.'

'Yes, yes, that's what I meant.'

'What's going on, do you think?' I asked.

'I have no idea. Unless she dislikes Milly so much that she's trying to sow seeds of suspicion ...'

'So it could be possible that Renu hid the nam pla in order to blame Milly?'

Ma was nodding her head slowly as she fit the pieces together. 'My god, how low of her. She was accused of stealing in an earlier job, so she is using that now against someone else ... It's all beginning to make sense.'

'What do you mean: stealing in an earlier job? What job? Stealing what? Why didn't you tell me before?'

'Again, this is something I heard, I don't remember from whom. Or I pieced it together. Or maybe when Renu told me that she used to cook for the ONGC homes near Reclamation – you've seen those ugly buildings many, many times, I'm sure – and that they fired her, I made up the bit about false charges of stealing.'

'What false charges of stealing? Did you just pluck it out of the air?' My confusion was increasing rapidly.

'I think she was accused of stealing and was thrown out of one of those homes where she used to cook. But she's very trustworthy. I have left money and jewellery unlocked in the house several times while she has been here on her own. She has even had the keys to the flat, when we were out of the city. I would trust her with everything. I'm certain that those charges of stealing were trumped-up ... You know how it is here: anything goes missing, the first person the blame falls on is the servant, who may well be innocent.'

Oh yes, I knew all about that. I remember watching, when I was a child in Calcutta, one such servant, accused of stealing money and jewellery from the family for whom he worked, being beaten in public as a way of extracting a confession. I had run to join the watching throng. It wasn't only the men of the accusing family who had a go at him; neighbours, residents of the street, distant friends, even strangers joined in. News that a thief had been caught and was being beaten brought a huge crowd to watch the entertainment; the punishments got more extreme, more cruel. At one point I remember someone lifting him by his ankles and swinging him around in a circle, his head so close, during each revolution, to a pile of jagged, broken bricks that it repeatedly hit that mound, tearing open his forehead and the back of his head. He shrieked every time the collision happened, and I saw blood on his face.

I could no longer recall what I felt as a child witnessing this: thrill? Sympathy? Pity? Outrage? The man was howling, 'Babu, I didn't steal anything, I swear on my children's lives, I haven't touched a thing, please let me go, I beg you, please.' What I did remember very clearly was my mother turning up and saying to the family in question that she had come to protest against their barbaric behaviour. And I remembered the reaction: the woman leading the accusation and chivvying on the beating and the cheerleading had rounded on Ma, jeered at her and said, 'If you had had your own stuff stolen, would you have come here to preach? Keep your high-mindedness to yourself.' Then she had turned round and tried to do some rabble-rousing against my mother. Ma had caught hold of my hand and dragged me away. I could still hear the vulgar Bengali equivalents of the taunts 'Goody-two-shoes', 'Holier-than-thou', which were thrown at our retreating backs.

I briefly toyed with the idea of first finding out in which flats in the ONGC buildings cooking-aunty had worked, then enquiring about the episode at each of them, but gave up on the idea as a foolish one.

The following evening, halfway through her cooking, Renu poked her head out of the kitchen and announced, 'The nampa bottle is back.'

My mother looked at the floor; I got up to go to the kitchen, largely to avoid meeting Ma's eyes.

Renu pounced the moment I entered: 'See, I told you, she's brought it back, I told you, she took it, did her thing with it and now she's returned it. I told you.'

That high-pitched voice, grating my nerves raw; I felt the pop of an ache beginning behind my right eye. I didn't know what to say. The bottle stood on the counter. It was unopened.

I forced myself to ask, 'Where did you find it?'

'In the cupboard, where it was supposed to be. She brought it back this morning, when she came to clean, and slipped it in there. I know how she works.'

I had had no reason to open that particular cupboard all day, so I couldn't disprove her. Besides, my embarrassment was so acute that I made some kind of non-committal sound and left the kitchen.

The food at dinner that evening was perfect.

In my remaining couple of weeks in Bombay, I increasingly engaged Renu in conversation; in the mornings, especially, because often my parents would be out, but also in the interstices of giving her instructions in the evenings.

'Find a job for me in your country,' she would say, only half-joking.

I would say, 'There are no private cooks where I live. Only restaurants have cooks.'

'How do you eat, if you don't have someone to cook?'

'We make our own food.'

'Huh, how is that possible?'

'We learn how to cook. Everyone there knows how to cook at least a few things. Then there are shops where you can buy ready-made meals. You bring them home and heat them up.'

That silenced her. Then she came back with a shy question: 'They are as good as aunt's' – referring to herself, of course – 'cooking?'

I didn't answer this point. Instead I said, 'Besides, where will you live?'

'Why, don't you have room in your place?'

The thought of explaining immigration, labour, living, houses, wages, class occurred to me for an instant; I felt defeated almost immediately.

She got in through that tiny gap: 'I can sleep in the kitchen.'

Before I could find a white lie in lieu of an explanation, something emollient, I burst out with 'That's not possible.' Ashamed, I retreated to the living room, worrying that I had hurt her feelings.

Another time: 'Will you take a dal tonight?'

I said, 'No, no need, there's a lot of food already, I don't want to upset my stomach.'

'I am your aunt, this aunt's food will never cause an upset stomach.'

Over those weeks, she told me she came from Medinipur, from a family of rice farmers. They owned the land they cultivated, so they were not poor, or certainly not the kind of poor one associated with the term 'Indian farmer'.

'You go visit my village one day?' she asked.

I made polite noises. She told me about her brothers and widowed mother, how the land had been divided among the three children after their father died. Her brothers cultivated it now.

'Did you not get your share of the land?' I asked.

'Yes, I did, but I sold it to my brothers. How could I cultivate it myself?'

'You didn't marry?'

Her face shut down. 'Oh, a long time ago.' The dismissive gesture again, without any of its usual complements. 'I've kept a bit of land to build my house after I stop working and leave Bombay.'

'Great. You know when? And you'll go back to your village? Why not stay in the city?'

'Naaaah, this is not our country. I'll go back when I have saved enough money to build a house. My own house.'

So she had savings. I didn't know why it surprised – and gladdened – me. I had no idea what her outgoings were, but if she worked in six homes, earning anything between four to six thousand rupees a month at each, her income wasn't insubstantial. Was that why she lived in a slum, so that she was saved from the lion's share of her earnings being devoured in Bombay rent, one of the steepest in the world? I found myself strangely invested in this aspect of her life, willing her to work longer, in more homes, to live frugally, so that she could save more, to the extent that I caught myself clenching my fists and my jaws, imagining a speeding up of her efforts and a commensurate escalation of the figure in her bank account. And I thought about what it must be for her to experience the kind of working life that she had, every day the same, yet each slightly different, all her actions repetitive, yet sometimes with a minuscule possibility of uniqueness.

'You go there and see my old house and the land where I want to build my new home,' she said in a tone of warm, easy familiarity, even intimacy.

Often, when she came in the morning to cook breakfast and lunch, I would ask her to cook lunch for exactly two, Ma and Baba, since the fridge was groaning with leftovers. I loved leftovers and I could happily eat them for lunch every day, but Baba wanted to take something freshly cooked every morning to work, something simple such as rice, a vegetable dish and some fish. Ma, too, I think, liked something different from what she had the previous night, although she was slightly nervous about confessing this to me. Renu, naturally enough, often cooked enough to serve between four to six people, since that was easier to do than cook for one. The outcome was such a surfeit of cooked food at home that we all struggled. But Ma explained, 'Eat what you want, no need to feel the pressure to finish everything. We can always give it to Milly.

She is always happy with the season of plenty that happens when you visit, I can tell. And she can also take the excess food for her children.'

One such morning, around eleven, when it was time for Renu to leave after her stint, she came out to the living room and said to me (Ma was out), 'The fridge is full of food. Why aren't you eating anything? You must eat up the stuff in there, otherwise it'll spoil, then I'll be scolded by your mother.' Her tone was playfully chiding; taking some liberties and sailing riskily quite close to a few unbreachable boundaries of class; it was a measure of how easy she felt with me, and how fond she had become. We still addressed each other using the most respectful form of 'you'.

'Why don't you take some of it with you? Honestly. There's so much . . . I can put it in tiffin boxes for you,' I said.

'Naaah, I don't need it, I eat only one meal a day, rice and boiled vegetables. I have no use for all that.'

Here was my opening to ask about her living arrangements. But before I could open my mouth, she had achieved a complete tonal shift: 'I know everything, you give it to that person.' (It took me a while to work out who she was referring to, since third-person pronouns are not gendered in Bengali.) 'I caught the person in the kitchen the other day,' she said, 'eating the food that I cook. I cook it with my sweat and with love – and you give it to her? I felt my whole body sizzle when I saw her. How dare she?'

She had suddenly become like a storm confined in a room. Her ugly voice had ratcheted up in pitch and volume. 'She knows her moves – the way she worked her way into your mother's life . . . Why is your mother so fond of her? That woman must have done some witchy thing, some kind of spell. She's exactly that kind. She leaves her children at home and goes out every day, what kind of woman does that? Her husband works, why does she need to?'

'Enough,' I cried. Perhaps I hadn't said it loudly, or urgently, enough – she showed no sign of abating but her tone changed from angry to pleading.

'You come back home from foreign. Your parents' lives are empty without you. I know, I see them every day. Before you arrive, they only talk about you. "Renu, my son is coming, he likes to eat this, he likes to eat that, you have to cook well every day," your mother says. Your father goes and gets all this fish – they don't eat so many kinds themselves when you're not here. I know what it is to have the jewel of your eye live in foreign. My brother's son, he lives in a far-away country. You come back, it's not good for you to be away from your parents. They're getting old. You're a young man, we'll find a good girl for you, you marry and have children, your parents will live the rest of their days in happiness. I say that to my Dulal as well, but who listens to me?'

By the time she reached the end, that slightly forced tone of jauntiness had come back. It was her insurance, should she have found herself accused of stepping out of line in her conversations with people above her station. Whether, this time, the return of the tone was the result of her awareness that she had allowed herself to take liberties, I couldn't tell.

I returned to India a year later.

The book had changed personality during work on it in London in the interim: it was no longer centred on breakfasts; its full title, *Real Indian Food: Recipes from Homes Across India*, gave an accurate idea of its nature and contents. The idea still was that the recipes should be reproducible outside India without making the cook or the browsing reader nervous about recherché ingredients and labour-intensive processes, and, for a completely different kind of reader and cook, without making anything appear watered-down, inauthentic, giving cause for the bitter *ressentiment* crowd to wield that age-old stick used to beat Indians who resided abroad – 'tailoring things for Western tastes and sensibilities'.

The time for my annual visit to my parents came round. I had already decided that I would travel to four or five different cities and towns, meeting up and staying with people, getting recipes from them and, most importantly, eating their food. My editor joked that I was following in the footsteps of Matthew Fort's *Eating Up Italy*; I had to be mindful of making our book different.

It was inevitable that Calcutta should be the first city on the itinerary. I stayed at my uncles' home in Shyambazar. It was a huge three-storey house: each of my two uncles had an entire floor to himself and his family, while the ground floor was rented out. The cook, whom I've always known as Thakur, the generic Bengali term for a cook, because everybody called him that, was still in charge of the food, as he was before my father left for Bombay with my mother and me. I didn't visit my uncles in Calcutta often; in fact, I had been back only about five or six times since I left for England. This gave rise to a lot of affectionate passive-aggressive banter ('Now that you live in London, you don't deign to visit your poor relatives', etc.), which I used to find enervating but had learned, over time, to negotiate light-heartedly. What made it all worth it was Thakur's cooking, despite the food torture that goes in the name of hospitality in Bengali homes. (My mother resented the fact that Thakur didn't accompany us to Bombay as our family cook, choosing to stay on with her brothers instead. In a way, she was forever looking to find a Thakur whom she could install permanently in her life. Everyone would always fall short of his standards; Renu had lost even before she had joined.)

Thakur surpassed himself again; I felt he did exactly this every time I visited. The food wasn't dressy; far from it. Things just seemed to come together alchemically in his hands, the final thing far greater than the sum of its parts. Rice-flour pancakes, delicate as muslin handkerchiefs, served with coriander chutney for breakfast;

a simple lunchtime dish of potatoes, prawns and spring onions; a teatime snack of very quickly deep-fried flattened rice, served with fried green peas and chillies on the side – it was difficult not to talk about these things using suspicious words such as 'magic'. If I were to get the recipes from him and pass them on to Renu in Bombay, would she have been able to get them right? No doubt she could have replicated them, perhaps even exactly, but that surplus Bengalis called 'hand', would be missing – by the very fact that she wasn't Thakur meant that his food cooked by her wouldn't have his 'hand's' touch.

I spoke to Ma every evening on the phone and one evening, while I was giving her news of her brothers and sisters-in-law and nephews and nieces, besides of course a detailed account of what we were being served at breakfast, lunch, tea and dinner – 'four meals a day' was a Bengali idiom – I heard someone talking in the background and Ma responding, 'Achha, enough, you go to the kitchen now.'

'What's going on?' I asked.

'Ufff, Renu. She's saying that you must go visit her home in Medinipur. I mean, *really.*'

Why not? I thought. 'All right. Why don't you ask her to call her brother and let him know? We can work out a date.' It was instinctive, not thought through, but suddenly seemed like an interesting idea.

Ma was first incredulous, then aghast. 'Are you out of your mind? What will you do there?'

'Why? I'm here on holiday, sort of, and it'll give me a glimpse of small-town India. It'll be interesting, no?'

'But there's nothing to see in Medinipur!'

I failed to convince Ma that my visit was going to be a different kind of tourism, not about pretty or famous sights.

'But it's not going to be comfortable,' she wailed. 'Where are you going to stay?'

'Why, in cooking-aunty's home?'

I knew what was bothering her – the traversal of class boundaries, the queasiness that derived from the dissolution of certain
impermeable, separating membranes that the intimacy of the
son of a master going to stay in the home of a servant entailed. It
brought out the rebellious teenager in me; I pushed back.

Two days later, the driver who worked for my uncles, Jishnu-da,
was taking me to Garhbheta, where we were going to be met by
Shankar, one of Renu's nephews, at a locally well-known sweet shop,
Mouchak, and he would direct Jishnu-da to the village, Putihari.

After the hell of driving through Haora district and the squalid
small towns of Medinipur, things felt less dirty, less squashed in and
claustrophobic, the more we got away from human settlements.
The road began to cut through large stretches of countryside with
nothing, for considerable intervals, to mar it. We had to get out at
a point about five or six kilometres from the village; Shankar said
the narrow road was not fit for cars; he had organised people to
carry my luggage. I only had a small backpack; I didn't need any
help at all, but Shankar was adamant. I knew I had to put up with
this intense servility that passed as hospitable behaviour; the guest
was a god in Bengali culture. I still hadn't got over the moment
when the car stopped to pick up Shankar and he fell at my feet to
do pranam.

Jishnu-da was going to return the following day to take me back
to Calcutta. The car, conspicuous in a place like this, had brought
out people, mostly men and children, who stood gawping with
undisguised curiosity. Some of the bolder children came forward
and gathered close to the car, looking up at me unblinkingly. An
old man at the door of a one-storey brick house about twenty feet
from where we were parked called out to Shankar and said something that I couldn't catch. Shankar said, 'Na, na, pishi's people, he
has come from Calcutta. He lives in London.'

'Dulal's friend?' the man asked.

'Arrey, na, na. I said, he's from London.'

'That's very far away. Ask him if he has come by ship or plane.'

I was desperately trying not to look at Shankar's face. The boy – he couldn't have been more than twelve – whom he had asked to carry my bag was sent ahead of us with my backpack. I fixed what I thought was a blandly pleasant and interested look on my face and followed Shankar. I could hear the boys behind us getting a bit manic. One of them broke into completely unintelligible chatter in a non-language, which I later understood was his attempt, maybe, to imitate English. Two of them started to sing a current Hindi film song that featured a phrase of English – 'Will you be my chammak-challo?' – but they sang the first four words as an aurally approximate gobbledygook. They kept saying 'hello' repeatedly and breaking into giggles. The word began to saw through my right temple, which had started throbbing.

Shankar must have read something in this because he turned to the boys and shooed them away. It took some tenacity; the boys retreated a bit, but carried on with their antics from a distance until they got bored of it and dispersed.

Putihari came as a pleasant green surprise: trees, bushes, creepers everywhere, neat courtyards with mud and thatched huts, ponds, banana flowers on trees, huge, spiky lumps of jackfruit low on the trunk, date palms, tall coconut and betel-nut trees, bamboo groves, and fields surrounding the village on all sides, dotted occasionally with a built structure, sometimes even brick houses, a lot of which looked either abandoned or half-finished. The winter sun was delicious. I saw bori drying in the sun, and some reddish-brown grain or seed set out on kulos in a courtyard flanked by flowering red hibiscus. The fields which had crops on them were the colour of golden sand in the sun. Other parcels of land looked waiting for something to be sown on them, or were dotted at regular intervals with what looked like tough hay-like stubble. Shankar kept up his patter, calling me 'sir', which I asked him not to do several times. Shankar had hardly any English but he insisted on dredging up a word here, a word there, and throwing them at me randomly: 'Flower', he would sing out, pointing to a tagar bush, 'Duck' when we passed a green pond, 'Hen' at a particularly showy rooster preening in the sun. He had clearly been to school, where he had had some rudimentary English lessons. I was still not making eye-contact with him.

Wherever we passed a home on the way, people came out to stare. Shankar pointed to a low L-shaped house of exposed brick and tin roof about twenty metres away and said, 'We're nearly there.' It stood on the edge of a vast rice field traversed by raised earth aals. The house had grown up piecemeal, concrete rooms added as and when resources had permitted. The earth courtyard was impeccably clean, with a border of flowers at one end, at the bottom of a low wall, and two trees on either side of the residential quarter, one a sour plum and another one I couldn't identify. The veranda in front had wooden pillars on which the roof-awning rested. A green parakeet in a cage hanging from a cross-beam eyed us sideways. There was a blue-painted tin gate, rust smudging it generously, where one of the arms of the L ended and the low wall began. Beyond it lay two squat, rectangular structures, unconnected to each other, it seemed, one with a tin roof and ventilation crosses towards the top of the wall, the other a thatched one. They seemed also to be separated from the main building by an empty stretch; what lay in it I couldn't see because my view was obstructed.

A whole reception committee was awaiting us; exactly what I had feared. Leading the charge was a dark man with greying hair and moustache, somewhere in his mid-fifties, I guessed. He was wiry but had a paunch. Another man was standing a few steps behind him; his younger brother, it was obvious. I assumed they were both Renu's brothers, although I couldn't discern any resemblances to her. Five children, three boys and two girls, of varying ages from six to twelve, I guessed, were standing in the courtyard, staring at us unblinkingly. A woman at the doorway quickly covered her head with her aanchol. Two men in their thirties or forties stood by a tree in the courtyard, one on either side of an empty plastic chair. The boy who had been sent ahead with our luggage, clearly the domestic help, came out of the house, looked at us and ran off.

The dark, wiry man came forward with his hands folded in pranam, head slightly bowed. 'Come, come,' he said (using the highest form of 'you', although I was nearly a quarter of a century younger), 'how kind of you to bring the dust of your feet into the hut of the poor ...', then, turning to the children, his tone changing, he barked, 'Ei, you lot, don't you see who is visiting, touch his feet immediately, he has come from London.' I retreated, lightning-quick, as if I had seen a snake approaching, almost shouting, 'No, no, no, absolutely no need, really, no, I forbid you, no, NO.' The children halted, looking at my face, then at the face of the man, in ping-pong manner.

The older man was Raja, his brother, Ratan; Renu was the middle sibling. The woman I saw when we came in was Ratan's wife, Mamoni. Raja's wife, Lakshmi, was inside, busy with chores in the kitchen. I was introduced to the women as 'my wife' or 'my sister-in-law'. I learned their names later when I heard their husbands call out to them.

We were taken to a dark room to be introduced to Raja and Ratan's mother, a frail woman who looked very old and clearly couldn't hear very much. Raja-da shouted, 'Ma, he's come from London.' His Bengali was accented, I had noted earlier, but not in the way Renu's was, which was slightly closer to pidgin, with the odd Hindi word here and there.

'No, I've come from Calcutta,' I said over my unease, adding a strained laugh to neutralise what could be construed as a corrective sting.

The woman could neither hear nor understand what was going on; her watery eyes were focused elsewhere. Even on this cool afternoon, I was sweating. As we were leaving the room, I heard her croak, 'Dulal, eli naki?', *Dulal, is that you?*

I had not paid much heed to Renu talking about Dulal being the apple of her eye, but his name had repeatedly come up in the last hour. I was so dreading the imminent discussion of sleeping arrangements, and the state of the toilet that we were about to be shown, that the question about Dulal got pushed to the background.

Raja-da said, 'You take some tea? Would you like to wash your hands and face first? Let me show you where the bathroom is.'

I followed him through the L. There were only three rooms, two of which were each occupied by a brother and his family; in fact, the room in which the old woman lay dying was shared by Raja, his wife and the two oldest children, a boy and a girl. The third room, in the corner where the two arms joined at right angles, was the size of a box, used for some purpose I couldn't identify – storage? A room in transition, about to be used as another bedroom? This was when I noticed that the floors were not concrete but compacted mud. Did I imagine the slight smell of cow-dung at that very moment of realisation? I didn't understand how rooms could be so bare and so cramped simultaneously: there were few possessions; the whitewash was peeling; a calendar from a shop in Garhbheta, Sri Bishwakarma Hard-Ware Co. & Sons, was hanging from a nail at an angle; a lizard had stationed itself on the top of the wall where it met the tin roof; a long, brown graph of a termite colony made its way close to where two walls joined. There was nowhere for me to stay, but there wasn't any conceivable way I could apologise for putting them to so much trouble – and, I would imagine, embarrassment and shame, too – without draw-ing attention to my understanding of their stretched lives. Better to go through the remaining hours feeling like an insensitive ogre of privilege, trampling through their hardbitten lives. Not for the first time I wished I had listened to my mother; I had failed to imagine how other people live. But why did Renu insist on me visiting if she knew, as she must have done, that this visit would fairly bristle with all kinds of awkwardnesses and contretemps?

Behind the short arm of the L, at the back of the house, lay a large vegetable patch and a pond. The larger part of the pond was obscured by the low brick box with cross-shaped windows that I had seen from the front courtyard; this was the bathroom. It had an unpainted tin door riddled with rust, which ended a good eight to ten inches above the floor. Inside were a latrine set in the floor, three buckets and a tin drum filled to the brim with water, and a large red plastic mug hooked to the rim of one of the buck-ets. There were no taps. A thin coir rope, attached to two nails on opposite walls, hung in a slack convex along the breadth of the bathroom. On it were slung two thin gamchhas.

Raja-da said, 'We bathe in the pond. We filled buckets for you in case you are not up for jumping in. Can you swim?'

Then he stopped and looked at me and gave a laugh, part invita-tion, part dare: 'Want to try it?'

I hesitated.

He said, 'It may be too cold for you … it's the month of poüsh, after all. Anyway, the buckets and drums have all been filled up for you.'

We went back to the front room; I was going to sleep there, he said. 'The bed's big enough for you? You'll fit in, yes? If not, you can sleep on the floor – we have enough shataranchi, duvet, blankets, sheets. We'll make it really comfortable for you, don't worry about it.'

'No, no … not worried at all,' I hastened to say.

'Think of it as your own home, do you understand? Your uncle's home, mamar-bari. You call Renu "cooking-aunty", so this is your mamar-bari, right?' He laughed at his own witticism; he was as uncomfortable as I was, perhaps even more.

The boy, Chanchal, brought in tea, and trailing him came Mamoni and Lakshmi, bearing huge bowls of puffed rice – they looked like white hills – and an enormous plate of fresh batter-fried aubergines.

Lakshmi said, 'Eat them quickly, otherwise they'll get cold, they've been taken out of the hot oil just now. There's more coming.'

I thought of doing the typical Bengali coy demurral act, faced with so much food, but dismissed it almost as soon as I had thought it; greed was too powerful.

'Eat up, eat up,' Raja-da urged. 'You don't get this kind of food in London, I bet.'

He was right. The aubergine fritters were perfection of their kind. The crispness of the kalonji-flecked batter giving way to the near-oozy softness of the aubergines, the puffed rice adding its own different crunch to the mouthful, the sharp heat from the powerful green-purple, squat local chillies . . .

'Enjoying it?' Ratan-da asked. 'I can tell that you are.'

Yes, he could: I had closed my eyes while munching.

Ratan-da's children were lined up against the wall, watching us as they would a gripping circus act: mouths slightly open, eyes huge and round as owls'. The youngest of the lot, an intrepid girl of six, came forward and handed me something: a picture post-card. I turned it over, saw the German stamp before realising that I might be seen to be reading the words of the sender, so I turned it back again: a picture of an old, beautiful bridge over a river with a castle in the background, with the words 'Heidelberg Old Bridge and Castle' on the bottom left edge.

'Tell him, who sent this?' Raja-da coaxed her gently.

The girl had reached the end of her courage; she ran back to join her two brothers.

'Who sent it?' I asked.

'My elder son. Dulal. He studies in Germany, in Heidelberg.'

I stopped chewing and looked up. Was he joking?

'He's been there for three years now. This muri-beguni that you're eating is his favourite. He eats it every afternoon when he is visiting.'

'What does he study?' I brought myself to say. My voice was hoarse.

'Orrey baba, now you've got me!' he laughed. 'I don't understand that stuff, it all goes over my head. We are foolish, unlettered farmer-types' – he used a common Bengali expression, mukhyu-shukhyu chasha bhusha manush – 'how can we tell you what he studies?'

'But what is his subject?'

'Phee-jeek, he studies phee-jeek, that's all I can say,' he said.

I took this to mean Physics.

'My younger son may be able to tell you better,' he said, then hollered, 'Khokon, ei Khokon, come here for a minute.' In the time that it took for the boy to arrive, Raja-da said, 'He, too, goes to school, the same school that Dulal went to, Ramkrishna Mission in Narendrapur.'

It was a highly reputed school in Calcutta, with a long track record of academic success, and apparently difficult to get admission to. Before I could phrase any questions – and I knew I would have to do so carefully – Khokon came into the room.

'Tell him what Dada studies. You know I don't understand such things,' his father said.

'Physics,' the boy said. 'Particle physics. He's doing a PhD. He'll be called a Doctor at the end of his degree, but it's not a medical doctor.'

He stood taller as he was saying this. I even imagined his chest was puffing out. Education had leached away some of the accent that his father and uncle had. Maybe he, too, would go abroad to study, or become a real doctor, a medical one.

In the event, I didn't have to ask anything; the story came out over dinner. They could barely stop talking about him; all except the women. Dulal's mother, while serving me food, mentioned him for the first and last time: 'He is my son, he lives so far away, my mother's heart is restless and anxious. I can't sleep at night. I worry about him all the time – is he eating properly? Is anyone looking after him? What'll happen if he falls ill? So many worries in my head. It's all very well that he's studying, that he's going to make a name for himself, but all I want is for him to come back.'

We sat out on the veranda to eat. A long sheet had been laid out on the floor, against the wall, so that we wouldn't have to sit on the cold floor. I wondered if they ate in the bare, poky inside in the winter and whether they were making a sort of celebratory ceremony of dinner tonight – eating off banana leaves instead of ordinary plates, for example – because they were at pains not to let their handicaps impinge upon my comfort. The children and I were fed first. They wouldn't listen to my repeated requests that all the adults should eat together; this, in reality, meant only three men, since the women would have eaten only after all the men were done; it was an unshakeable rule. Again, I read this to be hospitality doubling as a diversionary tactic, turning my attention away from the more ordinary food the family would be eating, fewer dishes perhaps, after the guest had been given the best that they could barely afford. The food wouldn't go down my throat.

My mother would have called the menu vulgar but it pierced me: breaking all rules, they had cooked fish ('From our pond') and egg because they couldn't perhaps stretch to meat. The fish wasn't special and the cooking was workaday, uninspiring. I deduced that Lakshmi and Mamoni were functional cooks. Shame and pity made my eyes prick; I stuffed my mouth with more food; everything was more delicious than I could have imagined.

Raja-da said, 'We brothers went to our village pathshala, we didn't have much education. I was determined to send my boys to school. I want them to have a different life, a better life. This life of a farmer, cultivating rice, growing a few vegetables … it's a difficult one. We struggle. Our days are not easy. I don't want this for my boys.'

'Your daughter goes to school too?'

'No, we can't … can't afford it, after sending the two boys. Dulal's education was taken care of by Renu. She loves him more than anything else. More than her own daughter. When Dulal was born, we were dreaming about how we wanted him to grow up and have name, fame and wealth, and Renu said, I am going to take care of his studies, I will work and earn money and put him through school. That's why she went to Bombay. Someone told her that in Bombay they paid cooks lots of money, thousands of rupees. So she said, Dada, I'll go to Bombay and earn money and save and send money home for Dulal's school.'

My hands were shaking. I couldn't keep them steady enough to pick the bones of the fish, to mingle the flesh with the gravy and the rice, form my fingers into a spoon to bring the mixture up to my mouth.

Raja-da continued, 'She earns a lot of money now. She works at a lot of places, four or five or six. Your home, too. Saving has become a habit for her. She has very few needs, she lives very simply, spends very little. She saves everything. And she sends money to Dulal in German country. He got a full scholarship but the plane ticket, the clothes – it was a lot of money.'

He paused, thoughtful now, as if the very memory of that amount was sobering. He brushed it aside and said, 'All that money, Renu provided.'

I had to say something. If I didn't say something, I couldn't trust myself to speak again in the company of my hosts.

'He must have been an exceptional student to go to Heidelberg on a full scholarship,' I said.

'Yes, he is very bright,' Raja-da said. His face was aglow in the dim yellow light of the sooty hurricane lamps. 'He got a scholarship from Ramkrishna Mission to go to IIT in Kharagpur. Then he came first in IIT, got a gold medal. His teachers at IIT said to him, You must go to foreign land to study. All his fees were paid for in IIT, we only had to pay for his food and clothes and hostel and transport. Renu took care of everything.'

A star student at the elite IIT. Something in this broken country worked. I had reached a place of what I could only call wonder. The parakeet, which I thought was dozing, began to shuffle about on its perch. Ratan-da's son got up to feed it whole chillies. The bird made a noise that sounded like a cross between crooning and tsking.

'Didn't she get married? Where are her daughter and husband?' I asked.

From Raja-da's slight stammer when he began to answer my question, and the way his wife and sister-in-law exchanged a glance, then looked down, I got the impression that I had stepped into awkward territory.

'Yes, she got married, but ... but she left with her daughter,' Raja-da said. 'The man ... turned out to be ... n-not good, he drank, gambled, so she left. We brought up the girl, Champa. She was five years younger than Dulal. We married her off last year, she's moved to Muchipara with her husband. Renu always wanted to go to Bombay and find work, I told you. She thought only of Dulal, how she could make the words of the astrologer, who came to see the boy when he was born, how she could make his words come true. The astrologer said, "This boy is going to grow up to make a big name for himself one day." The words scored a deep line in Renu's mind.'

I noticed how the moment the conversation came back to Dulal, the ease and flow returned. I had so many questions about Renu but I could hardly ask any of them now.

At night, under my slightly oily-smelling lumpy duvet, I worried that sore over and over: how much had it cost them, and not just in terms of money, to host me? Was someone going without a duvet, or even a bed, because of me? Who slept in this room? Where were they sleeping tonight? And then more shaming thoughts. The rice had been the cheap, thick-grained, reddish rice of the area. The food had been the paradoxical combination of oily and watery. Were the sheets and pillowcases clean? There was no running water, so they had been washed in the pond, in which they bathed, washed their dishes and did god knows what else. How was I going to use that bathroom? They had no electricity – how unbearable did it get under a tin roof in the summer? The sweets after dinner – there had been three different kinds – had been of bad quality, rancid and stale, from a low-grade sweet shop. Why didn't they serve the sandesh, made from the new season's date molasses, that I had brought as a gift from Girish Ghosh? I felt ashamed but couldn't stop myself from thinking the small, mean thoughts; the mind really was the unruliest and basest of human attributes.

I returned to Calcutta, spent one more day there, went to Bangalore and Kochi to visit friends as part of the research for the book, then returned to Bombay. I had given my mother an indication, in our phone conversations, of what I had learned about Renu in Medinipur, but I hadn't asked Ma any of the questions that were bothering me. Now they came gushing out.

'What I can't understand is this: wouldn't that ne'er-do-well husband have claimed Renu's portion of the land after she did a runner? Or the money that she sent home for Dulal's education? He must have kicked up a fuss,' I asked.

'Difficult to know,' Ma said. 'Maybe the brothers closed ranks against him. Remember, they needed Renu's money, so it was in their interests to fend him off. I wouldn't be surprised if they helped her run away.'

Yes, of course; that hadn't occurred to me.

'That could be the reason why Renu sold off her portion of the land to her brothers. So that her husband couldn't claim it,' Ma said.

'But what about the daughter?'

'If he was a useless drunk, maybe it was a relief to him not to be saddled with the responsibility of looking after a child and providing for her.'

'No, I'm talking about something different. How did Champa take it, being brought up by her uncles, her mother away, sending money for her cousin's education? It must have been obvious to her that her mother preferred Dulal to her.'

'You are forgetting something – she's a girl, she's got no expectations.'

It was true; I couldn't say anything to this. I tried another angle: 'But she is Renu's daughter, while Dulal is her nephew. Isn't blood supposed to be thicker than water and all that?'

Ma made a face, as if to say all things took second place to a talented boy in a family, especially if they were poor. She said, 'Who knows what they worked out between them?'

'And you don't think I could ask Renu to her face?'

Ma whinnied like a panicked horse. 'No, no, I absolutely forbid you,' she said. 'You will go away in a couple of days, it's I who will be left to deal with her every day. I don't want to field any consequences of you and she becoming friendly.'

'But what consequences? What do you mean by friendly? I'm only going to ask her a few questions about her life. She may respond positively to someone taking an interest in her. God knows, the people who have domestic help don't exactly treat them as their equals.'

'Ufff, this "equals" business again. You live abroad, you don't understand the culture here, you shouldn't come trampling in with your fancy notions. There will be difficulty for us to clean up afterwards.'

'You still haven't managed to explain the nature of the difficulty,' I said heatedly.

She replied with equal irritation, 'I have said several times before. It'll only set you off on your word-chopping and equality high horse. We'll be going round in circles.'

With that, she left the room. I was too riled to see her point of view.

When Renu arrived that evening to cook, I thought I discerned a curiosity on her face that made it almost mobile. I also knew she wouldn't say anything in front of my parents; she understood that I had a different, more informal and, yes, friendlier dynamic with her, which was a world apart from how she related to my parents or, indeed, to all the people in whose homes she worked.

A fine tension had descended between my mother and me. I went into the kitchen, drew the sliding door shut and said, 'It was wonderful. They fed me till I was bursting. And such good food. I ate fish from your pond, aubergines and chillies and cauliflower from your vegetable garden. It was all so so delicious. I met your family, your brothers, your sisters-in-law, your nephews and nieces ...' I knew I was babbling but I couldn't seem to stop myself.

Renu continued to acknowledge impassively what I was saying with a curt nod or an 'Achha', but without once looking at my face – she was busy taking stuff out of the fridge. I had the impression that she was either embarrassed by the gush or didn't know what it was and, therefore, what to do with it. Or was I talking so much as a way of preventing her from saying anything that I would have found embarrassing?

'All right, tell me, what are you going to take for dinner?' she asked.

I said, 'I heard about Dulal.'

She looked up sharply.

'Why didn't you tell me about him all this time?' I asked.

She didn't reply – she had gone back to arranging the vegetable drawer in the fridge.

I didn't know what to say after this or, more accurately, what to say to her. Anything would have come out as platitudinous or sentimental or false, but perhaps those things only to my ears and not to hers?

What came out after this internal debate was no less stilted, although I meant every word: 'He studies in one of the best places in the world. I know you're all very proud of him. You should be: he has achieved extraordinary things. I was very happy to hear about him. And very proud, too. And ... and ... you made him.'

She dismissed it with that gesture of hers, that performance of half-joking impatience: 'Arrey, leave all that, tell me, jaldi jaldi, what will you take for dinner?'

I ignored her, reading her words and gesture correctly for once, I thought. 'Do you know what he'll do after he finishes his studying? Will he come back?' I could imagine a successful future for Dulal as a professor in IIT, or at the Tata Institute of Fundamental Research, or even the Bhabha Atomic Research Centre, but being the person I was, I thought he would be better off working at CERN or any number of European or American universities.

'Who knows what he'll do? We've never been able to tell what goes through his head. He says he's going to come back in two years.' Pause. 'Two more years of sending money,' she said, then quickly tried to dispel the burden of the last few words by her usual dismissive tics.

'I said to him: stay as long as it takes to finish what you're doing, you don't need to think of money ... But who listens to me?' The shift in tonal gear this time was to mock-carping, a time-honoured Bengali way of expressing deep affection.

Then, another shift with: 'He says he's going to come back and build me a house. We shall see.' She said it shyly, almost coyly, with a touch of self-deprecation, as if it was his fault for choosing her, of all people, to be a beneficiary of his generosity. But there was a grain of disbelief in there, too: would she be so lucky to have that come to pass, in reality?

'I'm going back home day after tomorrow,' I said.

She turned her face away but not before I saw a dimming on it.

There was a long silence before she said, 'You'll come again when?'

'After a year. Maybe before that. I don't know. Shall I give you your money now?' I left money for her, Milly and the driver after every stay at Ma and Baba's.

She nodded; she had, refreshingly, never been coy about money. I took out two five-hundred-rupee notes and stretched out my hand. She indicated the big tin of puffed rice on top of the fridge and said, 'Leave it under that, I'll take it on my way out.'

She came in the next day, my last evening in Bombay, cooked in total silence except to say to me, while I was giving her my usual instructions, 'You come back home. Nothing doing, all this living far away.'

On her way out, she turned at the threshold to face me, said, 'Travel safe. Dugga dugga' and shut the front door behind her.

I call my mother on a blowy, wet November afternoon. We talk about nothing in particular for a while. I tell her about things from my life in London that she will find interesting. I ask her what they had for dinner, something I always do when I call her at this hour, just as they're about to go to bed. Soup, she says; chicken soup.

'You've taught Renu how to make chicken soup?' I ask. 'That's quite an achievement.'

'Renu doesn't work here any more.'

'What?'

'I had to let her go.'

I can't speak; Ma, it seems, isn't inclined to, either.

'But why? When?' I ask.

'Last month, just before Pujo.'

Contrary to her character, she isn't volunteering any information.

'But why?' I repeat.

'She was behaving very badly with me.'

Silence. I have to wring everything out of her.

'What do you mean, behaving badly?'

'Shouting at me. I've been putting up with it for a good while now. Even the minimal dealing that I have with her, telling her what to cook and, sometimes, how to cook something . . . she managed to be hostile and unpleasant even about that.'

'God! This is unbelievable.'

'One Sunday she came in to cook lunch and had some kind of a meltdown, shouting that I had messed up her whole day. Bringing things out of the fridge and setting them down with a clatter, banging the fridge door . . . it was quite something. I was speechless.'

'But why?' I'm a damaged vinyl, the pin stuck on a scratch on the surface.

'Who knows? Maybe because I asked her to come a little later than usual? I was really taken aback. And you know what her voice is like . . . Your Baba came out of the room and . . . and just asked her to leave, said: All right, if this doesn't suit you, leave – leave right now.'

My chest is hammering.

'And?'

'She left. She looked shocked, as if she had been slapped. She hadn't expected what was coming.'

'Then?'

'Then what?'

'What happened after that?'

'Nothing. I rang a few days later to ask her to come collect her outstanding salary, she didn't pick up her phone. I sent a

message through Milly . . . apparently she slammed her door shut
on Milly's face.'

I can tell Ma is uncomfortable talking about this. How is she
reading my silences, I wonder? I can spare her. I shouldn't put her
through this. I change the subject with 'Anyway, what's happened
has happened, no use thinking about it now' and talk about other
things.

But it is she who asks, 'How's the book coming along?'

I can't answer but I must say something, talk. The November
late afternoon has darkened and I need to turn the lights on.

III

No one knows where it has come from. Some children discover it against the big burunsh tree on the corner of the track that turns behind Sattu's house and leads eventually to the paved road going down to the valley.

– Look, a puppy, someone says.

– No, that's not a dog, it's too big, look at its face, someone else says.

– Look at its paws, another one.

– It's shivering, he says. No, it's too young to walk, it hasn't learned how to walk yet.

They throw stones at it, sticks and pieces of twig, to see what it will do or if it can run off. It shivers and looks at them, then frantically away, left and right and forward, as if searching for an exit. Its confusion tickles the boys – they laugh and jeer and throw more stones at it. It wobbles, runs a few inches, then stops, runs another few inches, stops again and shivers. The boys laugh and laugh.

They pick it up – will it bite? will it scratch? – and take it to Puran's father because he will know what the creature is. It trembles and whines and nearly leaks out of the large, shallow bowl of Puran's enclosed arms.

On the way they see Lakshman returning to the village down the path from Deodham, carrying a load of kindling on his back. The boys have a name, the whole village has a name, for Lakshman and his brother, Ramlal – shyal jyonlya, the fox twins. There is a rumour in the village that their mother, now dead – she died shortly after childbirth – was a witch, or had some kind of unhealthy relations with animals, which is how the brothers had come to resemble pointy-faced foxes.

– What do you have there? Lakshman asks Puran.

– An animal. We don't know what it is.

– Let me look, let me look.

– It's a puppy, he says.

– But it has very big claws, a boy says.

Lakshman notices that they are unlike any puppy's claws that he has ever seen. The nails are huge and curved, like miniature swords, but its face could be a puppy's. Or even a calf's, yet it is smaller than a newborn calf. Then it strikes him – could it be a bear cub? He is so surprised that he thinks it out loud.

The boys are thunderstruck. Bhaloo? they keep saying.

– Where did you find it? In the forest? Lakshman asks. – Here, give it to me, he says, setting down the stack of kindling.

The trembling, blinking creature is slightly larger and weightier than a fat dog. The pelt is dark grey and short, hugging the skin close. The snout is white in a line up to the bottom of the forehead. The animal will simply not stop squealing, despite the calming sounds that Lakshman makes.

A dog with a tail like a pennant comes barking and circles Lakshman, its head held up, its barking turning more and more manic. He knows this dog – her name is Jhumru and she belongs to the people who have built the new guesthouse on their plot, separated from their own home by a section of terraced land. They spend the larger part of the year in Morabadi, where they have another house. He orders the dog to stop barking, but the smell of the bear cub is stronger than a human shout. He takes a stick and threatens her but she retreats only half a dozen paces, barking continuously. Then she follows Lakshman, a few steps behind him.

The boys speed off to herald the approach of something different from the ordinary run of their lives. Minutes later, Lakshman reaches the old baanj that passes as the centre of the village; there are about a dozen people congregated there and more keep coming, once the cub is set down. Two other dogs join Jhumru and the chorus of barking becomes maddening. He has to shoo them away several times, but they position themselves outside the circle of people and continue to bark. Opinions, questions, comments fly about.

– Haan, haan, bhaloo hain. I know it, I saw one like this a few years ago.

– Where did it come from? It's too far up in the hills for these animals.

– Where is its mother? It's too small . . . do you think she lost it?

One of the children breaks off a little stick from Lakshman's bundle of twigs and prods the cub repeatedly. This gives the other boys an idea and they too make for Lakshman's stack, but he barks and waves them away. The cub mewls for a bit, tries to shift about, then gives up on both.

– Do you think its mother is looking for it? Will she come in the night to get it?

– It sounds like the mewing of a cat. It's a cat, pretending to be a bear, ha ha ha ha . . .

– How did it survive the night? How come a panther didn't get it?

– We saw it near Suraj's home, just outside it, one of the boys pipes up, hoping this is going to help others answer the big question.

– A bear is a good omen, no? It's a gift from Golu.

– It must be hungry. Give it something to eat.

No one can spare anything for the animal. Someone at last manages to get hold of a dry chapatti, tear it up into little bits and throw it in front of the cub. It doesn't react. This is a trigger for one of the boys to start poking it anew with a stick, while indicating the pieces of bread with the reiterated words – Eat up, eat up. The cub remains where it is, trembling, uninterested in the food being offered.

The woman who had asked about its mother now says – It's too young to eat bread, it doesn't have teeth, it only drinks its mother's milk.

– Mash up the roti with water then, someone suggests.

Once again, this gives the children something to do. A glass of water is found, the fragments of the roti brought together on the ground, and the water poured on it. The boy wielding the stick uses it to prod the bits of bread to mix with the water and turn it into pulp. But the earth has already soaked up the water, so his efforts yield only a muddier version of pieces of chapatti. The prodding of the cub and the mantra of 'Eat up' begin again.

– You are a fool, someone scolds the boy – the mashing needs to be done in a bowl. How can you do it on the earth? You have now wasted a perfectly good roti.

A woman frees herself from the swelling loose ring of spectators, slaps the boy and drags him out of the circle to lead him home. Ramlochan's son collects the soiled remnants of the bread pieces and runs off to mash them in the proper way. More observations are made.

– The bear could be a bad omen. A lost young one, with no sign of its mother ... this is not good.

The dogs try to nose their way past the human legs into the clearing in the middle. A kick is delivered to the most persistent one; it runs away, yelping.

– What if the cub brings bad luck on our village?

– How can it bring bad luck? Lakshman asks.

Ramlochan's son comes back and sets down a dented plate in front of the cub. In it is a dark-grey pulp. The cub moves its head away. The boy keeps turning its head to the food, sometimes forcing down its mouth on to the muddy sludge on the plate. The cub lets its snout be held against the plate – it has no option – but it won't eat.

– Let it go, it'll eat when it wants, Lakshman says.

Then there is a breakthrough. Ramlochan says – Some qalandar could have left it behind.

– Qalandar? There are no qalandars in these parts.

– Maybe the animal poachers working for them passed through our village and left a stolen cub behind by mistake.

No one can respond with anything to this possibility, but the mention of qalandars sparks off a chain of ideas in Lakshman's head.

– I could sell him to a qalandar. Where do I find one?

– They don't live in our part of the country. You'll have to travel far to find one. Down in the plains, the towns there.

Someone says – But we have seen them pass through our village, with their dancing bears. I don't remember how long ago. These people are always on the road, that's how they earn money.

– What are you going to do with the bear until we find a qalandar to take him off your hands?

– Where are you going to keep him? What are you going to feed him?

Lakshman's bright plan to make money from the bear has put in the shade the middle stage between now and that future: how would he afford the animal's upkeep when he struggled to feed his wife, Geeta, and his three small children, Sudha, Munni and Ajay, and now his brother's wife and two children, too, since Ramlal had gone to the plains to seek work on building sites. It was Suraj from the village who had planted that idea in the brothers' heads; not that any planting was needed, since a handful of men had already left to find jobs elsewhere, either in nearby towns and villages in the hills or much further down in the big cities of the plains – work as housekeeper, or security guard, driver, cook, and if any of those didn't pan out, there was always a job in construction. So Suraj had said – a job in construction.

– They are always building in the cities. Roads, houses, shops, building work was constant, one after another, it never ran out,

never stopped. There was always work to be had, even in the monsoons. Buildings coming up everywhere, in every available space or
land, nothing empty for long, the thirst for buildings was unend-
ing. So many people, you couldn't count them, they were beyond
numbers, they all had to live somewhere.

– Year-round work? Ramlal and Lakshman had asked in wonder.

– All round the year, year after year. So much money to be made
that your begging cloth will tear from its weight.

In one month Ramlal was gone.

That was two years ago. In that time, he hadn't returned to visit
his wife, Radha, and his children, Jeevan and Meena. He had sent
money – two hundred and fifty rupees once, five hundred another
time and four hundred another, all three times through someone
Suraj knew in a neighbouring village on the other side. Just over
a thousand rupees in two years – he might not have bothered to
move to the cities if that baby's-piss trickle was all that he had to
show for it in two years. And how was Lakshman supposed to feed
three additional mouths on five hundred rupees a year?

There are times, especially at nights, when Lakshman's youngest, two-year-old Ajay, and Ramlal's youngest, Meena, born two
months before Ajay, start up every couple of hours, unable to sleep
with hunger, or pain, or whatever bothers them, and the thin,
angry wailing, like the rain during the monsoon that does not let
up for days and days, becomes a fist that pummels and pummels
Lakshman until he, too, is screaming, his lungs and throat white-
hot with the will to stop that fist of noise coming down upon him
and flattening him to husk. He screams curses and abuse at Ramlal
for saddling him with the yoke of two families and wishes a painful
death on him.

His children are indifferent at first – no one knows what a bear
is. His oldest, Sudha, asks Lakshman if it's going to become a
dog when it grows up. His two other children stare at it for a bit,

then get bored – the creature doesn't seem to be doing anything. Ramlal's oldest, Jeevan, a boy of four, desultorily throws whatever he can pick up from the ground – bits of straw, leaves, snippets of twigs – at the squealing cub; most of them don't make it any-where near.

Lakshman's wife, Geeta, asks in despair – Where will you keep it? There's not enough space for us inside.

As if in response, the cub pisses – a brief dribble, over before anyone can exclaim – and from its arse lets out an equally brief squirt, which lands on the floor and runs. The children laugh in scandalised horror.

Geeta says – Put it in a box and keep it outside. We can get a rope tomorrow to tether it. Without a box, a panther will get it, maybe even a dog.

An empty fruit crate is found. The cub is put inside and three heavy logs placed on it to keep the animal confined. It does not have the necessary strength to push against them from the inside and escape, but Lakshman worries that the logs won't pose much of a challenge to a big dog or a panther intent on getting to it.

– If we raise it, I can go around the towns here, or even to the cities, and make it dance on the streets and get money. There is a lot to be made in the cities, there are many, many people, more than you can count. They will all pay to be entertained. There is no work here in the monsoons and winters.

Geeta is sceptical – How will Radha and I look after the children and the home? How will we feed them?

– I will send you money, and Ramlal will, too. He stops, hearing the wrong note that he's struck, and tries again – I will send you money, I will come back in the summer, it's too hot in the cities then. And at other times as well.

All night he has his ears pricked to catch the sawing, rasping sounds that give away the presence of a panther on the prowl.

In the morning the cub is still in its tiny wooden cage, which reeks of excrement.

A month after this, Salim Qalandar arrives; the local veins of news have worked successfully and fast. It's almost as if he's sniffed out, like an animal on the hunt, the presence of a bear cub in one of the precarious huts perched on the outer rim of a village in the hills.

– Yes, it's a bear cub all right.

Salim's eyes are round with wonder and something else. He has a confident and seasoned way of handling the animal – the way he holds it, lifts it up by the skin of its neck, carries it, stretches it out, all speak of experience and ease. There is a white ruff under the cub's neck. Lakshman thinks it looks as if the animal is wearing a garland.

– It's a boy bear, Salim says – just a few months old. Any other time, we would have paid you good money for him.

He cannot stop touching and stroking and playing with the cub, but with a kind of absence of intent or concentration.

– Why not now? Lakshman asks. He is prepared to let go of his idea of using the bear as a stream of income if he can get ready money for it now. The animal seems to be a godsend, not a bad omen.

– Impossible to do it now, Salim says.

– Why? Lakshman persists.

– They've banned bear-dancing. If they catch you travelling with a bear now, making it dance, like we used to do, our livelihoods were dependent on this, all our community did this, but now if they catch you, they take the bear away and put you in jail for seven years.

Lakshman had not thought of this possibility, so the novelty of it makes it easy for him to treat it as something trivial.

– You give them something, some tea-snack money, and they'll leave you alone, no?

– Yes, we did that for a while, but they have become stricter and stricter. Who knows, someone powerful may be sitting at the top, asking the police and people to catch poor folk like us.

Salim falls silent, ponders a while, then says – They caught my brother, Afzal. He's breathing jail air now. They asked him to hand over his bear and even offered him a job in return.

– What job?

– Some useless shop or the other. Putting spices in little plastic packets and selling them. They offered the same to another man from our village. He went bust in three months – how many people can you sell spices to in a small, poor village to make a living? Who has money there to buy spices in little packets? In three months he made less than half the money he drew in from a good week's bear-dancing. From crowds who gathered to watch his bear dance, who threw money and clapped their hands. But the bear was now gone ... Afzal knew what happened to this man. He said – no, I'll run away with Bilkis (that's his bear), I'll run away with her to a town far away, they'll never find me, he had laughed.

– What happened then?

– Find him they did. They took away Bilkis. Allah alone knows where she is now. They sent Afzal to jail.

A long silence descends.

– He's still there, Salim adds at last.

Lakshman can't find anything to say. He still cannot quite bring himself to believe that someone can go to jail for making bears dance in public. It had been done for ages; he has known about it ever since he was little. Besides, what he cannot understand is why it should be prohibited now. It wasn't robbing, or killing, or stealing. Where was the harm in it? Before he can put the question to Salim, the qalandar has swerved him along a far easier track.

– But if you want to keep him – Salim says – I can do what needs to be done. He will then dance for you for ever.

This is what Lakshman wants to hear, this is what he has been hoping for from the beginning.

– You'll do it? Lakshman's eyes shine. What needs to be done?

– A rope needs to go through his nose. Then some of his teeth must be broken. You have to do them when they're very young, when it is easy to handle them and keep them down. You'll also need a special stick, the one that we qalandars have. But you'll have to pay me to do all this.

– How much? To Lakshman, the actions are of far less moment than their price.

– Five hundred rupees.

Lakshman looks stricken. Where is he going to get that amount of money? He feels oddly irritated: what does this qalandar think, that money falls from trees?

– Where will I get five hundred rupees? Are we emirs or sheikhs?

– How can I work without money? It's hard work I'll be doing, not anybody can do it. Very few people, only qalandars, understand it.

– But I cannot give you so much money, I don't have it.

Salim mutters something under his breath, then goes quiet. The cub seems to be gnawing on his wrist; Salim shakes him off. There is another long silence.

– All right, then – he says at last – you owe me money. I will return to collect it, don't ever forget that.

Relief makes Lakshman rashly generous. He says – All right, come back when you want, after the bear has grown a bit and I've made some money. I will pay you more than two hundred rupees now.

– Remember this, because I will be back. This bear-dancing is our work, Muslim people's work. You are not one of us, you will never prosper in it unless you repay your debt. Do not forget this.

*

A fire is lit with kindling and, after it catches properly, a log placed on it; Salim wants it to be a deep, slow-burning fire. When it reaches the desired temperature, which Salim seems to be able to gauge with his eye, he inserts one end of a long iron rod in it. He has already cut some thick oak branches into different lengths. There is a piece of rope, generously lubricated with mustard oil. Over the time it has taken to procure most of these things, the people who have given them have come over to see what is going on. They do not know what it takes to make a bear dance; it will be a unique experience. Salim chooses four men, one of them Lakshman, and explains to them what they need to do. Each of the four men wraps a length of cloth – a vest, a sweater, rags – around his hand.

As if impelled by some deep instinct, the cub has scuttled off into its box to hide. Salim reaches a hand in, pulls it out and places it on the open ground, then tethers it with a short length of rope to a sturdy stick planted deep and firmly in the ground.

– Now, he shouts.

The four men turn the cub on its back – it's squealing now, a thick, squeaky noise – and stretch out its four legs, holding down the paws with their wrapped hands so that its claws can't inflict any damage. It moves its head manically, but Salim soon puts a stop to that. He inserts the thickest of the sticks into the cub's open mouth while the two men pinning down the front paws hold down the ends jutting out, effectively fixing the head to the ground. Its mouth looks like an improbably pristine pink hole seeded with small white teeth. The sound that comes out of it now is some kind of a hoarse attempt at a whisper from the throat.

– Don't press down too hard on the stick, Salim shouts – just enough to keep its head from moving.

But it isn't moving any longer, unless the convulsion going through its exposed underside, rippling that white garland and issuing as a staccato hiss, can be counted as movement. The spectacle of a tiny cub and five big men is a mockery of scale and proportion: it's as if a cannon has been deployed to deal with a fly. With four quick but forceful taps using a shorter stick, Salim knocks out the cub's canine teeth. The hiss changes to an odd rasping. The pink streaks with thin ribbons of red. They spill out, mixed with saliva, from the open corners of the mouth. Salim winds a long piece of cloth around his right hand, then removes the iron rod from the fire. He holds it for a while, one end of it glowing red, briefly, before it turns an ashy black, closes his eyes and begins to mutter something, as if he's in a trance. The crowd that rings around this business has fallen into a total hush. The surrounding pines respond in unison to a passing breeze with their own swishing sound. Children form the innermost circle, the children from Lakshman and Ramlal's family, the toddlers on the hips of their mothers, a scattering of boys and girls from the village. Salim opens his eyes – they're unfocused, as if see-ing through everything in front of them to something invisible beyond or under things. Even the pines hold their breath now. He lets out a demonic cry and with a short, thrusting movement, which seems bathetic coming after that sound, he drives the hot end of the rod through the area just above the dark grey tip of the cub's nose, pierces it in one go, brings it out, then drives it in again a few centimetres above that point, punching a hole through the bone.

The wail of a child punctures the hush with unexpected force. The cub cannot writhe or move – it is pinned into place at every point where movement can occur. Lakshman feels the tug from the sheer need to move express itself as tiny jerks in the joints of the leg that he's holding down; a cyclone manifesting itself as a breath of air. The red-pink open mouth, leaking liquid, would look as if a moment of utter, grinning glee has been frozen in time, had it not been for the unearthly squeal, dotted with a gurgling rasp, emerging from it. Then a smell alerts Lakshman – he notices that the cub is shitting, and dribbling a few drops of piss, not enough to wet the ground under him.

– Keep holding him down, but not too much force, remember, Salim orders.

He fetches the length of rope, now generously dripping mustard oil, and begins to insert it through the hole he has pierced above the cub's nose. The heat has cauterised the wound, so there's no blood, but there is the faintest whiff of burnt flesh. Lakshman looks into the bear's eyes, inches below his own face; they alternate between squinting, squeezing shut and opening wide. The pupils swim madly, left and right. A bead of sweat drops from Lakshman's forehead on to the animal's shoulder. Salim's deftness seems to have left him, as he has trouble threading the rope through the piercing. He fails once, twice, three times, shouts curses, then manages to do it at the fourth go. The sound that comes out of the cub – something Lakshman has never heard before – becomes weaker, as if the creature is running out of energy. Salim draws the end of the rope that has emerged from the hole and pulls it for a bit from the other side until both ends are more or less equal.

– The pain, Lakshman begins, but the words don't come out. He clears his throat and rephrases what he had in mind to ask Salim – He'll be all right, no? Soon?

Salim smiles. It is tinged with contempt, or certainly superiority.

– They are animals, their pain doesn't last. All these animals that live in the wild, in the forest, on the streets, you've never known them to need a doctor, have you? He laughs at his own witticism, a dry, hollow, foolish sound, and continues – They heal quickly, they're strong. It's we, humans, who are weak. He'll be all right in a few days. Don't let anyone go near him for a while. Keep him in that box and only you look after him, no one else.

Then Salim warns the men that he's about to remove the stick from the cub's mouth; the men should withdraw their hands off its paws simultaneously and move away.

A curious thing happens after it is released – it immediately retracts its legs from the stretched into a more natural angled configuration, but remains on its back, blinking, those eyes swivelling.

The crowd stirs into life.

– It'll run away now. Don't let it escape. Stand close.

– Don't go near it, it'll bite, stay away.

– Arrey, why isn't it getting up? Is it dead or what?

– No, how can it be dead, its legs are moving, see?

– When will it dance? Will it dance as soon as it gets up?

And get up the bear does, after what seems a long time, after some of the people are beginning to give it up as dead: it turns on one side first, then on the other, then lies on that side for a moment or two before standing. It falls immediately. A sound of amusement goes through the spectators in a weak ripple. It stands up again, the rope through its nose trailing on the ground like a giant noose. It wobbles and falls again.

– It's trying to dance, someone in the crowd says – but hasn't learned it properly yet.

– No, no, it's got to be trained to do that. The qalandar will teach it.

The squealing has now changed to an odd whimper. Its jaws remain open, like a panting dog's.

– Now you give it a name, Salim says to Lakshman. It's your bear for life.

– Raju, Lakshman says. His name is Raju.

Salim takes Lakshman through what he needs to do over the next few days – the fitting of the band that will sit above the nose, how to connect the mouth guard to the leash, the necessary information about feeding and where to keep him, and how to make the special stick that Lakshman could tie to the leash in order both to lead him and to prevent the bear from turning on Lakshman and attacking him, although this was extremely unlikely because Raju would now acknowledge Lakshman as his master and lord and do anything that he bid.

– Can't you give me that stick, that special stick you use? Lakshman asks.

– How can I get one here? I could find one in my village, Salim answers. Besides, you owe me money.

Before leaving, Salim reminds Lakshman – Don't forget, the bear is the lord of the underworld. The idolators and kafirs worship him because they say he has powers.

With that he is gone.

At night, Lakshman dreams of jaws, with pine trees growing inside, trying to grind him. From there the dream slides elsewhere but when he wakes up, to the sound of a wailing child, he cannot remember it. The taste in his mouth is metallic. Could he have been dreaming of his brother again? The weight of the grinding seems to be on his chest, on his entire body now, as if a huge invisible stone is bearing down upon him with the slow movement of a pestle. He pushes against air and goes out of the room into the open. He navigates in the pitch-dark by familiarity, then pisses against a tree, legs wide apart so that the stream doesn't touch his feet on its run back. The sound of the warm jet perforating a hole in the soil is disproportionately loud. By the time he finishes, his eyes are becoming dark-adapted. In the faint starlight, he can see Raju in the vegetable patch at the back, tethered to a baanj, as a darker lump of the night.

Lakshman stands there, waiting for his peering eyes to become more attuned to the dark. The lump shifts. He hears something between a snuffle and a snort. He has positioned himself in such a way that even if Raju advances, the shortness of the rope with which he is tied will ensure that there is significant distance between him and the animal, but Raju makes no movement towards him. Lakshman stands and waits, he does not know what for. He wishes he could see clearly what Raju is doing, how he is observing Lakshman. He stands there for a long time, at the end of which he is still unable to establish if Raju has been looking at him in the dark. Then he goes inside. The weight settles back on him again.

Lakshman comes in one day to discover Geeta cooking egg-and-potato curry for dinner. The children get one egg each, Lakshman only potatoes and gravy.

– Arrey, where's my egg? he asks.

Geeta is silent.

– You didn't hear me? Where's my egg?

The pared-down reply – Only for the children – comes in a manner that makes it obvious to Lakshman that she is hiding something.

He asks again. The same reply is returned but this time impatiently, with some heat. Lakshman feels an old, familiar roiling start up in him, but it must get rid of the surface confusion before it can get going fully.

– Why didn't you buy eggs for me?

Silence.

– You want me to force the answer out of you?

– Didi gave me eggs for the children.

It takes Lakshman a while to work out that she is referring to her employer, the woman whose husband's house, the big new one with the terraced garden, past the old bungalow by the hedges near the turning for the road up, Geeta goes to clean every day. City people, rich, holiday home in the hills.

– How come? Lakshman's confusion has been swept away.

– Her wish.

– She thinks I don't give enough to my children to eat? She thinks we're beggars?

Geeta, who has sensed from the beginning the approaching combustion of the very air around them, remains silent; any words would be fuel.

– Why are you so quiet? Did *you* go begging? Did you go and say – here he mimics her voice – Didi, Didi, the children are hungry, the children don't have enough to eat?

The children have become still as stones. Their plates are polished clean. Geeta steels herself against what's coming and sends up a quick, desperate, silent prayer.

Lakshman is trembling. His eyes have gone small. The mimicry continues – Didi, I'm begging, begging you for my children's food, they haven't eaten for three days, Didi, save us. The palm of his right hand, fingers curved inwards to imitate a beggar's gesture, suddenly stretches open as he leans forward, thought-fast, and slaps Geeta full on the face. She utters a short cry and topples over from her sitting position. No amount of experience in reading the signals – the small eyes, the silent crackle in the air, the subtle tremor in his hands and voice – has ever prepared her for the first blow. The girl, Sudha, starts whimpering. Lakshman turns to her, she cowers, he barks out – Shut your mouth or you'll be next.

Just as suddenly the rage leaves him; maybe it's Sudha's crying, or Geeta's prayer. He says to his wife – If I catch you bringing in food, or anything those people give you, I'll break your face. Understood?

Silence.

– Understood? he roars.

Geeta walks out.

Raju attempts to chew the wood of the fruit crate, which he has now outgrown. Children and adults no longer congregate outside Lakshman's back garden to throw stones and prod Raju into dancing. His novelty value has almost dissipated and the long, fruitless wait to be entertained has edged into boredom.

– When? the children ask.

– Soon, Lakshman answers. He does not know himself; the qalandar, Salim, who knew all the secrets, didn't tell him. Does he need to train the bear? How? By dancing in front of him and waiting for him to imitate? By getting hold of a damru and playing it to him? He does not know, and at times this fills him with panic. Is he saddled with a useless pet? Instead of bringing in money, will it be a steady and continuing drain on what little he earns? Another mouth to feed?

Just before the onset of the rainy season, he builds Raju a makeshift shed of wood and corrugated tin – stolen from the next village – with plastic placed on the roof under bricks and stones. His family huddles inside their two rooms, sometimes for days on end. The vegetable patch is washed away; in its place, there is an irregular rectangle of mud and puddles the colour of milky tea from which they have to salvage the junal, which they grill on coals and eat every day. The insects are so numerous in the mandua flour that Geeta is defeated by the business of sieving and picking them out. Mould spores everything that can be eaten, and objects and surfaces and damp clothes, too. The dense vegetation cladding the surrounding hills manages to look not green, but one with the grey of the skies.

Hearing a crash one night, Lakshman is aroused from his thin sleep. His first thought is that Raju has been attacked by a marauding panther. He goes with a torch and in the weak, faltering light cast by fading batteries he can make out Raju standing on his hind legs and the roof collapsed on to the mud. Rain falls on the tin and plastic, making a sound slightly different from the noise of the monsoon on the shed when it was standing.

In the morning Lakshman discovers that Raju has chewed the upright pieces of the thin, long wooden sticks that had held up the tin roof to his shed; the wood is in splintered little pieces not far from where the four pillars had stood before. Raju's wet pelt is covered generously in mud.

They leave him out in the rain for days until his battery of grunts and yowls drives a hot knife through Lakshman one night and he comes out with his thin guide stick, which he has fashioned as best as he could, following Salim's description and guidelines, and brings it down on Raju's flank and head and face and sides wherever he can, and on the tree trunk too, for he cannot see to aim in the dark. Raju cannot run or hide because he is chained to the tree with the rope that is only four feet long, so he lets out a run of cries that span the spectrum from roaring grunt to high-pitched shrieking without any punctuation, one modulating into another seamlessly. The noise wakes up everyone and the children begin to cry. Geeta runs out and shouts – Stop now! Stop! He'll keep making that hellish noise unless you stop. She takes the stick from his fevered hand and flings it into the dark.

In the grey, drenched light of the following morning, Lakshman comes out to find Raju cowering and whimpering at the sight of him. But Lakshman hasn't forgotten or forgiven yesterday, so Raju goes without food. The cub whimpers all day, digs up the earth around him while emitting that sound between grunting and snuffling that Lakshman is becoming familiar with, then continues with the whimpering. Lakshman comes out, bent on teaching him a few rules: the beginning of his training. He shouts out the 'Shhh' so forcefully that it ends in him spitting. Raju goes quiet. Encouraged, Lakshman raps out – Stop that din. Stop. Raju blinks, looks down, then away. Lakshman feels a stirring of joy inside him. It is stubbed out the moment he goes inside and hears Raju begin his whining again. He comes out and repeats the shushing and shouting. Raju obliges by falling silent for the duration of Lakshman's presence. Today, I have won, Lakshman thinks.

Geeta says – He'll keep up this racket unless you feed him. He's crying from hunger.

– No, don't feed him. He'll get food only when he stops the noise. He needs to learn this lesson now.

– He won't stop, I'm telling you.

The lid, that familiar, grinding weight, descends early now, when he is awake and alert, watching his children and his nephew and niece and his wife and sister-in-law. He cannot bring himself to focus on any one thing for long – it's as if his attention, something inside him, is bent on wandering and will not, cannot, be moored.

Geeta reads the slackness and goes out to throw some cucumber and ragi rotis to Raju. Loud slurping-snuffling noises, like an army of animals at a trough, over in seconds. Then silence that lasts and lasts. Everyone inside is holding his or her breath, including the two toddlers, Ajay and Meena. Lakshman refuses to look at Geeta's face. Later in the night, with the sound of the rain dotted occasionally by a whimper or a guttural croak, an image comes to Lakshman, an image that helps him hold off the weight falling on him again. It is the recent memory of witnessing Raju standing on his hind legs. He holds on to it as sleep takes him.

Their walks have been troubled from the very beginning. First, the gaggle of children following them, stubborn, mischievous and disobedient, refusing to disperse despite his repeated threats. Instead of disappearing, they let a slightly greater distance open up between them. Lakshman and Raju walk ahead. The children stop throwing stones and twigs and whatever missiles they can aim at the bear. Sometimes there are monkeys overhead, leaping from branch to branch, tree to tree, following them, but from a height. The most persistent problem is the dogs and their unstoppable barking. At times Lakshman has to turn back and threaten the dogs with the stick, or bend down to pick a stone and hurl it at the pack. Still they continue, if hesitatingly.

It is for Raju that Lakshman is anxious. Raju had seemed afraid of the dogs and halting in his progress, but after the first few excursions, the bear appears more or less indifferent to the volleys of barks and the presence of other animals. As they move deeper into the forest, the dogs fall off, one by one. The ground is thick with pine needles. There is no undergrowth, only the occasional pine cone, and fallen branches, covered with lichen and moss. Raju strains at the leash towards a cone or two; Lakshman obliges by leading him to them. That awkward, lolloping gait, as if Raju is moving forward clunkily while simultaneously swaying from side to side, interests Lakshman – is this because he is young and will learn to walk properly when he grows up, or do all adult bears move similarly?

And then it happens, by accident, and takes Lakshman by such surprise that he is left wondering what caused it. On a steep slope along a track, on the other side of which a small house is falling to ruins and its orchard and trees running wild, the sizeable patch of land surrounded by slack barbed wire and up for sale, Raju lets out a whimper, stands fully erect on his hind legs and does a brief trot before resuming his original position on all fours. Lakshman lets the rope go slack and finds himself speaking to Raju – How did that happen, huh? Do it again. Go on. Stand on your legs and dance.

Raju sniffs the ground.

– Come on, do it again.

Raju gives no sign that he has heard. In his impatience, Lakshman tugs at the rope going through the bear's nose. Raju squeals, jumps up and hops about. Lakshman lets out a whoop of joy and pulls unthinkingly at the rope again. This time Raju emits a yowl, while springing up and prancing again. Revelation floods Lakshman – so it's the rope. He feels the joy as a hollowing-out of his insides; such a lightness. He lets out another shout, pulls the rope again, this time to test the new knowledge, and when

107

Raju reacts, the cry of – Shabaash! comes out almost involuntarily from his mouth.

After he gives a demonstration back home, the children want to have a go at making the bear dance. Word spreads swifter than the rain falls. Soon there is a crowd and Lakshman half-teases (but only half) – I should be charging you for this. The rope is pulled numberless times; Raju can barely recover from one tug before another unseats him. Someone has brought Lakshman a damru so that he can shake it to produce the traditional percussion rattle that accompanies animal shows, a rhythm to which the animal dances. Lakshman tries his hand at it and pulls Raju's nose-rope. The animal stands up and executes a dragging-hopping movement on his two hind legs, squealing, his head held up, his mouth open. Lakshman attempts to synchronise the hitting of the bead against the hand-held drum's skin to Raju's movements, but each time the animal cannot sustain the dance after a few steps, maybe eight or nine, and goes back to all fours. Some of the children mimic dance moves when Lakshman starts on the damru. A few of them, the adamant and intrepid ones, get very close to Raju and poke him, or kick him, and run away to a safe distance to see if he will react and get up to dance again.

Lakshman's order – Dance! Dance! – sometimes modulates to pleading, in desperation, then switches back to angry shouts again. His face turns hot, he feels he has been humiliated in front of all these people who know him, even children. There is a white flash behind his eyes, that familiar friend, and for a few seconds he sits still. Then he drags Raju to his station, tethers him to the tree, makes sure that the knot is secure and brings down the thin stick on to Raju's back in one swishing movement that cuts the air. Raju flinches and squeals and tries to hide behind the tree but he is exposed on all sides. This attempt at self-protection liberates Lakshman – held now in the blindness of that white flash, he beats

Raju with unstoppable energy, with infinite and perpetual motion, the stick becoming the engine that drives his hand, the soul animating his body, bringing itself down like a malignant rainfall on the flanks, back, mouth, muzzle, face, legs, head of the animal, wherever it can land and strike, and Raju squeals and whimpers and growls and shrieks, a demented singer possessed by spirits, and then rewards Lakshman many times over by rearing up and hopping and prancing on his two hind legs, clutching the tree trunk with his forepaws as if it were a dancing partner and Raju were a singing and dancing actor out of a film and he, Lakshman, the director and music-director and dance-director all rolled into one. And Lakshman laughs and laughs and laughs until the stick drops from his hand and, with his sweaty palms, he is wiping his snot and tears and drool and trying to stop the sobs that come out of the stranger that he has become.

There is absolute silence from outside at night as Lakshman lies awake, his chest alive with a threshing, and heavy at the same time. No snuffling or rooting or gurgling sounds, not even the sound of loud breathing. In the morning he comes out to give Raju his food. The bear starts a kind of staccato mewling before Lakshman hoves into view and, at the sight of the man, cowers and tries to hide behind the tree trunk. Lakshman cannot bring himself to start the process of befriending – a terrible lassitude grips him. He flings the rotis towards Raju and goes inside. When sleep arrives, it comes smuggling a weapon – those dreams of fire, again.

It happened when Ramlal and Lakshman were little, both just old enough to have begun school. The Forest Department, which owned all the land that was not private – the land on the hillsides, the forests of baanj and chir, the valleys and ridges and banks – had invited applications from locals to tap the natural resources: collecting oil from pine-sap, honey from beehives, cultivating bamboo.

Their father had put in an application and, much later Lakshman found out, when he was an adult, also a little something in the right hands to expedite the process. And he had been successful. The news had spread immediately.

A day or two after this, Lakshman and Ramlal had woken up to the sound of commotion and an orange glow outside. The forest was on fire and their father was missing. Of that night, Lakshman remembered odd things: the breathing, whispering sound the fire made as it spread, so much more soothing than the punctuation of crackling and popping wood; the rhythmic, lulling creak of the high branches, then the whoosh and thump and pop of them giving in to the fire in a spray of sparks; the smell of pine and burnt wood; the sound of birds, confused, fleeing, so odd in the dead of the night ... Hypnotised by it all, still caught in the net of sleep, he didn't think about their father until he had picked up on the talk of the villagers gathered to witness the spectacle. Apparently, their father had rushed into the heart of the burning wood, trying to extinguish the fire, trying to save the area that had been allotted to him by the Forest Department, the portion set on fire by a jealous, malicious neighbour who had also bid for the same contract but had not been successful. But maybe all the explanation and piecing together had come later, when the boys had been told that their father's body could not be found because there was no body, only a length of black something, part ash, part charred matter that could have been a tree trunk. Had they seen that thing or had Lakshman imagined seeing it?

And, then, the new term attached to 'the fox twins' – bin mai babok – whereas previously they had been only chhor mulya, motherless. He remembered how a wealthy man, a raees admi's car had passed by some of them sitting on the low stone wall outside the school, and the car window had rolled down and the man's son, no older than he and Ramlal and the other boys hanging around aimlessly outside, had reached out his hand and given them tangerines, presumably at the urging of his father beside him. Not a single word had been exchanged. The car window had gone up soundlessly as soon as the boys had taken the fruits, and the vehicle had moved on as silently. While they had sat, peeling and eating the fruits, someone among them – he forgets who now – had pointed out the little segments of a tangerine that nestle among the larger, regular ones, and said that the little cloves, chhora, were for motherless boys: they had secretly been put into the fruit by their dead mother's soul for her children. The boy had given his anomalous segments to Lakshman and Ramlal.

The bear's pelt grows long as the days get crisper and shorter and nightfall arrives more quickly. Lakshman builds Raju another shed with wood and salvaged tin and even a scrap of tarpaulin, which he installs over the tin roof and secures with large rocks and bricks positioned so that they don't get dislodged in high wind or heavy snowfall. The tree to which Raju remains chained is inches away from the entrance to the shed. The eldest boy, Jeevan, his nephew, comes back from school and says that bears live in caves, that's what they were told by the teacher.

– See, I've built him a cave, Lakshman says to Jeevan, forcing himself to smile. He has always felt that he doesn't know how to talk to children, not even his own; not just what to say to them, but what tone to use, what manner, what kind of voice. The feeling has increased lately and it sometimes changes form to become that familiar lid again, a shutting-out of light and air.

– See, doesn't it look like a cave? Lakshman asks, baring his teeth.

The boy turns his face away.

Geeta grumbles that they will now have to find money to pay someone to come every day to clear the bear's shit from the shed.

– How was the shit better, lying outside, near the tree? Lakshman asks.

One day, before the weather turns really cold, Lakshman sees Jeevan feeding Raju by holding a roti high enough against the tree trunk so that the bear has to stand up to get it. This Raju does. Then Jeevan moves the second roti around the trunk, making Raju move on his hind legs to get it.

The following day, Lakshman takes Raju out to the woods, ties him to a tree and moves himself away a distance of eight or ten feet. Facing Raju, he goes down on all fours in an attempt to imitate the animal. From that position, balancing on one hand, he starts playing his damru with the other. At the first few beats, he gets up and does a little, hopping walk, then goes down on his palms and knees and stops playing the little drum. He keeps saying to Raju – You saw that? Now you do it. Go on, you do it, I'll show you again – and repeating the short suite of actions over and over. Raju blinks, yawns, scratches the trunk of the tree, circles it once, twice, sits down, sniffs the ground, looks towards Lakshman without betraying any signs of seeing him, lets out a series of different sounds, including a huff-puff one, but does not imitate him. Lakshman moves slightly closer and does his routine all over again. Raju watches him, impassive, blinking frequently, then walks back slightly as if to re-establish the original optimal distance between them. Lakshman grits his teeth; his mantra to Raju now comes out less gently coaxing, more impatient, more commanding. The second time Raju moves away – this time it seems that he wants to bring the tree between them – Lakshman takes it as a slap to his face.

– I'll teach you, sisterfucker, he spits out and lashes Raju with the stick. – You will learn, you will learn, he shouts, then, seeing Raju leap up and try to scurry away upright, in so far as forty-eight inches of rope could allow him to, even trying to hide behind the tree, Lakshman exclaims – See, sala, see! You can do it, you're just being difficult. What do you take me for? Soft in the head, haan? I'll teach you – and keeps hitting Raju. The bear whimpers and shrieks, tries to bite the stick, catch hold of it with his paws, but Lakshman is too quick – there's a fiend in him. The stick catches the bear's face twice, three times. Raju howls and tries to charge at him, upright, front paws held up, mouth a-snarl, a white thread of spit flying out from one corner, but is pulled back almost immediately by the limited length of the rope. Lakshman howls, too; with laughter.

After what he considers to be a period substantial enough for Raju to have forgotten the previous training session, Lakshman tries a different tack. He attaches a carrot to a long piece of thin coir rope and fills his pockets with several more carrots. He picks a different spot this time, far from the earlier location – a large tract of land, bounded by a low stone wall, with rusting spiked wire strung out here and there to mark it out as private, designated for some future use, probably a large house and gardens around and behind it. It has an orchard – the peach, apricot and apple trees all look dead, but they can be rejuvenated – and it is this phalanx of dormant trees that he has in mind for today.

He tethers Raju to a pear tree. To his great relief, Raju doesn't baulk at it. He ties the free end of the coir rope to his qalandar's stick, hiding the carrot end from Raju. The bear looks mournfully at the base of the tree. Lakshman plays the damru, slowly, hesitantly; an alertness comes upon the bear; he makes a brief whining noise. Lakshman moves back and aims the tied carrot to a point more or less four feet in front of Raju. The bear moves forward immediately, Lakshman pulls the carrot just out of his reach, Raju rears up on his hind legs. Wiggling the vegetable on the ground but still keeping it out of bounds, just so, stepping up the beat on the damru, Lakshman watches Raju strain at his leash, jig where he stands, walk around the tree to approach the carrot from another side, all the while erect; Lakshman is flooded with hope. He baits Raju a little bit longer, letting his own chatter fall in with the rhythm of the beats from the damru. At last he allows the bear his reward. Raju, ravenous, does not bother to sit down to eat it from the ground, but instead grabs hold of it and puts it in his mouth while still standing. Lakshman nearly leaps with joy. No sooner has he done that than a seed of doubt plants itself in his head: does this limited success mean that Raju is going to become habituated to dancing only when a carrot or something edible is dangled in front of him? That would make the actual street performances ridiculous. Who cannot make an animal dance by starving it a little first, then tempting it with food?

Lakshman repeats the first act but this time without the carrot. Raju works out soon enough that there's nothing in it for him, so he stands for a little while, ultimately settling down on all fours and returning to the vacant blinking and yawning. The hope leaches out of Lakshman. He waggles the rope a little bit more, even play-whips Raju with it half-heartedly, but faced with all the different combinations and exclusions – damru and carrot and chatter but no stick; or perhaps damru and chatter and carrot but the last only as something shown, not given; or maybe damru and chatter and stick but no carrot at all; or carrot right at the end of the day, not during training – Lakshman's mind reels. Deflated, he pauses the training. The same frustrated anger against the dumb, stupid beast begins to grip him again. He tames it in the only way he knows: he unties the coir rope and uses the stick to beat Raju into understanding what it is that he's trying to make him do. A monkey, which has been watching the entire proceedings from its perch on a tree, perhaps in the hope of stealing the carrot, lets out a chatter and runs away, leaping from the high branches of one tree to another.

Something behind the house catches Lakshman's eye, he doesn't know what, but it creates a moment's tense haze for him and lifts as swiftly. He walks back a few steps, scouring the ground with his eyes, trying to pin down what it is. It keeps eluding him, even though some sense tells him that it's staring him in the face. Stones of ber fruit, scrunched-up plastic, vegetable peelings, crumpled paper, grass, earth ... then he has it. Eggshells. Small white fragments of eggshells. There's a large piece with the curvature of either the top or the bottom end intact. He stands very still for a while, the next moment almost felled by the swell of pity that buffets him: pity for his children, who need the eggs, who perhaps look forward to the days when an egg might appear, and pity for Geeta, for persisting stealthily in defying him. The thought of her defiance disperses the sympathy as if it was so much dust held out on a palm to the wind.

Over the next few days he watches, silently and secretly. He goes out, bides his time somewhere out of sight until Geeta goes out to clean, then returns home to hunt for hidden eggs. He wants to know if Radha is in on the plan, but decides it will be unwise to confront her – it will be so much more effective if Geeta doesn't get wind of his strategy and is caught red-handed. For the same reason, he doesn't ask any of the children a straightforward question. She must be boiling the eggs and giving them to the children to take to school. But when does she do it?

He waits by the hedges next to the old bungalow, waiting for her to finish the day's job and come out. He does not reveal himself. He crouches behind a hedge as she passes by, counts to twenty, then peeps out. She is carrying a plastic bag. He lets her walk towards their house until he is certain that she is no more than a few paces from their front door. He sprints like a man possessed and enters his home before Geeta has had a chance to hide the plastic bag. She looks as if she has seen a ghost; her face goes slack and bloodless.

– Give me that bag, he pants.

She doesn't – cannot – move.

– Give me that bag, he thunders.

He snatches it out of her hands. Inside, there are four white eggs, one of them just broken from the force with which he has taken the bag. There are some stale chapattis in it, too, and a small plastic tub of leftover rice and another one of some sabzi, probably cabbage; crumbs from the rich people's table.

Geeta tries to run into the kitchen, in a foredoomed, pitiable attempt to get away; a mistake. He holds one of her wrists and, with his free hand, takes out an egg and smashes it against her face. He takes out the second egg, she turns her face away, he catches hold of her hair and twists her head to face his. He smashes the second egg on her nose with so much force that he can see a thin trickle of blood coming out of her nostrils, under the slimy drip of the transparent albumen and the opaque yellow splatter of the yolk. The tears and the twisted mouth add to the ugly mess that is her face.

Her wailing brings out Radha, who shouts – Stop it! Stop it now! Don't you have any shame?

Her relational seniority to Lakshman insulates her from being in any danger of receiving similar treatment, but this doesn't prevent him from threatening – If you don't stop screeching, it's going to be you next.

– How dare you? she retorts – Don't you have any shame?

Lakshman effortlessly modulates from rage to acid contempt. He says – What will you do? Complain to your absent husband? He fled the coop a long time ago, leaving me to deal with this zoo.

Radha has no answer. Geeta, too, has stopped her loud crying. His mention of Ramlal, however, has the effect of turning Lakshman's anger to ashes. A bitterness fills him, and a desolation. He has to force himself to complete what he has begun, but his heart is no longer in it. He says to Geeta – If this happens again ... He doesn't have the energy to finish it. He goes out to wash his hands of eggs and the disgusting smell.

*

By the time spring is giving way to summer, Raju has mastered a sustained dance to the playing of the damru. Lakshman had already worked out that all he has to do is pull on the rope through Raju's nose to make him leap up instantly and prance about as if red ants were biting his arse, but the trick has been to make him learn to hold that for five, ten, twelve minutes.

He waits for the big festival of Golu. There is bunting strung out here and there, and three different amplifiers, positioned in different parts of the village, blare out Hindi film songs throughout the day and evening. At night, the mountains seem to distort the sound in such a way that it's here one minute, gone the next, only to reappear from an unexpected direction, as if the sound had been torn into tiny paper fragments and scattered from the sky and dispersed helter-skelter by the breeze.

He feels lucky to have an unobstructed view of the high point of the worship – the sacrifice of fifty-three goats. He has waited outside the temple overnight to secure this prize position. The crowd is so vast that had he left it until morning, he would have been no nearer than the arches leading to the front courtyard of the temple. The saffron, yellow and orange of the low pillared structure and the sea of marigolds wherever he looks – marigolds in garlands and festoons and baskets and strewn about everywhere around the temple – meld into a blinding sun. All of life is here, with all its noise and colours and suffocation. Lakshman has a fractional view of the enclosure behind the temple in which the goats are penned. A whole field of black goats, a sea of goats, like the sea of people around him. He can smell them from here. The animals look docile, resigned, as if they have sensed what's coming. They have bright vermilion marks smeared on their foreheads, between their eyes, and marigold flowers around their necks or horns. Golu is almost hidden from his view, behind columns and the press of human bodies and heads in front of him. He can catch the occasional flash of the god's enormous white turban, or a segment of his white, squat body on the white horse, if there is a chink in the wall of people in his line of vision, or if he leans his head at a difficult angle, but there is no space to do even that.

A man leads the first goat, the biggest, fattest of the lot, reared for twenty-one days only on the fruit of the baanj and glossy jackfruit leaves, to the forked iron peg that has been permanently staked into the front courtyard, directly in front of the small, orange-framed door to the sanctum. What a blessing to be the first animal to be sacrificed, and what blessings will accrue to the young man who has been selected to bring the animals to the point where they will give up their life for Golu. Lakshman has long coveted this post, believing that such a service every year will make the god smile on him and remove all the giant boulders that sit in the middle of his life, obstructing its free flow. But, as in everything else, he has been unlucky. One chance at something, anything, just one chance – is that too much to ask? There is no getting away from Fate, but there is also no way of telling whether the story of his life is bound to continue in the same groove that it has run so far. What if there is a change? Is the god reading his thoughts?

The fattened goat, its head down, comes obligingly almost up to the peg, then seems to understand something and wants to turn back. Lakshman can tell this, because the man has to drag it for the last few feet. The drums are loud in the foreground, and the manically ringing bells, hundreds and hundreds of them, strung out on the red arches that mark the long approach to the front courtyard and on the red-painted wooden beams at the edge where the roof meets the columns, some rung by devotees and worshippers, other, lighter ones set off by the brisk breeze, mingle with the purohit's mantras, the shouts from the gathering, 'Jai, Golu Devta ki jai', the smoke from the incense, and Lakshman finds himself at once a part of this ocean and removed far from it, weightless, tiny, watching from above. When the feeling of suspension takes hold, there is a faint tingling in his fingers, accompanied by the sensation of every limb becoming thin and long like sticks and his head ballooning to a huge bubble while losing every weight it has, every mooring. He has to touch something, the shoulder or arm of the person nearest him, and clench and unclench his fists in order to remind himself of his tethered corporeality. Then he is back in the ocean again until the weightlessness tolls back and untethers him.

The man pushes the goat's neck in the space between the two tines of the peg. The animal has stopped thrashing. It doesn't even kick back with its hind legs. That perfect balance of absolute contraries again: in the thickness of the chanting, the drums, the bells, a stilled heart of hush. Waiting at the iron fork is the man from the Nath sect who will bring his sharpened khukri down on the goat's neck and sever it. The purohit is in a trance of chanting. The worshippers hold their breath – the blow has to decapitate in one stroke, otherwise thirteen years of bad luck will be sent down by Golu upon the village. The drums are now the aggregated percussion of the heart of every human gathered.

The khukri comes down in such a swift arc that there is no process, only the before and the after. The goat's head is not severed in one clean cut but hangs at the neck, making it look like a toy animal that a clumsy child has broken during play. The spurting jet of blood, the purohit's shout and the devotees' collective exclamation of horror are all one in Lakshman's senses. The man who had led the animal now brings the hind legs of the thrashing torso together, then the front legs, gathers it up as if it were an old mattress, hugs it to his own body and carries it out, his face and clothes sprinkled with blood. Lakshman sees his retreating back, as if he is fleeing a scene of crime, and the uncut head dangling from the crook of his arm like a dainty handbag picked up as an afterthought to the main spoils. A trail of shiny blood follows him.

The man with the khukri has turned to stone, his weapon down, its blade almost black with the fresh blood, and a small colony of dark spots directly under it on the green-and-white tiled area on which he stands. A group of people on Lakshman's right tries to move, jostling each other, and in the temporary space allowing some freedom of movement, he shifts, too, and catches a glimpse of Golu's marble-white face and full lips the colour of kaafal. The god's face, pleasant in its huge-eyed expressionlessness, is marked by something – Lakshman cannot tell what exactly – that makes him look offended. Then Lakshman is jostled too and he has to move with the segment of the crowd that he is in. The flash of vision is gone.

The restless people are stilled as the young man leads another black goat to its slaying spot. This time the animal is refractory, straining to turn back, trying to dig its hooves into the unyielding tiles. It lets out a single bleat, then stops, as if realising that no amount of crying will save it. The sound conveys something to the other goats in the waiting area and is echoed by creatures that have remained strangely silent. But here, too, the responsive bleats are half-hearted, resigned, and after a dozen wavering and low 'meeh-eh-eh-eeh', the restiveness is extinguished. What survives, at least for Lakshman, is the much sharper presence of their suffocating odour.

The second goat is dispatched in one go, and the third, and the fourth … A new smell begins to assert its metallic note, mild, almost evanescent compared with the cloud of goat-odour, but present nevertheless. Lakshman knows that this is the smell of blood. Years ago, when he was a boy, Ramlal had seen his twin's eyes water at the overpowering stench at this annual sacrifice for Golu Devta and had explained the different smells to him.

The lopped heads are quickly taken away and arranged in a circle at the feet of the god's milk-white horse. They look deader than dead, separated from the bodies, with some of the bluish tongues

sticking out slightly from a corner. A small wick is lit, between the
horns, on each of the heads. Some of the wicks catch, others don't;
those that do burn with a small blue flame for a short while, then
go out. The runnel, especially built around the tiled forecourt, is
filling up with blood, but there's more of it on the tiles and all
around. The goat-usher skids more than once going about his work
but manages to balance himself steady each time. The rising smell
of blood brings back Ramlal to Lakshman's mind. He feels close
to suffocation. The flesh of the sacrificed goats will be cooked and
served to everyone in the village. He tries to catch a final glimpse
of the god's face to check if his look of displeasure has been erased
by all the blood that he has been offered. Some error of rhythm has
occurred in the dance that had brought everything together, the
flowers and blood and incense and bells and drums and chanting
and people, people everywhere, their sounds and life. The slackness now unbinds all the component parts and sets them off in
different directions.

Lakshman turns round and pushes his way out, his back
turned to the temple, until he reaches the thinning end of the
crowd. He picks up his pace as he walks past the stragglers and
latecomers, past the school-building with its grey doors and
windows and the playground on three small terraces, until he
arrives at the knoll on the edge of the wood behind Bhagwan's
house. Even at this elevated point, from which he can see the
valleys fall away and roll into the distance under their cladding
of forests, the lighter pine and darker oak coming together in
a dense weave and, sometimes, a colony of human habitation
that looks like a small cluster of doll's houses, even at this height
Lakshman cannot shake off his shortness of breath, his feeling
that there isn't enough air for him to breathe here. The mountains dazzle in the distance: he sees popping dark-and-coloured
spots after staring at them for a while. He can't find what he
always searches for, almost involuntarily, when he looks at

them – the nearly shut, heavy-lidded eyes, the long mark for the nose and the faintly, inscrutably smiling lips of Shiva imprinted on the slope of Nanda Devi that Ramlal had taught him to discern when he was little.

On a golden afternoon when the boys were eight or nine years old, Ramlal had pointed out and named all the peaks – You see that blunt one, just along from the flat line, that's Mrithugni, and the one after that, with the two dips, the two curves, do you see? – here he had shaped the indentation with his hand, to make his brother understand better – that's Trishul, because if you see it from the other side, we're seeing it sideways, if we see it from the front, it looks like Shiva's trishul, do you see the three prongs of the trident?

And Lakshman, dumb with wonder, had nodded. Whether he had actually understood it at the time he no longer remembers.

Ramlal had continued – Then the one after it, on the right, here, follow my finger, that one is Nanda Devi. That is where Shiva lives.

Then a dramatic pause, after which – You can see him. Do you want to see him? I can show you how to spot him.

Still silent, Lakshman had barely been able to nod.

– Follow my finger very carefully now. First close your eyes and think of Shiva. Now open them and look hard at where I am pointing. See that front slope of Nanda Devi? You see it, with snow on top and on the front, with rock showing where there's no snow? You see it? Now look directly under that long, thin line of snow, just under that shadow. Do you see his two eyes? They are the curved lines under the shadow, one on each side of that black ridge that has no snow on it – that's the nose. Do you see the eyes and the nose? The eyes look a bit sleepy, no? That's because he has just woken up from his meditation. Why are you so quiet? Can't you see?

Of course, Lakshman could see – he could see the god's beautiful, lotus-like eyes, more closed than open, and the mouth, almost smiling . . . there he was, the great god Shiva, his face imprinted on

Nanda Devi, his abode. And there he, Lakshman, was, gazing on it, a wonder revealed to a boy, and all the air, all the light and all the days were his to do what he wanted.

That evening Lakshman drinks four glasses of the bhaang-laced saffron-and-pistachio lassi they whizz up near the temple, an annual ritual at this time of the festivities for Golu. The hand with the bhaang is generous, in keeping with the mood around the occasion, and Lakshman finds himself, first, slowed down to the dragging, underwatery beat of his heart, then giggly in an escalatingly uncontrollable way. After a while the marketplace cants at an uncomfortable angle and he loses the ability to command any of his thoughts or the way a wildly rushing and random stream of them seem to make a playground of his mind. He is sure he saw Golu frown. That white, white skin, like wax made out of milk. So much blood. And that smell. The meat the day after at the communal lunch has always had the whiff of goat for him. His wife and children will love the mutton. A heavy shroud falls on him, and he is suddenly fighting for air and light, for breath. He heaves and retches and the grass beside him gets covered by a small, viscous patch of yellowish-green liquid, still smelling obstinately of pistachios and saffron under the sour overlay of sick. And yet even after there is nothing to bring up, not even the last drop of his bitter, green bile, he still finds himself under that recognisable lid. Now there is an immovable stone upon it, getting heavier by the minute. There is nothing to do, nothing that can be done about it.

When he wakes up, the helter-skelter film in his head has stopped but the weight hasn't shifted an inch. He observes himself, from a distance, watching the children play danda-gulli outside and feeling nothing. Geeta complains about the piles of bear-shit at the back of the house and how the man she is paying to clear it away has not showed up for the last three days and the stench is unbearable, this used to be a human house, not a zoo, and the children are distracted all hours by the bear, and the creature is going to eat them out of house and home, where is she going to find the money to keep feeding him, too, when there is barely enough for the children and the three adults, particularly now that Lakshman has stopped bothering with even the basic work that their scrap of land demands and she has to look after that on top of everything else, how is she going to do it, does he think she has ten hands, how are the vegetables going to grow . . .? Lakshman's right hand itches to slap her right across the mouth, but the feeling lasts for the tiniest moment before that dark crushing takes over again.

He goes out to the back. Raju recognises him now. He is standing up, trying to bite the tree trunk, but on seeing Lakshman resumes his normal quadruped position and tries to advance towards him, but the four-feet rope pulls him up short. Undeterred, he makes that odd guttural sound, punctuated by short squeaks here and there, that makes Lakshman think Raju is trying to say something to him in his own language. He moves closer and strokes the creature's back, tentatively, gingerly, ready to leap back if he shows any sign of attacking, but Raju continues to emit sounds that can only be of appreciation, even affection, and for the first time in god knows how long Lakshman feels that lightening he has felt once or twice, in the company of Raju, or while contemplating his future with the bear, far away from this village.

The following day when Geeta is out working in the Bengali house he puts a few things in a small sack – his ration card in its blue plastic sleeve; a few items of clothing (he doesn't have much: his shawl, a sweater and a snuff-coloured, skull-hugging woollen cap, a lungi, a pair of pyjamas, an old white vest, now the colour of dust); a small tin of puffed rice; a coil of rope; two half-empty boxes of matches, anything he can take away without it being missed. He picks random things – there aren't many to choose from – without any thought or reason. He ties the sack, flings it over one shoulder, picks up the damru and his qalandar's stick, goes out, unties Raju from the tree, takes the rope in the hand that holds the stick and whispers – Come, we're off. The bear makes slobbering noises and roots around in the earth with his snout, as if looking for something that he wants to bring with him on the journey. The sounds change to what Lakshman thinks of as yawning ones: mouth wide open, a long glimpse of pink, and those dots of mewling notes.

– Yes, you're happy. I know. Let's go.

He doesn't really have a plan except to stop at each small town at the end of a day's journeying and make Raju dance the following day, collect the money and move on, repeating this routine until he reaches the city where Ramlal is working on building giant homes and river-like roads and arcing bridges. Three to six months at the most, he tells himself; he will be home long before the trees have shed their leaves, certainly long before snowfall fells trees and closes the roads to traffic.

They take the steep paths through the hills, eventually descending to the only road that connects all the villages, but at a point several feet below his own, and several kilometres away. From this juncture, marked by a shop that sells everything, from candles and batteries to Maggi noodles, car lubricant and strings of small sachets of Sunsilk shampoo, they stick to the road. The periodic truck unsettles Raju – he jerks around at the end of his rope, moves his head wildly, whimpers and growls.

– Shush, shush, it's all right, it's only a car, you're going to be all right, no need to be scared.

A driver rushing past leans on his horn, doubtless at the sight of a bear. Raju goes berserk and pulls at the rope so hard that he drags Lakshman along with him over the verge into the trees and bushes. Lakshman shouts. Raju blinks in a baffled manner, then looks down and, after a few seconds, into the distance. The narrow two-lane road falls away steeply, in a scree of rocks and earth, to the shrinking green ribbon of the Rishabh river, rushing along the rock-and-boulder-strewn gorge far below. After Raju's reaction to the loud, horn-tooting lorries, Lakshman realises that it would be safer to walk on the other side of the road, the one that banks against the slope of tree-dense land.

They make their way down to the river for a drink and for Lakshman to splash his face with cold water. In the dappled shade of trees they come across a still stretch of water, an overspill from the river and now cut off from its parent by a narrow bank of sandy earth and grey-green rocks and a strip of paler pebbles. On the surface of that island of water float many brown leaves that have fallen from the trees. No sooner has Lakshman seen them than he thinks there is something not quite right about them, but he cannot tell what. As if someone has read his thoughts, the dry leaves move in unison, in a blink-swift movement, and the folded-up undersides of the drinking swarm of butterflies change to a flickering mosaic of oranges, yellows, browns and blacks, stippled by the dance of spots of lights and shade. Lakshman finds himself unable to move. Before the reaction to pull back Raju to stop him has managed to travel to his hand, Raju has taken three or four steps. The sound and the movement disturb the butterflies. Like handfuls of coloured paper thrown upwards by a playing child, they scatter, then flit away. Raju stands up, chatters and reaches out his paws to swat them. But they are far away from him and in any case they are moving and, finally, all gone. The skin of the water is now just a green, shadowy screen for the swaying points of light and shade.

At the first hamlet they reach, Talla Panchgarh, which is a loose straggle of low houses with asbestos or tin roofs, all distant from one another, Lakshman buys a big packet of sliced bread from a small roadside shop, some stale, soggy biscuits and a small paper packet of groundnuts to eat with his puffed rice later.

– Is that a bear? the shopkeeper asks.

– Yes. His name is Raju.

Then inspiration strikes – or a canny calculation.

– He can dance. Do you want to see him dance?

The shopkeeper shrugs.

Lakshman calls out Raju's name authoritatively a few times, strikes the ground with the stick, then detaches the chain from the thick collar around the neck at the same time as he frees the rope through the nose and the hole in the snout from the knot into which it has been tied to attach it to the muzzle guard. He tries to do all these actions as swiftly as he can while crooning in a very low voice. Before Raju knows it, the rope is in Lakshman's left hand and the damru begins to sound its beats, arrhythmically at first, then settling to the rhythm of whatever tune inside Lakshman's head is animating his right hand. His heart thuds almost painfully against his chest; this is the first performance he is giving outside his village. The knowledge transmits some kind of keenness to him. He tugs the rope hard. Raju, who has been looking confused, instantly stands up on his hind legs, squealing, then drops down almost immediately. The action produces a soaring, followed quickly by a deflation, of Lakshman's heart. Maybe he is losing his touch; he needs to practise and let Raju have his daily routine more.

Suddenly the rhythm of one hand synchronises with the movement of the other, and the beats of the damru and the tugs on the rope going through Raju's nose are as one. Lakshman watches – more feels than watches – this unity of rhythm spread and make Raju a part of its entity: the bear, too, now begins to keep moving on his back legs, shaking his head, as if marking beat or signalling a gentle yet sustained 'no'. The squealing has stopped. He looks like a giant dog, not much like a bear. The shopkeeper is smiling. Lakshman keeps up a patter – Shabaash! Dance, my Raju, dance. Little bear, little bear, dance. Yes, that's it, my little bear, that's it. Well done. Forward, now. Now a few steps back, that's it – that seems not much different from the private, one-sided conversations with Raju that he has begun to fall into when they are on the move.

The rhythm breaks; Raju falls on all fours; or maybe it is the other way round, Lakshman can't tell.

He opens the packet of bread and throws four slices to Raju. Before he can tie a knot in the plastic bag, the bread has been snaffled up and Raju has ambled right up to him, his snout trying to press into the packet. Halfway through leaping backwards and tautening the rope involuntarily, to bring about a safe distance between himself and Raju, Lakshman thinks, no, let me show him I'm not afraid of him, even if deep down I really am, and tries to slow down both actions so that they are more casual, more natural. Simultaneously, another bright idea occurs to him.

– Won't you give me something for making the bear dance for you? he asks the still-smiling shopkeeper.

The man is unwilling to part with any money, so Lakshman asks for food and water for the bear. These materialise, and not only for Raju: sweet biscuits; laddoos, sour, on the turn; some stale rotis; a lump of jaggery; some oranges, even, and a couple of squishy bananas. Raju, overexcited, breaks into a whole choir of noises. Lakshman puts away the jaggery and rotis, keeps an orange and a banana for himself, and gives everything else to Raju. In less than a minute, it's all gone. He sniffs the ground where his food has been, avidly, as if there's more of the stuff that is oddly eluding him, all the while making his grunting-snuffling noises. He comes up close to Lakshman, raises his clawed paws – Lakshman freezes with terror; those claws are like miniature swords – and brings them close to Lakshman's ears, touches his head and brings it down to the ruff around his neck. The grunt-snuffle changes to a panting mew, with a few guttural notes mingled in it somewhere, while Lakshman, with a dry tongue cleaved to the roof of his dry mouth, is unable to move. But after the first few moments with his head in Raju's chest, he realises that the bear intends no harm, and it is over in seconds.

Lakshman and Raju do not get to the first town until the beginning of the summer. If he can spend the next three months in this town by a lake in the valley, its houses and shops lined along the road and hugging closely the hill-slopes on both sides of the lake, he will have saved enough money to find a shelter for the monsoon months. So far he and Raju have slept under trees or behind houses in the lower slopes of the densely vegetated hills. The more they progress south, the more the hills open up, allowing for wider valleys, more space, until he feels one day that the tight fist in which the mountains have always held him is correspondingly loosened, sometimes even absent.

The lake is green and where its edges meet the road there is the usual rubbish of plastic bags, food wrappers, cigarette packets, empty cartons, plastic bottles, flowers, paper, unidentifiable debris, shit, wildly coloured algal blooms, stretches of green slime, slicks of some viscous chemical or other, colonies of sedge, foamy scum, all so dense as to form a solid, ragged border, immovable, unlike the water further in, which is ripply and wavy in its ordinary way.

They attract attention – a bear is not a usual sight – and are soon followed, first, by one or two street-children and then, a bit later, by a bigger group of children, seven or eight, even a couple of young men and street urchins. A refrain begins – Bear, bear, show us how you dance. After a while it has the effect of something blunt slicing through Lakshman's head, but he ignores the retinue. Raju follows him docilely, undistracted by the clamouring children. It's only when one or two of them pick up stones and start throwing them that Lakshman turns round and spits out – Do you have money to see him dance?

A slightly older boy, maybe thirteen or fourteen, it's difficult to tell, swaggers forward aggressively and asks – How much do you want?

Lakshman tries to argue reasonably – I don't have a rate. People gather around me and I make the bear dance. Then more people come, seeing that. I take whatever they give me at the end.

The boy says – So you're a beggar then.

The words wind him but he recovers quickly enough to snarl – Do you know, I can set the bear on you and he'll maul you to shreds in five minutes. Why do you think there is that band around his mouth?

The boy's swagger leaves him. The entire gaggle steps back, then halts. Lakshman turns back and continues in the direction he and Raju were walking. His back prickles in the way it does when one is being watched, but he senses that the boys are no longer following them. A stone lands behind him, almost getting his ankle, and a second one, hard on the heels of the first, strikes the ground, bounces up and hits one of Raju's back legs so that he gives a little startled jump. In one furious movement, Lakshman picks up two stones, wheels around and, screaming, hurls them at the fleeing backs of the boys.

– Motherfuckers! Sisterfuckers! he shouts. The stones he throws at them come nowhere near. Does he imagine their contemptuous laughs from this distance? He realises that he is snarling, a thread of sticky spit dangling from his chin. From their assuredly safe distance, one of the boys turns back to face Lakshman, goes down on all fours and does a mocking mimic of Raju's walk for a few seconds before he joins his running friends. The thread of spit falls to the ground.

It is at the third performance in this town that Lakshman notices the boy who had called him a beggar and then, in close succession, he thinks he recognises some of the younger ones' faces too. He has had slim pickings at the first two events – twenty-three rupees and thirty-four rupees, barely enough to feed him and Raju for three or four days – and although this crowd looks bigger, he is beginning to learn that this does not always translate into proportionate takings.

The act is lacklustre; Lakshman knows this. It's not only Raju who is in need of being trained into a routine, with different numbers, but also Lakshman, who is a novice, all at sea. These street performances, on the other hand, are developing by a sort of impromptu trial-and-error. He plays the damru and tugs at the rope going through Raju's nose; the bear gets up and scampers around as long as the rope is being pulled; Lakshman chants some repetitive words – See, see, the dancing bear, now he'll get up on his back legs, now he'll dance, see, see, dance, dance, dance – and that's the pitiable extent of it. Today he wants to try out something new: make Raju go round and round in a circle around him. He will have to work out a way of doing this without the rope encircling him; the easiest solution would be to remain standing and rotate as Raju describes a circle; but he wants to keep sitting because he feels tired. Not for the first time he wishes that he could sing a couple of songs – any old, or new, Hindi film songs would do – to perk up matters a bit, give the audience the illusion that this is a rehearsed performance, that Raju is dancing *to* his singing.

The desultoriness is broken when a child, no more than six or seven, pipes up – Can I ride the bear? I want to ride him.

A man, presumably her father, brings her out of the surrounding circle to the centre where Lakshman and Raju are.

– He won't bite or attack? he asks.

Lakshman quails before the question, but the calculation that results in the lie – No, no, he's a total baby, a paaltu bhaloo, wouldn't even know how to hurt a fly – easily overrides the fear. This business of letting small children ride Raju could bring in more money than simple bear-dancing.

The girl comes hesitantly towards Raju, one of her hands tightly clutching her father's. She stands about four feet away from the bear, watching him intently.

Suddenly, a shout from one of the spectators – It's not a bear, it's a dog in a bearskin.

Lakshman knows who said this without needing to look; yet he does look and his eyes alight instantly on that boy, as if some kind of mocking destiny had singled him out and presented him solely, to the exclusion of everyone else, to Lakshman's vision. The pinning focus dissolves; Lakshman can identify a couple of the other, younger boys from that earlier day by the lake.

There is the beginning of a collective titter, then another voice – The bear dances, and the fox pulls the rope to make him dance.

The tittering explodes. A collective chant goes up – Dog, fox, dog, fox, dog, fox . . .

The people are all gathered up into a derisive laughter. How did it all degenerate so quickly, the time between the strike of a match and the conflagration so short? Lakshman looks up around him. There are construction sites everywhere, flatland and hillsides gouged out, piles of brick, cement, sand, machinery, one or two heavy vehicles. Hotels? Why couldn't Ramlal work here, near his village? Why did he have to go so far, no one knew exactly where?

Most of the spectators have left, leaving only a desolate handful. Lakshman is rooted to where he is sitting by a bottomless exhaustion. Raju has sat down too; docile, deflated, it seems to Lakshman. There is a single one-rupee coin on the cloth spread out to collect what people give.

Before they leave the town the following morning, Lakshman goes to a grocery stall right at the end of a road lined with tea shacks and places selling fruits and vegetables, grains, rice, onions, garlic, gourds, potatoes. He looks through the produce, making sure the man in the stall has noticed Raju.

– Is . . . is he a bear? the man asks, his interest stoked.

– Haan. A baby one. Raju, he's called, Lakshman answers pleasantly. His heart is beating madly. He knows he's taking a big risk but they need to eat. He lets go of the rope in his hand and nudges Raju's back with his foot. Raju wiggles his bottom a bit but doesn't move. Lakshman nudges him again, this time more forcefully, while keeping up a patter to sustain the shopkeeper's initial curiosity.

– He's just a baby, very quiet, very friendly, like a paaltu dog. Aren't you, beta, aren't you a little doggy-woggy? Go, go to this new bhaiyya, go.

The plan, such as it is, is unfolding on the hoof. Lakshman bends down and, with his hands on either side of Raju's rear flank, urges him gently to make friends with the new bhaiyya.

Raju takes a few steps forward, seeing which the shopkeeper blanches and exclaims – You've let go of the chain? No! Don't let him loose, tie him again, tie him!

Lakshman disregards him – He won't do anything, ekdum bachha hain – as Raju begins to advance, the blinking, resigned confusion on his face intact.

The shopkeeper repeats his injunctions, his voice rising, the panic in it becoming uncontrollable now. Raju sniffs the ground, a sack of dirty potatoes, another sack of tired pink bruised onions, looks up and yawns. The shopkeeper gives out a strangulated shout, edges himself out from behind his scales, with the stack of polygonal black iron weights lying beside it, and runs out of one corner, almost tripping over a huge basket of shrivelled gourds at the threshold. He retreats into the narrow dirt alley adjacent to his stall. Raju, perturbed by the perplexing feeling of not being on a leash, and the proximity of food, snuffles and grunts and ambles towards the corn near the mouth of the alley down which the shopkeeper has fled. Fearing pursuit, he runs further inside, leaving Lakshman, incredulous at his good luck, to stuff anything he can lay his hands on into the sling-sack that he has improvised from the large sheet that he spreads out for people to throw money on, when he is making Raju perform. Dark potatoes; onions slipping out of their papery skins, mushy here and there; gourds; sweet-corn; mangoes; bananas; packets of white, sliced bread ... until the thought of capturing Raju makes him pause and drop the sack, now impossibly heavy. But Raju hasn't worked out yet what the novelty of unshackled movement means; instead he is rooting around in a jute sack of half-rotting cold-storage carrots from last winter, snout in, gobbling them up with absolute abandonment. Lakshman cannot bring himself to disturb that unity of focus and concentration, so he carries on with his erratic pilfering. Then – while Raju is still lost to the world – Lakshman catches hold of the free end of the chain and gives it a tug, two pulls, three, before Raju registers and looks up. The sack is going to impede a fast getaway; fear is upon him now. He has a good idea of how easy it would be for the shop-keeper to raise a cry of *Thief! Thief!* and have a crowd of people instantly at his back. Slinging the sack over his left shoulder, he pulls Raju sharply and hurries to the mouth of the road and from there slips into the scatter of houses amidst the trees set back from the road, turns left and right and right and left randomly, in case anyone is following them, and at last reaches the final line of built structures beyond which lie only trees. He stops to catch his breath and ease the sack off his shoulder.

The town straggles into an isolated tea-shop or two, a tyre shop and the frame of a house being constructed, with iron rods stick-ing out of the foundation pillars like tall, thin reeds, and then gives out on to an empty road bordered by vegetation. A mile further on Lakshman comes across a small temple. Its outside walls are painted blue, there is a red pennant on the conical roof and gar-lands of drying marigolds festooned across the small grilled metal gate. Lakshman ties Raju to a tree, removes his own chappals and walks into the tiny courtyard in front of the gate. He expects to find an idol of Shiva inside but it's Hanuman instead, a mace in his left hand and a miniature mountain in his right, which is lifted up as if he is offering the mountain as a sweet to a particularly honoured guest. His face and body are painted blue too. Lakshman brings out the coconut, bows his head – more in concentration than devotion, for he has only one go at what he is about to do – then, with a force disproportionate to breaking the coconut in his hand, he brings it down on to the courtyard with something akin to fury, his teeth clenched. The coconut shatters and the fragments are dispersed wildly. There is a dark spray along the concrete where the liquid has exploded. Lakshman collects the coconut shards, reaches his hand through the metal grille and leaves the fruit on the floor of the sanctum. The prayer he says inwardly reminds the god that the offering is for the surprise gift of food, the blessing that had made his escape so easy, that he won't forget his part of the bargain and will remember the god with gratitude every time he looks after his servant.

The heat is beginning to bare its teeth, and by the time he and Raju have walked another mile, Lakshman, wet from head to toe, feels he is going to faint. Raju has the self-possession that only an animal can have.

They cleave to the shaded areas, following the movement of the sun, until that is no longer feasible. At its zenith, the sun has full, ruthless command over everything under it; nowhere to hide. There is nothing to be done except find some cover and while away the time until sunset, at which point they can begin walking again, but he cannot think that far ahead without drinking some water. An image flashes through his head: the water tank in Golu's temple back in his village, shaded partially by a neeli-gulmohar tree with its small grain-shaped leaves and, sometimes, the blue flowers strewn on its calm, green surface. After an hour of searching, when they reach what he thinks could be a stream, he discovers only a curving line of boulders and rocks, with a rare patch of yellow-green silt where the water has evaporated more recently.

Raju pulls him along, sniffing the rocky ground and, uncharacteristically, pulls at the chain around his neck, as if he wants to break free or lead Lakshman somewhere. Stumbling over stones, he follows Raju to a tiny puddle of water hiding in the dark opening under the point where two big boulders join their rotund stomachs. Before Lakshman can negotiate his footing on the stones and get down to it, Raju, flexing the chain to its tautest, manages to perch on one of the fat boulders, push his snout down into the opening, his body at a mad angle, and lap up the water. Lakshman can hear the loud slurping, followed shortly by the habitual grunting sounds. He pulls Raju away and peers into the crack. All the water is gone. He shuts his eyes tight – he can see popping colours – and opens them again: no, no water. Raju's enormous pink tongue is licking the mouth that houses it. He looks unperturbed, unreadable.

The world around Lakshman turns dark. Before he can think of a suitable punishment for the ungrateful animal, he detaches the nose-rope from the collar and gives it a furious tug. Raju squeals and leaps over the boulder. At that moment the punishment presents itself to Lakshman's conscious mind. He keeps pulling the rope without letting Raju descend on to more level ground, effectively keeping him hopping precariously from one rock to another, or sometimes jogging on one large boulder, the pain preventing him from finding an even surface on which he can at least balance while being kept dancing.

Lakshman lets out a crazed laugh – See, haramzada, what I can do to you? How does this feel, eh? How does it feel?

With each word, the pulling on the rope becomes harder, more manic. The sounds now emerging from Raju change to an infernal combination of shrieking and yowling, the switch between the two random. Lakshman feels fear and relaxes his hold on the rope.

Will Raju now leap at his throat? Will he charge and attack him with his nails? Lakshman drops the rope to pick up the stick to protect himself in that eventuality, forgetting that Raju is temporarily untied and can easily run away, particularly after what has just been inflicted on him.

But Raju doesn't escape. He sits on a rock, emitting that frightening shriek, which peters out gradually. Lakshman waits at a safe distance, stick held ready in his right hand. He swings between fear at a potential attack and anxiety at the possibility of Raju's escape. Raju, his shrieking now over, looks down at the ground, as if he is searching for something he has lost. He clambers down and presses his snout between the two round boulders to peer at the spot where the tiny puddle had been, but there is no comfort to be had from there any longer. The chain is now stretched out slackly on the stones. There is a reasonable length between its end and Raju's neck. With thudding heart, Lakshman catches hold of it but doesn't dare pull. He will reattach the nose-rope to the collar later, when he feels safe.

Two weeks pass. They perform at a crossroads – Lakshman is now desperate; they've eaten once in the last two days. Traffic is desultory: a truck every twenty minutes, a few cars. From the open windows of a couple of them empty packets of crisps and gutka are thrown out. Lakshman runs to the spots where these land, hoping to salvage something, praying that the people in the cars made a mistake, or were getting rid of unwanted food. Raju licks the shiny salty-oily innards of an empty packet of Kurkure. Not a single vehicle stops, no one gets out to watch a bear and his owner sitting at the roadside, the man shaking his damru, the bear trying out a few steps. After several hours of this, the heat becomes too unbearable for this half-hearted soliciting to continue. When it's dark, Lakshman makes his way with Raju to the railway tracks. The heat is hardly any lower at night, when the baked earth radiates it back in its weak revenge on the sun.

There was a far higher density of people and their settlements along the tracks. They wouldn't starve around here, or die of thirst. But he works out quickly that these thin strings of slums, and sometimes even small villages, will not provide them with sustenance for more than a day or a night. Besides, there are too few people to make more than one bear-dance worthwhile; or even one – they do not have anything to spare for roadside entertainment.

Lakshman and Raju live off bread and tea, dal and rice, bananas, the occasional samosa or fried snack, pakoras, sweets, biscuits, fritters. How little one can get used to, he thinks, not for the first time, coveting the food of others, all the while trying not to think of food. At a depleted reservoir under a railway bridge, he strips off and washes himself and his clothes. He spreads out the wet clothes on scrub bushes; they are dry in minutes. He sees Raju, tied to a tree whose trunk casts a shadow as thin as a piece of loose thread, digging up the ground in the four-feet radius allowed him and apparently eating the dry dust and earth. When Lakshman reaches him, he notices, but only after close inspection, that Raju has discovered a long line of black ants and has eaten all that have been within his reach. He has dug up the earth around him hoping to discover a network of nests. Lakshman untethers him and leads him along to where he can spy more ants. They seem to be more readily visible to the animal's eye than to the human's. The glare of the burning soil doesn't make things easier. In a moment of both optical blindness and indulgence, he lets Raju lead him in a zigzag, spiral, circular dance, chasing tiny, scattering black insects, all of which the bear appears to be mopping up with the pink extended cloth of his tongue and devouring with sureness and ease. The grunts and unnameable range of sounds coming out of him seem to Lakshman to belong to the same arsenal out of which his pain is expressed. Would Lakshman, if he had his eyes shut, ever be able to distinguish between the two kinds? The unexpected gift is exhausted all too soon. He thinks Raju looks mournful.

– Chaley, he asks, we have a long way to go. He wants to stroke
the bear's head but holds back.

Scourged by the hot winds, they can barely proceed. The very air
has become an invisible fire. Lakshman has salvaged empty, discarded bottles of Bisleri along the way. He fills up whenever he gets
a chance, often from tea-stalls and roadside eateries. At least water
is one thing he doesn't have to pay for. Besides, the novelty value
of a bear prises open some people enough to offer food. But a substantial amount of their erratic and meagre supply of food comes
from foraging. It occurs to Lakshman that Raju is much the best
equipped to do this and it may be in his, Lakshman's, interests even
to let the bear free and follow where the animal's nose and instincts
lead him, but that, of course, he cannot do.

They find watermelons lying among their decaying leaves like
dark green boulders in a field. Lakshman waits until it is pitch-dark,
then gorges himself on four of them, breaking them open with
the side of his hand. He gets the runs through the night and soils
his trousers. He exhausts his supply of water cleaning himself, but
there's no way he can wash his pyjamas until he comes to another
pond or reservoir. Disgust fills him, and shame, until he feels he
can taste them as the rebellious ball of phlegm at the back of his
throat, impatient to come out. Like a helpless child, he surrenders
to tears, tears of self-pity and anger. How did he get here, squatting yet again to let another brief, hot squirt come out of his sore
sphincter, when he had a home, more to eat than he has now, his
wife to look after him, children to carry on his line and take care of
him in his old age?

The density of slums increases near the level-crossings and stations
of bigger towns. It feels as if the greedy, unruly sprawl is restless in
its desire to subsume the iron tracks within it. Pigs, dogs, snotty children with matted hair, rutted earth that will turn to large stretches

of puddle-pocked fields, sewage, open drains, narrow lanes with rickety houses closely huddled along them like too many bad, crooked teeth in a mouth, signage everywhere, on walls, on make-shift boards, on the front of houses and shops, signage in Hindi, which he can read, but often in languages he doesn't know but can tell are Urdu and English. And garbage, garbage everywhere, inseparable from the humans and animals and buildings and shops, each seemingly flowing into the other, with no lines to mark the boundaries. In the narrow roads and lanes, the thickness of traffic – rickshaws, cars, motorbikes, buses, lorries, bicycles, scooters – stuns Lakshman. How is he ever going to penetrate to the centre of these towns and make Raju dance? He can barely cross the road. An odd thing happens. So far on their journey, Lakshman has fol-lowed Raju, now this reverses itself; Raju seems to want to hide behind Lakshman, making it awkward for him to hold on to the chain with his hand behind him at an angle to his shoulder. And . . . and . . . who knows, what if the animal, in a moment of wildness, attacks him from behind?

But the sheer numbers mean that they attract attention, which, Lakshman is beginning to understand, he can attempt to harness. Set inwards a little distance from the railway-edge of the town, Lakshman and Raju put on their show under a tree near the crossing of three roads, in the narrow margin between an open drain and the stream of traffic, the band where fruit-sellers and snack-merchants sit during the day. A sizeable crowd gathers around them, impeding the passage of traffic. Encouraged by the number of people, Lakshman tries to up his game – he sings snatches of Hindi film songs which are currently all the rage and which he has heard blaring out of loudspeakers everywhere along the way. He doesn't know the lyrics, only the refrain or the catchphrase, but that seems to be enough, coupled, crucially, with Raju's antic movements, to bring some entertainment to the gathering.

Halfway through the act, Lakshman feels an odd sense of detachment steal over him after he inadvertently notices Raju's eyes – blinking, unfocused, looking at nothing, or seeming to be looking at something beyond what is in front of and around him. It is as if he is not present. Lakshman begins to feel that he, too, is looking at himself in a different way, from a distance: a man playing a damru, mouthing repetitive words of command or cajoling, singing snatches of popular songs, with a funny black-and-grey animal circling him on its hind legs, sometimes shaking itself rhythmically, sometimes bringing up its front paws to its face as if in a namaste. In this state of flotation, Lakshman feels that he has done this before many times, this roadside performance, including this very one, in this very place, at this very hour, so much so that he can predict the next few seconds of the action. All his life is becoming the repetition of the same few actions, unfolding in slightly different destinations.

A corpse is borne past them on a pallet with its retinue of mourners. Ram naam satya hai, Ram naam satya hai. Lakshman, pulled out of his reverie, instantly notes that the dead body passed him on his left side; an ill omen. His heart goes out of the performance. He tries to wind it down but a child, accompanied by her father, wants to ride Raju. Lakshman, pushing down his anxiety, asks for an upfront payment before he assents. The man gives him ten rupees. Scarcely believing his luck, he lets go of the rope pulling Raju; the bear sits down immediately. Lakshman attaches the rope to the collar – in a sign of how much he has been trained, Raju goes on all fours, thinking that it is time to go. The girl is seated on him gingerly, the father's hands on her, steadying her, unwilling to let go, should anything untoward happen.

Lakshman's heart is a mad drum only he can hear. The trick will be to keep Raju in this position. Will he be able to understand the change in signals – *leash* and damru, not nose-rope and damru? The corpse-bearers. He should not be attempting this on a day a corpse has passed on his left. The girl's legs come down the sides of Raju by only a few inches. She holds them out; she is not relaxed and clearly having second thoughts. The father keeps up a comforting patter. Lakshman adds his voice to it, but more to keep Raju comfortable and steady. Instead of playing the damru, he lets Raju see that he is standing up and tugs gently at the collar band, hoping, praying, willing that Raju is going to start walking slowly, thinking that they are moving on from here.

And Raju does exactly that. He starts walking, the girl balanced on his back, the father at her side, reaching out to keep his hand on his daughter, and Lakshman following no more than three feet behind, chain in hand, crooning – Chal, mera beta, chal, chal, mera Raju, mera chhotu, chal, chal.

Halfway through Raju's navigation of the circle, the crowd erupts into applause.

The following day, at around the same time, Lakshman and Raju begin their act again. But this time Lakshman advertises before he begins – Come, come, come one, come all, come to see the bear that gives children rides on his back, a gentle bear, a paltu bhaloo, a bear who is a child himself; come, come, only ten rupees a ride, ten rupees only. He shakes his damru as he chants this in a sing-song. Raju shakes his head. People think he is doing this in harmony with the rhythm of the damru. Raju gives ten children rides on his back. Lakshman has to turn away a few more because he judges them to be too heavy for the bear. He makes just over a hundred and eighty rupees that evening.

He orders two plates of dinner at a shack – rice, roti, dal, sabzi, egg curry – and gives one to Raju, then buys fruits and laddoos for both of them. Raju shits – an enormous pile – near where the pigs are wallowing on a spreading hill of garbage, sewage and mud as they try to find a slightly secluded spot where they can settle for the night. Lakshman picks the back of a dawakhana, shut for the night; a narrow ledge that forms the top stair of a flight of three leading to a collapsible iron gate, heavily locked, at different points, with five padlocks. The place has the great advantage of a gulmohar tree a few yards away on the lane that leads to the main street. Lakshman ties Raju to this tree, checks and rechecks if the day's takings are in the inside pocket of his trousers, and settles down to wait for sleep to come.

He dreams of fire again, vast, swift-flowing streams of it spreading out with absolute abandon, absolute freedom, and wakes up sweaty and terrified. His first thought is of his money. He takes it out of his inside pocket and counts it – it's all there, slightly damp from its proximity to his underwear, which is wet with the sweat from his groin and thighs as he had lain dreaming. Before his heart has stopped rattling, he decides he has to stow away the money in a safer place: so many people have seen him make money, who knows what is going through their heads, if one or two of them are not petty thieves, pickpockets – after all, these places are full of people who are up to no good. Who can be trusted these days? Certainly not strangers in a strange town. He has heard of thieves who can slit pockets with such a sharp knife that the sleeping man who is being robbed does not feel the slightest disturbance to awake him. It is so skilfully done that he doesn't even become aware of the theft as soon as he wakes up. Only when he searches inside his trousers or shirt to use some of the earnings does he find that his hand has gone clean through a hole.

The brainwave startles even him. He takes the money, folds each ten-rupee note on its horizontal axis and moves towards Raju, who gets up from his sitting position immediately. Lakshman crouches and contemplates him for a while, wondering how he is going to do it. Raju yawns – Lakshman can see the flash of his teeth and gums and tongue, and even his throat in the diffuse moonlight, and a brief gust of his rotten breath hits him. That view of the inside of Raju's mouth makes him even more nervous. Moving quickly,

Lakshman loosens the collar-band around Raju's neck, chanting meaningless words in his usual cooing sing-sing tone all the while, and inserts the thin strip of folded money carefully under the band. He realises that he has forgotten the stick. His hands shake as he keeps one firm finger pressed against the notes, tightens the band and eases his finger away. There. The money is now safe. No one will ever dream of that as a hiding place, should they want to rob him. Besides, even if they guessed, who would dare approach a bear?

The early hint of rain is beginning to touch the sky and the air when Lakshman and Raju arrive in the outskirts of what seems like a small, contained town – Varadapur, the black letters against the yellow-painted stone sign says. It is too small for trains to stop here. The afternoon fills with the milk of mist, low-lying in the open fields before the human habitations begin. Lakshman can smell it mingled with the odour of cow-dung – it is not mist but smoke from the chulhas being lit for the evening cooking. The sky turns a dark purple at the hinge of dusk and darkness; Lakshman fears a tremendous downpour, but it only spits for a few minutes, just enough for the dry earth to release that subtly rotting smell, then stops. Lakshman reads it correctly: the end of summer is here. He is lucky that the imminent monsoon coincides with his arrival in Varadapur, where he can look for some kind of shelter for the next three or four months.

A walk down the only paved road running as the spine of the town reveals something unusual: a series of almost identical buildings on either side of the road, near the centre. They are each four storeys high, with the outside of the curved front verandas all painted a rectangle of yellow, which must once have been the colour of ripe mangoes but is now closer to muddy shit. But still, compared to the greyness of the exposed concrete elsewhere – the paint must have been erased by years of rain, sun and neglect – the tenacious yellow is startling. Surrounded by overgrown ferns and weeds and set back from the road in what looks like a thinning jungle of pines, the buildings are all in such a state of dilapidation that Lakshman cannot tell at first if they had once been occupied and are now abandoned, or if the construction work had been discontinued at a very late stage. Floors and railings of some of the balconies are missing; the short, flying-bridge-like stairways connecting one building to another on each storey are broken and dangling in mid-air; leaking pipes have left indelible lines of rust, all exactly in the same spots on the different buildings; broken and missing windows, some boarded up, some like hollowed-out eyes, give on to the darkness inside, others have rusted or missing grilles. The buildings have compounds abutting them and shared with the others; clearly a housing complex. The yards are cracked, rife with weeds, barely visible. It is a spectacle not of ruin but of the process of ruination. This is the kind of place where ghosts live.

Lakshman's first thought is that if these buildings are derelict, with no signs of inhabitation, he and Raju may be able to find a temporary home here, before moving on towards the plains after the end of the monsoons. In whatever state of disintegration, one of these could still offer a roof over their heads to protect them from the rain. But months on the road, one day here, the next day somewhere else, living like a bird or a wild animal, have sharpened a certain kind of instinct in him and he decides to wait until it's dark before exploring the buildings. In the interim, he walks around for a while, taking in the town, always on the lookout for ideal places where they might be able to perform, spots that are likely to attract the largest possible numbers, the location of the shops, the ragged streams of slums on the periphery ... The reconnaissance reveals a large school, set in its own grounds, now just a stretch of loose, level dust, and a BDO complex.

Lakshman discovers that he can get a square meal of dal, rice and sabzi every day at around one o'clock at the canteen of the

BDO for five rupees only. And he finds out the history of the ghost buildings. They were built to house the employees of a big national machine-tools company, which had to close down its operations in Varadapur after ten years. Most of the inhabitants had left, either because they got a transfer to another branch, or because they lost their jobs and could no longer live in accommodation that came with their work. The company had done nothing with the houses, letting them stand and rot instead. A few of the flats still have people living in them – who knows what their rights are? But a lot of them are empty, probably unsafe, given that time has eaten into them so thoroughly. Most are inseparable from the wild undergrowth surrounding them, even during the dry months, nests to insects, reptiles, animals. This much Lakshman pieces together while he and Raju have tea and samosas at a roadside stall. The usual group of stragglers and curious people with nothing to do, nowhere to go, hang around asking questions – Doesn't he bite? Does he attack with his claws? How old is he? Where did Lakshman find him? Is Lakshman a qalandar? Will Raju dance now? When will they put on their act? He dodges and parries and gives partial replies, calculates what sort of answers are going to serve him best. They talk aimlessly for a good while – about whether the monsoon is going to arrive on time, about the school, about the temples in Varadapur. This last subject breaks down a certain invisible barrier; the men understand now that Lakshman is not a real qalandar – that is, not a Muslim. He knows he may have to stay in this town for some time, so he makes an effort to be warm and friendly and get to know the familiar faces. He buys matches, a candle, and tries to push away the thought of what he might need to live in one place for longer than a day or two, for that thought is a trap, the enormous lid.

When it's totally dark, he walks back with Raju towards the ghost housing complex. He steps over the low stone wall that marks the margin of the road and stands amidst the dried ferns, behind a tree, calf-deep in undergrowth, and watches, letting his eyes become adapted to the darkness. After what feels to him a long time, he thinks he can make out a light at a window on the second or third floor in a building east of where he is standing, a good distance away. The one closest to him has been entirely devoured by the dark. He ties Raju to a tree and makes his way, slowly and carefully, to this one, afraid to strike a match to see where he's planting his feet. The rustle of his footsteps is too loud to his ears. He can hear Raju sniffing around in the earth. He wonders how close he is to the building when he receives a small shock – he can suddenly see weak firelight framing the edges of an imperfectly boarded-up window. Someone is in there: a place to avoid. He cannot see anything around him, he doesn't know in which direction he can, or should, move. He lights a match and in its brief lifespan can only make out cracked concrete and weeds at his feet and shadowy details of a corner of a wall, maybe even a door or a doorway, but all is shadow and flicker before darkness reasserts itself. It doesn't seem like such a good idea to have come here in the dark. The thought of criminals and miscreants using this as their den occurs to him and he wants to run away swiftly – it doesn't look as if it's going to rain tonight, another night under the open sky would be perfectly possible.

He doesn't understand what pulls him along, surmounting the fear, to explore. He lights his candle; impossible to move without it, now that he is almost within the housing complex. In that weak yellow glow, he navigates himself away from the house in which he had seen some light to a building diagonally behind it, across a cement compound shared by both. In this one there is an electric bulb on one of the top floors. There is a doorway to his right, leading into pitch-darkness. He enters; the candlelight is as useful as a wet paper bag; still, it's the only thing he has. He trips over a raised bit – a stair – and falls. The candle escapes from his grip and rolls away, but fortunately continues to burn. Lakshman grabs hold of

it and looks at where he has fallen: two stairs, leading to a landing, on either side of which are two identical doors, or rather one
set of doors, shut, and another doorway with its doors missing. He
enters and finds himself in a large empty room. The floor is littered
with dried leaves, bits of broken brick, inches of dust, unidentifiable
debris and rubbish, broken glass near the window, which is missing all the panes from the wooden frames, a strew of dried pellets
that look like goat-droppings . . . Something scurries away across the
floor. A rat? The walls are stained and cracked and, in places, oddly
furry. There is a dark patch in one corner of the floor, near the window, where the room seems to slope, or it could be a shadow, an
area where the candlelight doesn't reach. There is a doorway next
to it, presumably leading further inside the flat to the other rooms.

Lakshman has exhausted his supply of fearlessness; he cannot
bring himself to explore the whole place in the dark. He wants to
check if there's anyone living, or hiding, here but doesn't know
how to go about it: should he call out? Should he bring in Raju first
and then go looking with him? The presence of a bear could protect him from all manner of things. Besides, he feels lonely without Raju. He turns and heads out, candle in hand, his neck and
back prickling with fear, an atavistic fear of something getting him
from behind. It's odd that dark open spaces, such as fields, copses,
forests, roads, do not hold this terror for him, only dark interiors,
rooms, the insides of houses.

He tries to retrace his steps but is certain that he is losing his way.
In desperation, he lets out a loud whisper – Raju, Raju.

Nothing except a general rustling.

He calls out, now using his whole voice – Raju, Raju.

An answering sound reaches him, something between a chatter,
a yawn and a squeaking. Lakshman's fear dissolves.

The spectacle that greets Lakshman at first light, after a sleepless
night of fears and discomfort, gives him a shock. The interior

is filthier and more dilapidated than candlelight had revealed. To Lakshman, who has some sketchy knowledge of buildings, renovation and decoration, everything in here has crossed that line beyond which it cannot be cleaned, restored or repaired but has to be destroyed and begun, from scratch, again. That dark area he saw yesterday is not a shadow but a huge tongue of slime that has survived, wet and gleaming, all through the blood-evaporating summer. There is a bloom of orange mould – or is it rust? – occupying one-third of the ceiling. The wall in which the doorway is set is spored by a rash of black spots. There are paw prints in the dust and splotches of paan- and gutka-spit on the floor and splattering the lower third of the walls. Through the doorway that leads inside he crosses a short passage that gives on to what used to be a kitchen and an empty room beside it; the wall between the two is broken. Doors lean off their hinges and the wood at the bottom is eaten away in wildly serrated curves. The sink in the kitchen looks dry – there is no running water, Lakshman checks – yet all the pipes are corroded by rust, some sections into a fine filigree work. How could everything be so dry and yet marked so much by the wet at the same time? The small window in the bathroom, missing all its glass, looks out on to the side of the adjacent building that is a mirror image – a vertical series of identical tiny bathroom windows with the rusty, disintegrating cages of the grilles protecting the small bedroom verandas two or three feet away from them, repeated on each level. The rust scars from the metal bars outside the bathroom windows and the veranda grilles score the side of the building in thick orange tracks. Lakshman takes in the bathroom. The rajma-shaped toilet on the floor, with a raised, ridged rectangle on each side to plant the feet on, is full of dried leaves and has turned the colour of dried blood from, presumably, white; a huge colony of cockroaches on the walls, some scurrying about, most of them still and waiting; again, that strange mixture of opposites, slime and mould on one hand, extreme aridity on the other. The bed-room, while of a piece with the rest of the flat, is comparatively less afflicted. In here Lakshman sees the first and only piece of furniture in the entire place – a broken chair, partially burnt, with a large lick of soot on the wall behind it. Apart from this, the flat contains only the gathering rubble of its own slow disintegration. It is this room that Lakshman decides to make his home for the rainy season, and the front room, Raju's, with the bars on the window serving as the tethering post. If anyone tries to enter, a bear just inside the entrance will serve as an effective deterrent, Lakshman hopes.

There is a tiny nub of panic in him: he has to make the bulk of his money for the next three months in the days – no one knows how many – before the rains begin. He goes out with Raju and finds a temple. A blue-faced Shiva, smiling subtly, is enshrined there, sitting on a cow, one leg raised and folded over, the other one hanging. Lakshman buys a garland and a water-melon from one of the men who have spread out their wares on jute sacking or baskets just outside the temple, on the verge of the road. There's much excitement among them – Look, look, a bear's arrived! Lakshman offers the flowers and fruit to the doz-ing priest, who wakes up, takes in Raju with a glance, then sits up and says – Stay away, stay away, this is a temple, can't you see? It's not for people of your kind.

Lakshman retorts – I'm not a qalandar. I come from Deodham, I'm a kayasth. If I were a Muslim, I wouldn't have bothered to come here. Which Muslim brings offerings to Shiva?

The priest looks suspicious but accepts the marigold garland and the watermelon, if reluctantly, then rings a little hand-bell, sprin-kles some water on him and murmurs something hurriedly that sounds like a mantra. Lakshman sits, feet tucked under his bottom, and brings his head down on the first step of the three leading to the tiny vestibule where the priest is stationed, looking at him with unmasked distaste. Against the wishes and hopes of tens of millions of people in the country, Lakshman prays for a big delay in the onset of monsoon.

When he raises his head, the priest asks – A bear, huh? Let's see him dance.

Lakshman says – There aren't enough people here.

The priest says irritatedly – If you put in some effort to get people here, there would be. It's a temple, there are crowds here at certain times.

Lakshman understands why the priest is keen to have him put on a show in the temple precinct. He weighs it up and finally says – Thik hain, I'll do it, but not now, it's getting too hot, we won't be able to get many people. You tell me when the crowds come, which times of the day, and we'll be here.

The priest, too, does some kind of inner calculation before he agrees – Come on Friday, come early in the morning, six or seven. Friday is the big day of worship here.

Lakshman and Raju are at the temple early on Friday morning. The flower-sellers, fruit-sellers, vendors of relics and puja paraphernalia are all there. The purohit doesn't show any sign of recognising him. There are, however, around eight or ten people, mostly women, who have come to worship. They are all distracted by the presence of a bhaloo and a bhaloo-wallah. Lakshman sets up his station a few yards from the temple. He begins playing the damru and the sing-song chant inviting people to come and see the dancing bear. Lakshman keeps this up until enough people have gathered, maybe twenty or thirty. A couple of cars have stopped and their passengers have come out to see what's going on – who knows if they'll stay? These people have more money, Lakshman knows, than the townspeople. He begins to sing his incomplete film-songs while tugging on the rope that goes through Raju's nose. Raju jigs and cavorts and walks round in a circle. How dirty and dusty his pelt looks, Lakshman thinks, but look at his claws – they look like miniature swords made out of grey iron. The butterflies on that stream: how beautiful they were; and Raju enchanted, too.

On a whim, Lakshman says – If you give him something, he will take it, he knows how to accept things.

He knows he is tempting Fate but hopes that Shiva, so near him, will send him his blessing. Lakshman leads the upright Raju around in a circle. The bear's front paws are held near his throat, as if he is a supplicant in this court of spectators. Lakshman picks out a man from the inner circle and says – Give him something, go on, something small, a fruit or a vegetable, he'll take it. The man looks embarrassed; he doesn't move. But the man next to him says – Here, take – and fishes out a banana. Lakshman gently touches his stick to Raju's front paws. The animal extends one of them towards the fruit and, miraculously, as if Shiva really has seen what is going on in Lakshman's head, Raju makes a bowl of his paw – Lakshman can see the grey pads, like stones held in the bear's palm – and lets the man give him a banana, which he wolfs in an eye-blink, even as the people are clapping and expressing their amazement at his darling cleverness. Lakshman is, to begin with, stunned; he recovers himself quickly – it wouldn't do to let anyone guess what a fluke the trick was – and lets his heart swell with gratitude for Shiva.

At the end of the performance, Lakshman goes around collecting money – Show the joy you had from clever Raju. Give with open hearts and open hands. Give from your heart. Make little Raju happy.

As soon as the people disperse, the purohit approaches Lakshman and asks for his 'fee'.

– Fee? Lakshman falls from the sky.

– That prime space beside the temple, you think it comes free?

– But . . . but you didn't mention anything about money that day. Had I known, I would never have come here, I would have gone somewhere else.

– Gone where? Where else would you have got such a crowd in a town like this? The fee is hardly for my use, it's for him – the priest indicates the idol inside.

Lakshman doesn't have the opportunity to hide part of his takings and offer a fraction of the remainder to the priest, for everything unfolded right under his nose.

The priest says – Give it as an offering to the god. If you don't, he'll be angry. And you know how terrible his anger can be.

Lakshman capitulates, initially out of a vague sense of fear, but later, while nursing the sore from being stung by the priest, he thinks that perhaps the bribe was not such a bad thing, for it bound the priest into a certain tie of obligation. Besides, he really needs the god on his side for the rains to be delayed.

Back at the ghost building, he secretes most of the money he has managed to retain under Raju's collar, keeping on his person only what he thinks is necessary to buy food. That evening, indoors, Lakshman feeds Raju and, in a rare moment of intrepidity and affection, strokes his neck and back while keeping up a chatting and crooning. Raju answers with his own spectrum of sounds, more eloquent than usual. Lakshman has never been able to read them, to understand the emotions or wants behind them, but tonight he takes them to be Raju's pleasure at being stroked; the bear's expression of gratitude and friendliness for the human who looks after him. Raju's vocalisation of whatever he feels doesn't let up; instead, it gets louder. Lakshman is afraid that anyone living in these buildings – so far invisible and inaudible – will pass by, hear it and come over to investigate. He tries his usual twin approach, soothing followed by threatening, but tonight Raju won't be placated. What on earth has got into the cursed creature? It doesn't take long for Lakshman to find out – the diminishing of the noises and the appalling stench are almost simultaneous. He swings between despair and rage: who will clean up the mess? His living quarters are now defiled. And the only reason he hadn't kept Raju tied to a tree or post outside was because he was afraid of being discovered. Because Raju had always done his business outside, it had never occurred to Lakshman that such behaviour was not fixed or regular, governable by rules that applied to humans. What keeps him from punishing Raju is the fear that the resultant yowling might attract attention. He bites down on his fury.

The following day he has a choice: whether to set up near the temple again or find a new spot. He weighs up the pros and cons of each option and decides to go for the former. The priest wants a bigger cut of the day's income. Lakshman has no negotiating power.

He knows he is getting good at the performances, with his patter and singing and soliciting, but his heart is not in it today. The heat and the humidity are pressing against him like a wall on either side. He wants to smash the priest's head against the concrete stairs on which he had laid his own to worship that first time. The man's spilt brains would be a suitable offering to the god. Lakshman gives him half of what he has made and asks him to exchange his, Lakshman's, handfuls of loose change for paper currency. Away from the public, he hides the notes under Raju's collar. The sky has darkened.

He is beside himself with worry. At night, he wakes up every twenty minutes or so, waiting for the sound of rain, which doesn't happen. The mugginess is suffocating. He has covered Raju's shit with newspapers. He worries about Raju, now tied to the nearest tree outside, being discovered. Then he catches the distinct sound of a child crying somewhere in the building, or maybe in the adjacent one, and freezes. Rustling and creaks and taps, ordinary night

sounds that would have gone unnoticed before, now become mag-
nified to his ears as preludes to imminent discovery and disaster.
When nothing materialises, he ventures out to check on Raju. A
low chatter greets him, as if Raju understands the need to be quiet.
The moment disappears as Lakshman looks up and notices lights
at no fewer than four windows in the housing complex and one on
a higher floor than his in the building he is in. Fear and incompre-
hension jostle for supremacy inside him. How could anyone live
in his building? The staircase leading to the upper floors is broken
and ends in a huge yawn of suspended jagged concrete halfway
up the landing above his floor. Absent-mindedly, he strokes Raju's
head, forgetting to be afraid of him. Raju raises his paws and tries
to bring Lakshman's head down. Lakshman, now alert, gently tries
to move away but Raju positions himself closer to him, brings his
lowly chattering head to his master's chest and holds him in a brief
hug before letting go.

All morning it drizzles weakly. Lakshman avoids the temple and
walks in the direction of the school. He is surprised to discover that
the loudspeaker broadcasting the latest film songs, which he has
been hearing since waking up, is located within the school prem-
ises. Preparations for some kind of a festival or function are under
way. There are more snack-sellers, balloon-wallahs, drinks-sellers,
sherbet-wallahs than he had noticed the first time he walked past
it. Raju is overexcited, as are the vendors and other people who
see them arrive. A stage has been set up beside the school building. In the wings of the stage, entirely open to the view of people
on the road, a girl, in garish costume and make-up, is trying out
dance moves, oblivious to being watched. She looks very pleased
with herself, then she breaks into a grin and a giggle, as if she is
about to play a big prank on someone. She disappears into the
building. A gaggle of girls comes out next, each one dressed to the
nines. They, too, dance to the song that's blaring out of the sound

system – 'Aankhen do' – until an adult, presumably a teacher, comes out and admonishes them. They scatter, helpless with giggles, and run inside. Lakshman discovers from the cold-drinks-seller that it's a three-day festival to celebrate the founding of the school.

Raju and Lakshman are a huge hit when they perform. The crowd is the largest they've ever had. Lakshman throws himself into the act, singing along to some of the songs that are playing on the public address system, much to the delight of the girls, their teachers and guardians. People buy Raju all kinds of things – chana garam, ber, cucumber, peanuts – to have the pleasure of watching him take them in his paws and eat them.

For three consecutive days, Raju and Lakshman repeat their gig. The takings are beyond any of Lakshman's previous imaginings. Raju's collar band swells; Lakshman thinks he will need to replace it soon with a wider, tougher one. He wonders if he has enough to send home – he will have to take it all out one evening and do a count – but how is he going to send it? Through whom? Someone once told him that a post-office could arrange these things.

On the third day, as they walk towards a roadside eatery on the way back to the housing complex, a day almost tremulous with the weight of the stillness and waiting that come before the skies open, someone calls out to him. He turns round. A man he doesn't immediately recognise is saying to him – Salaam, ji.

Then the wave of recognition crashes over him. Salim Qalandar.

Salim says – So. He's grown big, hasn't he? But he doesn't make a move to stroke or pet Raju, only looks at him intently.

Lakshman still hasn't managed to gather his thoughts.

Salim says – Yes, very big.

Pause.

– And I see you've put him to good use. He's making good money for you. Here he hums a line from one of the songs that Lakshman has sung in the most recent gig – My name is Lakhan, mera naam hain Lakhan – and lets out a great cackle. It sounds so sinister that Lakshman loses what few words he had scrambled together inside his head.

– You owe me money, Salim says. The transition from laughter to business is like the crack of a whip.

– I can't give you the entire amount, Lakshman at last finds himself able to speak.

– Why? For three days you were raking it in with both hands.

– It's not as much as you think. Most of it is loose change, in coins. You know well how it works.

– You can pay me some of it. You can be sure I'll come back for the remainder.

Lakshman does a quick calculation. It defeats him: he cannot be certain of the amount he has stored under Raju's collar. Then another thought strikes him, more terrifying: does Salim know about his hiding place?

Just to be rid of Salim as soon as possible Lakshman says – You can have everything I've earned today. Here you go. I'm keeping back ten rupees for chai-paani, here, see.

– I know these tricks, you forget that I was a qalandar. A real one. This is not *everything* you've taken today.

– On my mother— Lakshman begins.

– Cut it out. Who'd believe a fox like you? All right, I'll take this now, but don't forget . . . He leaves the rest unsaid.

When he is gone, Lakshman feels that the whole encounter was a dream. He has only the disappearance of the day's income to show that it was real. As he walks past the low stone wall, he cannot tell if it is the wall's shadow, cleaving to it, on the road, or a shadow-coloured stain running alongside it.

At night, he hears the crying of a child again, followed, shockingly, by the muffled sounds of a couple quarrelling. All kinds of tumultuous thoughts go through his head: has Salim informed the authorities? Are they already on his tail? Are they biding their time, waiting for the perfect moment to catch him? Is he being watched by some of the people who live in this complex? Has the crooked priest shopped him, out of spite because he moved his act elsewhere, depriving him of his cut? How will he ever find Ramlal? Is he alive? Everything is curdling.

In the morning, he and Raju go to the school. There is no music over a loudspeaker today. The number of itinerant vendors has halved. Inside, there are men dismantling the stage – the bright-orange cloth that was its outer skin has already been removed, exposing the skeleton of bamboos and planks. Chairs are stacked in discrete piles all over the dusty ground that is the school's playing field. There are no girls, no teachers, no guardians, only the silence of their absence.

– It's closed today. The school's closed today. Nothing for you here – the tea-stall owner tells him.

He makes his way with Raju to the temple, anxiously, reluctantly. A thin drizzle begins, more fine spray than rain. The purohit ignores him. Lakshman has no energy to do his usual prelude to drum up business, no interest in making Raju dance. He hopes that the sight of the bear tied to the tree will be enough indication to passers-by to gather.

The spray becomes more substantial, a proper drizzle. The tamarind tree, in resplendent leaf from the killing summer sun, offers them a comforting circle of protection. He notices the trunk of the tree for the first time: there is a strange pattern of huge eyes, much like Shiva's on the slope of Nanda Devi, on the bark, eye above eye above eye. The trunk is watching him with dozens of those eyes. His world cants around him. After an hour, or two, or three – Lakshman loses track of the unmoving mass of time – he has made only ten rupees, and his clothes and hair are damp. When the priest pokes his head out of the temple chamber and hollers – You bring bad luck, you look like a jackal – he knows that it's time to go. Everything is curdling.

And, as if in confirmation, the skies really do open this time and the rain comes down in lashing sheets with such force that the drops seem to perforate the ground on which they fall. Before he knows it, he's soaked. Raju looks shrunken, with his dripping wet pelt. He lets out a set of low squeaks and grunts and keeps opening his jaws wide, as if yawning, and shaking his head repeatedly. The road turns into a swift-flowing stream in no time, and the earth margins dissolve and flow into it. The trees offer little shelter from the strafing; in any case, the movement towards home, from one tree to another, gets them so drenched that it becomes pointless to seek shelter any more.

At the housing complex, Lakshman cannot decide whether to bring Raju inside or leave him out in the rain all night. Maybe it'll stop, he thinks, and leaves the bear tied to his tree outside.

All night it rains. The sound of it, first loud, then musical, ultimately monotonous, keeps Lakshman awake. Then he hears the drips inside, over that unchanging background of water pounding everything in its way with steady, focused obstinacy. Rain is coming into the flat through unseen cracks and holes, a few of them seemingly quite near him. He lights the candle to investigate. At first, nothing, except the sound of two sets of drips, out of step with each other. Lakshman discovers them after some strenuous searching – one at the threshold, from the top of where the door-frame had been, and one from the ceiling, a few inches away from where Lakshman sleeps, but near his feet. He goes out to bring Raju in – the animal is a sodden hulk, which keeps shaking itself vigorously and spraying huge quantities of water around him – and while rushing back, soaked himself now, he notices the lights at exactly the same windows where he has seen them on previous occasions. Who are the people behind those windows? Why has he never seen them outside? Do they know he is here? Have they noticed Raju? He wants to scream into the pouring night and ask them to come out and show their faces.

In the morning, he catches a split-second's glint on one of the walls in the front room where Raju is. It's on that stretch of dark slime, explaining its presence – water is thinly and steadily seeping down the wall. He looks up at the rust-coloured stain on the ceiling: could that be the point of entry? But that means that the water could be penetrating through the floor of the flat above and, in this manner, all the way up to the roof of the building. When will it all cave in? While they are here? On him and Raju?

It is raining relentlessly, his world now trapped between mud at his feet and unbroken grey above. From now on, there will be no hope of regular work. He'll have to take his chance in the gaps, if any, between downpours, and it will be the most difficult thing in the world to set up, solicit, get a crowd in this weather, because it is against the vital thing his trade needs – time.

Over the next seven days Lakshman and Raju manage two shows; or, rather, one, because it starts raining one-third of the way through the second gig and what few people there are run off to find shelter without paying. He spends the last of his ready money buying tea, samosas and sweets at a shack inside which he waits for the rain to let up. The woman behind the huge kadai does not allow the bear to come inside. Lakshman goes out to share his food with Raju. He comes outside and stands beside him, holding his leash, in the sliver of mud under the narrow-est of awnings formed by the jutting tin roof. It offers almost no protection from the pelting rain. The runnel of dirty dishwater at his feet swells with the steady, generous run-off from the roof until the sliver of mud on which he is standing begins to be swal-lowed by the drain. He will have to break into his savings under Raju's collar band if they are to survive. The thought of nibbling away at the packet, which he has been meaning to send home, does not bother him as much as he thought it would. Different sorts of calculations go through his head, such as how much he would save if he were to buy a chulha, a pot, rice and dal, and cook for himself in the room that used to be the kitchen in his flat. He would have to check how much money he has saved. The thoughts of housekeeping instantly summon up, as if they are words of magic, the presence of his old friend – that invisible boulder, lately absent from his life, presses down on him. It's that familiar feeling of being buried alive, of light and air all around him being squeezed out inexorably. Would it have been better without Raju if, for whatever reason, he had been sheltering in these ghost-haunted ruins on his own? He knows the answer, but denies it in the argument he is having with himself – Raju is not a burden to him even though being chained to an animal, who is his responsibility, is burdensome on a day-to-day basis. Instead, it's the only freedom he has ever known.

It's dark and still pouring when he and Raju return home. He strips off all his clothes, wrings them and hangs them out to dry. He will need to buy another pair of trousers and a shirt, maybe a large sheet for lying on or covering himself with.

Raju tries to get away from the small puddle that has dripped off him, but four feet of rope will only allow him so much manoeuvring space. Lakshman ties him to a different spot and loosens his wet collar band to take out all his money. What comes out on his fingers are wet shreds, almost a pulp. Incredulous, he takes off the band entirely – Raju is free of his leash for the first time since he was found by humans. Lakshman runs his hand first along the inside of the collar, then along Raju's neck. The paper money has disintegrated into wet confetti. Even the notes that seem to be whole come apart in his hands the moment he tries to lift them out of the soggy mass. The band lies on the dark floor, knotted to a length of rope, which is tied to a metal bar on the window. Raju sits beside it obediently, not yet aware that he can move around at will. Lakshman shifts through the chyme of paper – how meagre it seems now – looking for something, anything, to salvage; even a ten-rupee note will do. No, nothing.

If he doesn't sit down, he feels that he will be blown away, out of the barred window, like a mote of dust or a feather. He holds his hands to the sides of his head and sits on the floor. Then he howls. Unmindful of who may be listening, whom he awakes, what unwelcome attention he may be attracting, he screams. He screams not from his throat but from his lungs, his navel – the sound comes from somewhere deeper than where the voice is. He screams and screams and screams until there is no sound left in him. It is only when Raju, chattering lowly, comes up to him with hesitant steps and tries to take his head between his paws that Lakshman comes out of himself to realise that Raju is free.

Through the murk inside him a single thought rises to the surface – what does the animal think?

IV

I: *Axe*

The first image that came to her when she thought of that day was the way the blood had arced and sprayed as they threw her brother's right hand into the surrounding bushes. Her eyes had followed the flying curve of the drops of blood as the severed hand flew into the bushes and disappeared. What else did she notice? That blood on green leaves in the shadow was not red but black. And even on the green that had the sun on it, the blood was also black until you looked carefully, very carefully, and then it would appear to be red, but only if you already knew that it was blood and, therefore, red, not black. Milly remembered all this.

This was when she was little, before she was called Milly, before the conversion. She was still called Manglu then, because she was born on a Tuesday. And her eldest brother, the one whose hand they cut off, was born on a Wednesday and so called Budhuwa. They had come into their hut and dragged him out. There were six of them and it was winter, their faces covered in shawls and woollen hats. Budhuwa didn't shout or cry. They took an axe from the corner where all the farming implements and tools were kept – the sickles, the ploughshares, the tangi, the chherkha. The lohar had visited recently and sharpened the tools of all the families in their tiny village. He had sat outside in the courtyard around which all the homes were built – he was not allowed to enter any of them – and sharpened scores of these tools and knives on a whetting stone and on the pedal-driven sharpener that was ingeniously connected to his rusty bicycle. The more furiously he pedalled, the more generous the spray of orange sparks from the sharpening edge against which he held each tool. The children all gathered round to watch the fireworks; so exciting they had been. The lohar brought his own glass for water and a plate for his food. Someone gave him roti and pickles for lunch, all of which he ate quickly, wiping his plate clean. Milly, transfixed, like all the other children, by the presence of this magician who could send such short-lived flowers of fire flying at will, remembered that he had sharpened their family's axe right after he had finished his food.

This was the axe that the men grabbed that afternoon. Four of them came in and got hold of Budhuwa and pulled him out. There were two more outside. They must have already been to the rice fields to look for him and knew that he was at home. It was terror that had silenced Budhuwa, she understood now, not courage. The only person crying was their mother, crying and falling at the feet of each of the men, saying over and over and over, 'Please let him go, he's my son, please, I'm falling at your feet, please spare him, let him go.' Their father, too drunk, even at this hour, to plead, had tottered around the place, barely able to keep his eyes open, or to string intelligible words free of slurring. There was a crowd in the courtyard – people had come out of the surrounding huts to see what was going to happen. Even the children were there. Two women chased their little ones inside, lifting the crawling babies on to their hips. Milly's mother didn't have the presence of mind to do that, and neither did their father, so Milly and her six siblings witnessed everything.

Two men held down Budhuwa's neck, one his feet, while the man wielding the axe said, 'If you don't hold out your right hand, I'm going to let you have it in the neck.' Budhuwa held out his right hand – the fingers were trembling, Milly could see even from far away, where she was standing, almost hidden behind the legs of one of their neighbours stationed at the edge, near the bushes – then withdrew it immediately. She couldn't see her brother's face. The axe-wielding man shouted, 'You choose, then, is it going to be your head or your feet? If you can't hold out your hand straight and still, you choose.' Budhuwa held out his hand, still shaking. Milly thought, was this going to be like the time she saw the slaughter of the cockerels for Sarhul, the head of the red one, meant for Luthum Haram and Luthum Buria, chopped off in one blow, the thin jet of blood first sprinkling the pahan's face, as he had turned his head away, then his clothes, and the headless torso of the bird spinning and spinning and spinning around on the ground, getting blood everywhere. Why could he not have held it down and cut it into pieces?

The axe came down, Milly didn't remember if she saw that, only the flinging of the hand, which flew past her into the bushes, and her head followed that arc and her eyes got fixed on the brief agitation and parting of the leaves and branches and the blackness of the blood on the green. She couldn't turn her head back to the source of the terrible sound: her brother. Something had frozen her neck. Or her eyes. After a long time the howling changed to whimpering and she could turn her head. The first thing she saw was the axe, which they had left behind. The sparse amount of blood clinging to the edge of the blade was out of proportion to the cries that she had just heard.

2: *Friend*

The youngest daughter of the woman from behind whose legs
Milly had watched the mutilation of Budhuwa was her dearest
friend. The girl's name was Soni and she and her family lived in
the same village. The girls played in the dust together, ran along
the narrow aars of the rice fields, chasing each other, sat under
mango trees to shelter from the rain and made up songs about the
way raindrops or downpour sounded on the leaves. 'Jhim jhim
jhim, it goes,' Milly said. 'No, jhum jhum jhum,' said Soni. They
climbed trees and made reeds out of the long leaves of palms.
They discovered that the stem of the papaya tree was hollow; they
dipped it in soapy water and blew bubbles. They saved tamarind
stones after eating the ripe fruit off the trees in the summer, or
tamarind pickle at other times during the year, cleaned them and
put them to use in invented games. They lay on the ground, balanced a stone each on their foreheads, exactly between their eyes,
and a garland of the brown seeds around their necks, and kept
very still so that the stones didn't fall off, and pretended that they
were both brides, decked out on their wedding day. The girl from

whose neck a stone slid off first would be the first to get married. There were no shop-bought toys or dolls, but they made do with painted clay birds that someone in the village made – they had dried palm leaves for tails and ears – and little carts made of sticks and dried sal leaves, and garishly painted carved sal-wood or bamboo creatures: humans, animals, once even a bus with wheels. They had to be told what it was because they had never seen a bus before. They played with leaves and stones, arranging them in pretty patterns, sometimes strewing flower petals around them and singing the songs from Ba-parab: '*Rupa lekan ba chandu setera kana / Sona lekan ba chandu mulua kana*'.

They sat next to each other in the local school, which was three miles away, and a few metres off a tar-metalled road, in the middle of open land with nothing around it except a long, low knoll on the horizon to the east, a few trees dotting the red earth, and some bushes, scrub and other vegetation. Children from all the villages within a radius of ten or twelve miles had to walk to, and back from, this school, the only one in this particular block of the district. They didn't mind; it didn't occur to them that something such as minding existed; this was the way things were and they knew nothing else. Sometimes the long journey in all seasons meant that they missed class, but this was infrequent. There was certainly a lot less absenteeism among students than among the teachers.

The school was painted pink and had two large rooms, a blue 'kitchen shed', where the students' midday meal was cooked, and an outhouse, which was the latrine and had a wooden door that did not reach all the way to the floor. It had to be shut with a hook lock, which had begun to rust. This toilet was a new thing for all the children because their homes didn't have any – everyone did his business in the open – and they had to be taught by the teacher how to use it. Much embarrassed giggling had accompanied these demonstrations. Milly and Soni had been the most helplessly tittering of the lot.

Everyone between the ages of seven and eleven sat in one classroom, and the older children in the other. They sat on the floor, cross-legged, facing the teacher and the blackboard. There weren't enough chataïs for all of them – anywhere between thirty and forty-five – so some had to sit on the bare concrete. Sometimes as often as fifteen or twenty days a month the children walked to the school and the teacher didn't show up; or she did and left around noon. Over time, this had the effect of thinning student numbers, too – who would want to walk so far, especially during the merciless summer and monsoon, to sit in a room, waiting, waiting, until it was time to walk back again? And when they tenaciously continued to come regularly, it wasn't because of the lessons – there weren't many – but for other reasons: a close friend or two; an escape from being sent to the fields to work; or simply a way of keeping at bay the weight of endless days of nothing. And the biggest reason of all, the one square meal they got in school, regardless of whether the teacher was present or absent.

But Milly's case was slightly different. She had her best friend not very far away in the village; there was no need to do a round trip of over two hours every day to be with her. True, the midday meal was a big attraction but there was something bigger than this. Milly was on fire to study, to learn to read and write, to go to a bigger school where she would get to wear a uniform and carry a pile of books in her hand or in a bag, books she would be able to read easily from cover to cover and retain in her head everything they contained.

But after barely two years at this school, Milly, at the age of eight, was taken out and sent by her mother to work as a housemaid in distant Dumri, eight hours by bus from her village. The family desperately needed the money, and her mother, who tried to hold everything together, couldn't see how they were to hold off starvation if Milly wasn't sent away. She was going to need every paisa from those extra two hundred rupees a month that were going to be Milly's wages. Her mother had nine mouths to feed – herself, seven children and a drunkard of a husband, who instead of earning money was a drain on what little they could pool together. They struggled to raise the bus fare, which was one hundred and twenty-five rupees. The money necessary for a return ticket for her father or one of her older brothers to accompany Milly was beyond their means, so they had to wait until someone else was travelling to Dumri. Arrangements were made for Milly to be met when she got off the bus. This was all done without her knowledge; not because her mother thought that the girl would be upset, but because the idea of consulting a daughter on a decision already reached by her mother was unimaginable.

Milly was told two days before she was scheduled to go. At first, she thought she was going to see a town far, far away, a different world altogether, so there was some excitement mingled with the fear that she felt, excitement especially about travelling by bus, which she had never done before.

'How long will it take to get there?' she asked.

'Six, seven, eight hours,' her mother said.

Milly did not have any notion of time to understand what this actually meant, she only knew that it was a very long time.

'Oh, that's very far. When will I come back? After how many hours?'

'You won't come back, you will stay there,' her mother said.

'Stay? Stay where? Many days?' Milly was baffled.

Even after the situation was explained to her – that she was going to be living in the home of a couple in that far-away town – and a consolatory lie, that she was going to come home every month, added to the mix, it only dawned on Milly by slow degrees that she was being sent away to work. She looked at the healed stump of Budhuwa's arm, its end gathered together in a tiny knot-like pucker like the kind she had once seen at the end of an inflated balloon, and realised that it would look a little bit different when she saw it next time; and something went in a sweeping movement inside her child's chest, emptying it.

'And school?' she asked in a small voice. 'Studying?'

'Nothing doing,' her mother replied impatiently. 'Studying. What good is that for a girl? You'll be more useful bringing in some money. Now shut up.'

The pictures in her school book, with the words written large under them – ainak (glasses), kachauri (stuffed pastry), titlin (butterfly), aurat (woman), gilhari (squirrel) – went through her head. There would be no more books, no more pictures. She looked at the faces of her brothers and sisters; Budhuwa's was turned away. Three of them were too little to understand what was going on. The faces of the other two looked small. Or so it appeared in the shadow-casting flame of the sooty hurricane lamp. Then a different thought struck her: Soni.

When Milly said that she was going to a different country to earn money, and that she was going to come back every month in a bus, bearing gifts of tinsel, sweets, pictures, and red, blue, green and yellow ribbons, all things she considered beautiful and desirable, it wasn't at all clear that Soni understood the full implication of what her friend was saying. There were no goodbyes, no promises or expectations to see each other soon, because there was no understanding of absence and not hav-ing each other's company. There was no wrench, no exchange of tokens or mementoes. The day's play ended as it did on any other ordinary day.

The next day, when boarding the bus, Milly was eager to sit at a window because Budhuwa had told her that she could see the world, the trees, the houses, the fields, all moving past her in the opposite direction when the bus was in motion. She sat at the win-dow and looked out. The bus was stationary, still boarding. She looked out at Budhuwa standing beside her mother, who had a toddler on her hip and one of the younger brothers holding on to her hand. Milly saw her father with his crumpled face. Someone was selling bananas. Budhuwa bought one, reached his hand in and gave it to Milly. The bus was beginning to fill up rapidly. Something shifted and she began to cry, not as a child cries, with its innocent and skinless complaint against the world, but as an adult, silently, trying to keep it all in, only just beginning to understand the weight of the world.

3: *Friend, part II*

Soni was the one who first noticed it. She said to her mother, 'What do you have in your mouth?'

'What do you mean? Nothing,' her mother said.

'You do. Open your mouth. Show, show.'

'Here, haaaaaa.' The jaws opened. Nothing in there. The jaws shut. 'See, nothing. I told you.'

'No, you're hiding it. See, here, here', and Soni touched the slight protrusion on her right jaw, low down, almost under the ear. It was as if she had tucked in a morsel of a treat, a sweetie maybe, and had stowed it far back in her mouth to savour it slowly. 'No, no, show again,' the girl demanded.

Soni's mother obliged. Soni stuck a finger inside and poked around. Teeth, wet flesh, but no hidden sweet. Her mother gently caught hold her wrist and moved her ferreting hand away.

'You're very naughty,' she said.

Yet that lump persisted: Soni could see it clearly the moment her mother shut her mouth again. Then she forgot about it.

Until her elder sister, older than her by seven years, noticed it too and pointed it out in front of the others.

Soni piped up, 'Yes, there are sweets she's hiding in there.'

Their mother, rushed off her feet, snapped back, 'Sweets, sweets! Where do you see sweets? Why have sweets got into your head? Where are we going to get sweets from, you mad girl?'

There was no mirror in their hut, so Soni's mother couldn't check for herself. She felt along her right jaw, pressing at and around the point her daughters indicated. Yes, there did seem to be some kind of swelling, but she didn't feel anything out of the ordinary. She thought of asking her husband but forgot about it. Then someone else, her neighbour, mentioned it as they were picking sal leaves and dead branches in the forest one afternoon. The two women walked back to the village to verify the matter in her neighbour's hand-mirror, a rectangular one framed in green plastic, which was so small that it showed only segments of the face, not the whole thing, if held too close. It took Soni's mother a few tries to get the distance between mirror and reflection right so that she could see her entire face in perspective.

Yes, there it was, exactly as her daughter, Soni, had said; it was as if she was sucking on a lump the size of a sparrow's egg. She opened wide and shut her jaws a few times to see if she could feel the thing. Nothing, except a few clicks. Anyway, it didn't hurt, so it was nothing.

That nothing became something. At first, the pain was a dull ache, sometimes flicking over to a throbbing, then returning to the steady state of ache. The monsoons had tricked them that year by not arriving and the rice in the fields had died to a brown waste. The only thing the villagers could salvage was bundles of hay and straw from the dried plants. Soni's mother had fallen over, face down in the sharp stubble, while tying a bundle she had harvested earlier in the day. An egret, watching the ground intently, strutted a couple of steps and flew off. The pain seemed to have come alive:

it was moving its hundreds of fingers up into her ear, her neck, the back of her head, her right eye, her throat. The sparrow's egg had given birth to an animal that was struggling to get out.

She gurned and drooled. The pain wouldn't allow her to speak. They gave her tribal remedies: a hot poultice of quicklime and turmeric on the growth; a paste of jumuri leaves; dried red berries of the ajarini infused in hot water. These did nothing to abate the pain. Soni watched her mother let out the screams of a woman possessed at night, when she said the thing in her jaw was moving. At other times she saw her writhe and thrash on the floor, once beating her head against the mud wall so hard that a small crack appeared on it. Soni's own heart thrashed inside her little chest. Why couldn't they take her mother's pain away?

The nearest doctor's clinic was three hours' walk away. She was never going to be able to do it, not now. Soni's father rode his wife pillion on a borrowed bicycle and took her to the doctor, worrying not so much about the reduced person he was pedalling into town as the doctor's fees. He only had thirty rupees with him. How would he pay for the medicines on top of the fees? The doctor waived his fee, wrote out a prescription and said, 'This tablet, number one here, give two to her every four hours. Then you need to take her to the hospital. This needs to be removed. She'll need an operation. Quickly. I'll give you a letter, show it to the people in the hospital.'

With the money he had, Soni's father could only buy fourteen tablets. He watched the young man in the dispensary cut out four tablets with a pair of scissors from a blister-pack of ten to add to the one full pack. The pills were gone in two days. The pain, which hadn't disappeared but had somewhat lessened, came roaring back, as if punishing her for daring to use something to battle it. Soni saw her mother return to becoming a wraith again, and her heart felt like it was rice being threshed. Her older sister stopped going to school to take over the duties their mother could no longer perform.

They went picking kendu leaves in the forest together. For every hundred leaves, they would get twenty-five paise. One afternoon they were late coming back: dusk had already begun to settle and soon it would shade into dark. Soni's sister led through a wider path, away from the denser jungle. They heard a vehicle not far away: forest officials on duty. The sound came nearer and nearer and, with it, the two beams of the headlights. Without exactly knowing why, the two girls tried instinctively to hide, but a beam caught Soni's sister as they were attempting to scurry into the interior. The Jeep came closer and stopped. Two men jumped out. The girls could hear voices.

'Who's there? We're forest officers. We've seen you. Show yourself,' one of them shouted to the trees.

The girls might have stayed undiscovered, but someone shone a powerful torch and the light caught Soni's sister straight on her face. Later, Soni would think, they could have run into the cover of the jungle; they would never have been found.

Now, Soni watched her sister transformed to stone. The men came nearer.

'What are you doing here?' one of them demanded. 'Why are you trying to run away?'

'Come here, move closer,' the other man commanded. They were holding lathis. 'What, you've swallowed your tongue?' he barked. 'What were you doing in the dark in the forest? Do you not know, it's not a good place for girls to be?' His voice changed with the last sentence; something else had crept into his tone, something slow and lazy.

The other man laughed. 'Yes, tell us, what were you doing?' he asked. 'What are you holding?' He extended his right hand and took the bundle of leaves that Soni's sister had collected.

'Aha, kendu. Do you have a licence to collect leaves? Don't you know it's illegal otherwise?'

Licence? Illegal? Everyone in the village had been doing it for as long as the girls had been conscious, and their parents and grandparents and ancestors before them. But Soni's sister was too cowed to answer them. What if there really was a new rule they didn't know about? Every day the government people made some rule that made their lives more and more impossible. They kept hearing talk about how they would have to leave their village and the forest and move far away because big companies wanted the land. Where would they go? What would they do?

'You have to come with us,' the man said, and grabbed Soni's sister's wrist. She seemed to have become stone, yet that stone was trembling, a tremor that was transmitting itself through the narrow gap of air to Soni standing by her side.

The man nearer the Jeep added his voice to this. 'Yes, you need to come with us. We'll see what we can do with you.' And then a laugh like a crow manically cawing its death.

Soni could feel her sister trembling. Why wasn't Didi speaking? Where were they going to take her? What were they going to do?

'Let's take the younger one too,' he said. 'There are two of us, and two of them.' That carrion laugh again, like audible gusts of rot.

Didi let out a cry – 'No!' So clogged, from the depths of a dream, it seemed. Then that stone-like inertia broke and everything happened so fast that it outran thought. Soni's sister reached out a hand towards her, pushed her away and said, 'Run! Run back home' in a ferocious whisper. She tried to wiggle herself away from the man who was still holding her wrist. The grip tightened. One beat, two beats. Then Soni moved sideways, turned her back to the men and her sister and started to run. She heard rustling, a cry go up from the men, heard one of them shouting and beginning to run after her. She was nine, light, fleet-footed, powered by fear; and she knew the forest, where she could slip into a brake or take cover behind a close-packed sentry of trees. And the light was going fast, particularly near the ground, up the trunks of trees now almost to the height of an adult. She ran like a spirit escaping the case of its body at the moment of death. All she knew was the particular small clearing, at the junction of two thin, almost invisible trails, that she had to get to before the dark devoured everything. If she couldn't, she would be lost for the night and eaten alive by a leopard or a bear. She looked back only once. What light was left was like ash. Through the screen of the tree-crowd, she saw, or imagined she saw, one of the men, visible only because of his white shirt, huddled on the ground as if weeping over a dead loved one. Or an animal eating its prey. The darkness, and the swiftness of her backward gaze, made it impossible to see what he was hunched over. The forest seemed to stick in her throat.

They sent a search party into the forest at first light the next morning. They couldn't find her. They came back to the village at dusk, in total silence. When Soni and her father entered their hut they found her sitting with her back against a wall, her face in the shadow. Their mother was crying, but to Soni's ears and eyes it was a different kind of crying, a different sound, not of pain but what she could only think of as anger. Didi was a stone again. Her knees and elbows were scabbed, her legs cut in places. In the darkness inside, Soni couldn't see what she would discover over the next few days – bruises everywhere, a slow, pained walk as if everything inside her sister had been broken. She remembered her mother saying only one thing when they returned from their search: 'She crawled back, she couldn't walk.'

Over time, Didi learned how to walk normally again. Yet something felt lacking – sometimes she bared her teeth in a kind of simulation of a smile but, lacking the corresponding illumination in her eyes, it couldn't be called that; it was a perpetually failing, half-hearted rehearsal for it.

Even as Soni's mother's body came to resemble a scarecrow's – she could barely eat anything – her face seemed to be sucking up all the matter in her body and storing it in that bulging angle. Her face changed shape: it was a small, empty, shrivelled sack from which someone had forgotten to take something out from a hidden corner. Her eyes were distant and out of focus all the time, as if they had become strangers to the head to which they felt they didn't belong any longer.

There were two trips to the nearest public hospital, a four-hour journey on a bus. The seventy-five rupees for the bus ticket for each passenger were out of their reach. Soni's father borrowed the fare and an amount he guessed he would need for medicines; the total came to five hundred rupees. He was told that he would have to pay six hundred rupees if he repaid after one month, seven hundred and twenty-five after two months, eight hundred and fifty after three, and so on. But he couldn't think ahead to the time of repayment or the reality of the incremental sums involved; they meant nothing to him; now was the only thing that mattered.

The hospital – how was he going to negotiate that? Who was he supposed to talk to? Who was going to guide him to the right person? He should have brought someone from the village, someone educated, someone who could speak, someone who would know whom to speak to. This place was going to crush him. Wherever he looked there were sick people, people with bandages or casts, the bandages sometimes with a visible blot of blood underneath, dark at the centre, fading towards the peripheries, people walking very slowly with the help of sticks, people lying flat on the floor and in the entranceway, people lying absolutely motionless, eyes wide open, in some cases, staring at nothing, people groaning, coughing, wheezing, people with missing hands or legs, with open sores and grisly protuberances. A man was sitting, back to a wall, the left side of his face a bulging hive of tightly clustered black berries. Soni's father's stomach heaved. He couldn't read a single sign, he didn't know how to. How stupid was it to have come without anyone to help him? This place was going to crush him.

He went from person to person, the doctor's letter clutched in his hand, asking for guidance, some kind of direction. The only word he thought could help him was 'operation'; the doctor had said she needed an operation. Someone said, 'Go to that table there, they can help you.' When he went to the table, he was told he had to go somewhere else. At a counter, the press of people clamouring to be heard, reaching forward pieces of paper, elbowing and jostling, defeated him. How was he ever going to get to the front? When he did get there, after an hour, he was told he had come to the wrong place. He had to go upstairs. They couldn't help him here, this was the ... then some unintelligible words. He went up two flights of stairs to the next floor. People rushing about, waiting, sitting, standing. Who was he going to ask for help? He fixed on a woman he thought looked like a doctor; she had that listening rope around her neck. She told him he had come to the wrong place. He had to go downstairs and ask at the main counter. He went downstairs again. He was a tiny piece of straw in the wind. When he jostled his way to the counter downstairs, he was told to go upstairs again. This time he said that he had already been, but had been sent back down. The man said there was nothing he could do, and could he move aside – he couldn't spend the entire day talking to just one person, there were others waiting behind him.

Soni's father turned away, came outside and sat down on the steps. Against his will, his mouth twisted, like a child's; he couldn't make it hold its shape; he failed to make his crying resemble a dignified adult's. His wife tried to comfort him. What a strange world, he thought; she comforting him when it should be the other way around. He was utterly defeated. People around them probably thought he was crying because some near one had died in the hospital and he had just received the news. What were they thinking? He had never felt so ashamed in his life.

An elderly woman, hobbling on her stick, came up to him to commiserate; it was all up to him, uparwalla, she said, and looked

up at the sky. It was she who accompanied him to the main desk
of the surgery section, on the other side of the building. Here the
collection of people waiting to be seen was even grislier. Some of
them hardly looked human any more. There were dogs sniffing at
sores and winding their way in and out among the humans. No one
seemed to have the energy to chase them away. It was the elderly
woman who spoke to the man in charge, who filled out the forms
for him and who conveyed to him the most important information:
the people here had been waiting for operations for days because
there were no doctors to do them. They would have to return the
following day, but there was no guarantee that a doctor was going
to be present to look at Soni's mother. They would have to keep
trying until they got lucky one day; how long that was going to
take, no one knew.

Soni didn't get to hear the details of what happened on her parents' first outing to the hospital, but only gathered a sense of how
reduced they were afterwards, like husk, without weight, without
any consequence.

They went again, after two months. Soni's father borrowed
money again, while the previous loan remained unpaid, accruing
interest. He could no longer bear to see his wife thrashing about
like a cow in labour. He felt his insides had become the floor on
which the thrashing happened. He had to save her and he had to
save himself. This time he asked the Christian man, Joseph, to
accompany him to the hospital. The fear, which had paralysed him,
of dealing with that huge, crushing, opaque world was mitigated
when Joseph agreed.

Joseph's presence certainly cut out the time wasted in the previous visit going around in circles. Soni's father let him do all the running while he followed him like a faithful dog. That same crowd of
afflicted people again, that same assortment of maimedness and
leprous sores and growths, skin like crust, arms and legs no longer

arms and legs but leaking barrels, withering branches, spongy sacks. And everyone waiting, some for days, months, who knew how long, waiting to be relieved of pain. Illness was a luxury for the rich. Illness had reduced everyone here to a beggar.

Joseph returned with news that there were no doctors in this ward who could perform an operation. Everyone was still waiting – there was a huge list – and no one knew when a doctor would show up; there hadn't been one for weeks. The last doctor in attendance, many days ago, came and did four operations: one of the patients had died, the other three had had to come back with aggravated problems. This information came not from the staff but from the assembled people, awaiting treatment, and their relatives.

There was nothing to do but go back.

Ten days after this, Soni's mother hanged herself. It was Joseph who discovered her; the tamarind tree from which he found her hanging by her saree was in the woods behind the clearing at the back of the church. It was only after they brought her down that he recognised who she was. She had tried to cut out the tumour at the back of her jaw, almost under her ear, with something sharp. They couldn't find the instrument.

4: *Paper*

The only thing Milly took with her on the eight-hour bus journey to her new life was her school textbook and some sheets of dirty, blank paper which she had saved from a small sheaf distributed in school earlier in the year. She knew that the book was called *Pratham Kiran,* although she couldn't yet read the first word, only the second. The clothes she had were what she was wearing: a pair of old drawstring pyjamas frayed at the bottom edge, the string replaced by her mother for the purpose of travel and held together by a safety-pin; and a shift, which was once white with a bold red paan-leaf pattern on it, but now looked like a greyish-brownish swabbing cloth. The rubber flip-flops on her feet had mismatched straps and were of slightly different sizes for each foot because they had been found in that state.

The people who employed her belonged to the same tribe: Munda. The man, Lewis, and his wife, Pendo, both Christian converts, like Milly, had moved from a remote village to Dumri because Lewis had bagged that ultimate prize – a government job. He worked as a clerk in an offshoot of the state government's Forest Department.

Milly's parents knew them, and the grandparents of both families had lived in the same village many years ago. This was how the job had come about. Lewis and Pendo wanted a Munda Christian girl and Milly's mother had put her daughter forward.

These connections were vital: while they did not treat her as one of their own – she was the servant-girl, after all – there was some fundamental commonality that linked them, a sort of tribal bond. Milly was fortunate; it could so easily have gone in the other direction: the hatred of the successful for the less lucky of the same group. Maybe it was this tribal sympathy which made them notice that Milly's sole possession was her school textbook and some cheap paper from an exercise copy, yet not treat her with contempt or cruelty.

While cleaning one morning after Vinti, the nine-year-old daughter of Lewis and Pendo, had left for school, Milly found herself alone and dared to reach out for the other girl's small pile of books by a chaupai on the floor. She thought of the possible consequences of touching what was not hers but the temptation was too great. She laid down the broom, picked the biggest book and opened it. A forest of words and pictures emerged, beckoning her in. Not a single word made any sense – none of them was in Hindi, the only alphabet she knew.

A shout from Pendo, 'Milly, Mill-ee-ee, what's taking you so long?'

Startled, she dropped the book, then replaced it hurriedly. 'Coming,' she called out, afraid that she had somehow been seen and was now being summoned to be punished.

For the following two days she cleaned around the books in a frenzied hurry, willing herself not to touch them, and ran out of the room. But in the evenings, when she was engaged in her duties – making roti, filling the buckets in the bathroom, helping Pendo with the preparation of dinner – half her mind was in the room in which Vinti was busy with her homework. On days when Vinti read aloud from one of her books, whether in Hindi or in their own play language, Milly felt an odd emotion tightening her chest – a mixture of restlessness, lightness and anger. She wanted to spit in the dough. The rotis were rolled unevenly and came out singed. On more than one occasion, a roti caught fire as she was holding it with a pair of tongs over the coals on the chulha. Pendo scolded her roundly.

One day Pendo discovered Milly poring over one of Vinti's books, rapt, her entire being elsewhere, softly mouthing something that sounded like nonsense to Pendo, but on close listening was deciphered as repetitions of certain words – ainak, aurat, titlin, gilhari – that made even less sense to her.

Pendo revealed herself. 'What rubbish are you up to?' she said. Milly looked stricken. Softening her tone, Pendo said, 'Do you know that speaking to yourself is a sign of madness? Do we want a mad girl on our hands? What are you doing with Vinti's book? You don't know how to read.'

Milly, who was on the verge of bursting into tears, felt proud of the little literacy she had and decided to defend herself. She said, 'Yes, I do. I can read from my book, and a few words in Vinti-didi's.' The avidity on her face was like a glow.

Pendo couldn't be much bothered with her maidservant's breathlessness about her incipient education – she had two small children to look after – so she let the matter pass. Milly, fearful of being caught browsing Vinti-didi's books, took to leafing through, again, the latter half of her own tattered book, the sections she couldn't read because she had been taken out of school before they reached them. She looked at them in the afternoon, when everyone had a nap and she had a free hour or two, then again at night, just before getting into her bed, which was a couple of thick sheets, folded over, on the kitchen floor, another bundled-up sheet for a pillow and an old, greasy mosquito net, the four corner strings of which had to be tied to a window bar, the tap in the sink and two nails on the wall opposite, to erect it. She sat outside this dented, misshapen parallelogram and looked at her book in the light from the naked bulb on the ceiling and wished her mother would fall face down on the burning chulha one evening, or get lost in the forest while gathering kindling or mahua flowers fallen on the ground and get eaten by a jackal or bitten by a snake, or have her arms and legs cut off by the men who had come for Budhuwa, the men (and women) who came to the village every night and had to be fed and given places to sleep. She looked at the opaque words on the pages and ripped them out, one by one, and scrunched them up and put them inside her mouth, chewing slowly and carefully, using lots of saliva so that the ink which created the words dissolved thoroughly and dispersed as a thin stream of disassembled words through her insides. In the morning she knew she would wake up knowing the words that had withheld themselves so far.

A week or so after this she was caught by Vinti, eating the balled-up pieces of paper that she had discarded from the fair copy of her school homework.

'Ma, ma,' Vinti shouted, thrilled and slightly appalled. 'Milly's eating paper, come quickly.'

Milly's mouth was full. She could neither swallow nor spit out in front of Pendo and Vinti – either would be an unacceptable thing to do right under the noses of the people in whose home she was a servant-girl. Her eyes filled with tears of shame and fear.

Pendo, stunned for a few minutes, found her voice. 'Why are you eating paper? It's a disgusting thing to do, you savage girl. Are you hungry? Don't you get enough to eat here?'

Milly nodded to indicate that she did. The bolus felt larger than her head. It was consuming her. Vinti looked at her as if she were something floating on a particularly toxic open drain.

Pendo said, 'You're not in your village any more. These kinds of junglee things are not done here. Is that understood?'

Milly, her cheeks swollen with the matter inside her mouth, nodded again. She had been caught in her magic ritual; now she was never going to learn the words that Vinti-didi had written and rejected.

A few days later, a moment of inspiration. Vinti, in Class III of Birsa Munda Girls' School (a private school, despite the name), was going through a phase of wanting to be a schoolteacher. It suddenly came to Pendo that, in Milly, her daughter could have the perfect companion to play games of Student – Teacher; Vinti could truly teach Milly the elements of reading, writing and arithmetic, not only in play.

Milly's first experience of two meals a day – two-and-a-half, if the morning tea and stale chapatti were counted – was at the home of Pendo and Lewis and Vinti-didi and the little one, Suraj. In the village, on lucky days, they had one meal, which was usually bajra ki roti and til chutney. A two-meal day was a rare gift; also a great struggle. There were days when they went hungry. Milly remembered those by the absence of smoke and its particular smell because her mother didn't light the chulha to cook – there was nothing to put on the fire. Even into adulthood, the smell of a chulha being fanned to get the flames to catch filled her with a simple joy, a sense of security. On smokeless days, Milly remembered her mother sometimes berating her father, drunk and stretched out in a stupor in a corner or outside, in the courtyard, but the more frequent scenario was of her mother crying silently and bitterly, her lip torn and bleeding, her face livid, one eye bruising up, from the thrashing she had just received from her drunken husband. On one of these evenings, with the smell of violence still hanging in the air, Milly had watched, with a kind of horrified fascination, the blood, snot, tears and saliva from her mother's face all mingle while she had cried out, twice, words etched indelibly in Milly's memory – 'The pangs of hunger are great pangs, it's a burning. God gave us stomachs to punish us.'

Still, this was the way things were, and Milly and her brothers and sisters, not knowing a regular or even occasional alternative where meals were numerous over long uninterrupted stretches, did not know to complain – this was the way their world was; there was no other. The glimpse of the alternative, village feasts and festivals, was not seen as such because, by their very nature, they were exceptions to the ordinary run of their days. A cow or a couple of goats were slaughtered, and all the families in the village paid for the meat, which was then distributed among the households according to how much each had paid. A meal of rice and beef was what they imagined heaven to be like. Even if what they got on their plates was gristle, tendon, a pucker of skin or fat, it was still flesh. Communal feasts were cooked and distributed centrally. These offered a higher chance of getting actual meat, not just a nub of bone and the translucent fat that clung to sockets. Milly sucked out the marrow from sections of the shinbone, if she ever got one, and was sorry to have to throw the cleaned and picked bone to the dogs roaming through the eating area, alert for scraps.

At the conversion ceremony, the church paid for the feast following the entry of eight families – fifty-five members in total – into the fold. Milly was too young at the time to have had much understanding of why their mother had decided one day to christen all the little children. She had asked, many years later, what impelled her to do it.

Her mother had said, 'They promised a big sack of rice. It was food for a month. I had reached the limit with not having enough to feed you lot. They also said all of you could go free to school in the big town, which would mean government jobs for the little boys when they grew up ...'

Then it had dawned upon her that school was a touchy subject between her and Milly and she had stopped and looked away.

The christening feast involved the sacrifice of two cows and a big fat pig: it felt as if the days of plenty had arrived. The feast lasted two days. Then, over time, there were the four days of Easter and Christmas Day, all of which included communal feasting. To a lot of people that was inducement enough to convert, although non-Christians were welcomed to these feasts, and sat down, side by side, with the Christians, ate their food, tried to sing their hymns. They could even go into the church, but not during service.

Here in Dumri, Milly was given lunch after the family had finished eating. In other words, she ate whatever was left over, which often meant that if the family had, say, a dal and two kinds of sabzi, she would get rice or roti, some dal and whichever vegetable dish had not been eaten entirely by Lewis, Pendo and Vinti, and Suraj, when he grew up a little. This rule of priority applied particularly to fish, egg and meat dishes: by an unspoken rule, Milly was not allowed to eat – or not given – these special things, the leftovers being saved for the children and Lewis and Pendo, in that order. If anything remained after they had had a meat dish several times, Milly was given the final residue, which often consisted only of potatoes and gravy with tiny shreds of meat here and there, or an inferior piece, all bone, gristle, fat and membrane, which no one wanted to eat, or when Pendo thought the dish was on the turn and couldn't be given to the family any longer. Milly didn't mind, didn't even notice most of the time. She had plenty to eat – plenty of rice, which was such a luxury back home and, crucially, a reliably regular supply of two full meals every day. She no longer went to bed, after writing out the difficult words from her one page of reading every night, wondering whether she was going to eat the following day.

A child breaks things. Milly was eight, going on nine, when she started working in Dumri. Her child's hands could not carry large, heavy objects, get a saving grip on a soapy saucer or cup intent on slipping from her grasp. They did not have enough span to arrest something from falling and breaking while she was doing the cleaning. Such accidents were not frequent; they were usually limited to dropped knick-knacks. The plates, glasses and bowls were all stainless steel at Pendo's, so there was no danger of breaking them. A set of four china cups and saucers arrived once. They sat in a cupboard and were taken out for very special guests, not so much to honour them as to advertise Pendo and Lewis's upward mobility. After one of these outings, Milly broke the handle of a cup while doing the washing-up. It was such a delicate little toy-ear-like thing, it simply came off in her hands. Pendo scolded her – 'Look what you've done, you clumsy pagal! My set is ruined for ever' – and Milly felt afraid for a day or two, then it all blew over. The lame set sat in the darkness of the cupboard and was forgotten.

The reprimands were, predictably enough, in direct proportion to the cost of the object broken. There were few expensive things in Pendo's home; usually the value was of emotion or attachment. Milly broke a terracotta doll belonging to Vinti once; Vinti brought the house down. Again, Milly was told off, but this time she felt that Pendo's words and tone had something of the performance about them, as if she felt she had to be seen by her daughter to be punishing the servant who had broken her toy. On this occasion, Milly felt far worse – and far more fearful – than the time she broke the handle on the cup: her lessons were dependent entirely on keeping Vinti-didi happy. This storm, too, passed; it was a children's quarrel, temporary and trivial, although clouded by the element of class.

Nearly four years after she started at Pendo and Lewis's, Milly was taken out of their home by her mother and sent to a Bengali couple in Jamshedpur, an even bigger town. By now she could read Hindi effortlessly, write slowly and haltingly but clearly, and do basic addition and subtraction. She knew the English alphabet and could read small words – 'cat', bat', 'car'. She read the word 'bus' one evening and smiled at her younger self, which had not known what a bus was, until the moment of the journey to Dumri.

5: *Fate*

Soni had known them to visit their village frequently; in fact, a few of the group were familiar faces. She was sure that she had seen the woman in the blue sari with the medicine van on the two occasions it had visited their village. The new water tank, behind the school, had been built by some of them. They gathered in front of the school, or on the neat green in front of the church, or the raised square platform under the circle of the eight giant trees by the river where the gram sabha sat. 'Samaj sewi', social workers, she thought they were called. She had heard them give speeches, long, fiery ones, and had tuned out; everyone who wanted to win elections gave speeches. Those men during election time came from big towns or cities, promised big things, smiled, bowed, then left. Everything carried on as before. But the social workers were different. She could tell by looking at them that they belonged here, were people like her and her neighbours. Word went round that they were putting on a play.

What was a play? She had only the haziest notion. She joined the crowd assembling near the well. She stood next to her sister, intent on watching her face during the play – maybe this could make her smile again? Would it have singing? Yes, it did. They were words she didn't understand. What language were they singing in? Would the play be incomprehensible too?

The song was over. The group disbanded and moved to the sides. Two women returned to the centre. They pretended to be picking kendu leaves. Or was it kindling? They spoke about how the forest was their home and protector, how it provided them with everything they needed. But the government wanted to move them out and give the forest to rich people, big companies, who wanted to cut the trees, sell the wood, dig up the land for the riches under it … The water of the rivers and streams would turn red from green and would no longer be fit for any use. They would lose everything, their homes, the forest, the air, the water, their freedom, and would be made to work as slaves on the land, no longer theirs but someone else's. Soni watched, unblinking.

They talked of adhikaar, haq, izzat: 'The government does not give us those things, rights and respect. We have nothing except the rights to jal, jameen and jangal. They're going to take our water, land and forest away from us.'

Then they shifted to talking about how much they were paid for every kilo of tamarind collected, or every pile of hundred kendu leaves, and how much the tamarind or kendu was then sold for. They said the difference could pay for a doctor's clinic at the village, or a month's supply of rice and lentils.

'Why have we been poor and hungry for decades? Why do we always hear of vikas, of crores of rupees given by the Centre for development, and never see a paisa of it? Where does the money go? Why has our situation not changed?' There was a lot of talk. Sometimes Soni couldn't understand what was going on.

Things perked up. Two men joined the women. The women announced, in loud, frightened whispers, that one was a forest official and the other a contractor. Why had they shown up? The two men started harassing the women. Did they have permission to pick leaves? Where was the piece of paper that gave them permission? How much had they collected? Did they know they would be fined for the illegal picking of leaves? Everything in the forest was government property. The women would have to come with them and pay a big fine, and if they couldn't ... here the men began to laugh. They caught hold of the women's arms and started dragging them away. The women cried for help. One of the men pulled at the clothes of the woman he was holding by the wrist. Soni felt a tremor passing through the skin of her arm where it touched her sister's. She looked sideways. How could anybody sitting so still – Didi's eyes were not blinking, she didn't seem to be breathing even – generate such a steady, low hum of trembling? Soni turned back to look at the actors. They were gone, but the audience could still hear the women screaming and crying, the men laughing. The sound held. She sensed an ultimatum in the play that she was seeing.

Two of the samaj sewi came onstage, a man and a woman, and asked how long the people here were going to put up with such humiliation, such indignities? Were they not humans, too, or were their lives as nothing to the big people?

She noticed that her sister's trembling had transmitted itself – it was she, Soni, who was now the core of the tremor. She was approaching the realisation of something fateful in herself. Something her sister had said after she had come back, something Soni thought she had forgotten, now inserted itself in her head – just a few words: 'I didn't put up a fight because they would have killed me otherwise.'

The meeting happened by chance. Soni and her sister had gone to wash clothes by the river when they saw a group of people appear out of the forest, on the other bank, and begin to wade across the water towards the village. It was winter and the river was a narrow green channel running through a wide expanse of sand and black-and-grey-and-white rocks that were now exposed. As they came nearer, Soni could recognise most of them. She was now better informed and thought of them as 'the Party people', not samaj sewis. They were the ones who organised the meetings and plays, the ones who had recently started visiting the village in a truck, with doctors who spoke to anyone who was ill, with injections for babies, medicines for fever and pain and stomach trouble, bandages for burns and bites.

They seemed to know who her sister was and what had happened to her. The woman who was always part of the medicine-van group spoke first. She said her name was Bela. She squatted at the edge of the water to be level with the girls, then she put both her hands on Soni's sister's shoulders. She looked at Soni and asked her to leave them alone. Three days after this, Soni's sister left home to join the Party.

Soni waited for a few years until she had finished with Class 8. Their school was now being used as a base by the Army to flush out guerrillas who had taken over the forests. She could wait for months, years, before the school was returned to its proper use. But it was too late for all that. She knew to whom to talk, now that she had seized – by both hands, it felt – the decision that she had made years ago. It felt like acknowledging someone familiar, someone destined, who had been within her sight for so long.

The Maoist activists operated in the surrounding forest and often held meetings in the bordering villages. They found a sympathetic audience in the villagers whose lives of unchanging poverty and misery and hopelessness needed a radically new kind of hope, which the militants provided. The Party, as the Communist Party of India (Maoists) – CPI(M) – was called, had two guerrilla wings; the group Soni joined was the People's Liberation Guerrilla Army.

She couldn't join the group her sister was in because there were strict rules against having family members and relations within one squad. 'Liberation' was a loaded word around these parts – all areas of forest in this state under the control of Maoist guerrillas were called 'liberated territories'. Their village meetings were well attended and one of their chief purposes, recruitment of young men and women, was often successful. Some were inspired to join because they wanted change, improvement to their lives of hunger and squalor. Others joined because they had no prospects – low education, no jobs, no possibility of changing their lives for the better. Still others, because the guerrillas paid money to the new recruits: an upfront payment of fifteen hundred rupees, then the promise of a monthly payment thereafter; besides, they would be fed and clothed and even given further education at no cost. And who wouldn't want to leave the dirt and mess of the villages, the open drains and sewers, the lack of sanitation, the river polluted by a mining factory upstream, its green water now the colour of the dark-orange soil? Soni certainly felt this new experience, of waking up in the forest and being the first to breathe in the air that smelled of dew and trees and leaves, as a wonderful thing in her life.

First, the new recruits had to undergo a year-long training session. Soni, along with her new comrades, got up at four in the morning and ran up and down the hills, did sit-ups and push-ups and presses. The squad commander drove each recruit to better his or her performance over the months, expecting him or her – there were nearly as many women who joined the guerrillas as men – to shave time off their personal best. She learned to crawl through jungle floors and was marked on, among other things, how noiseless she could be during the exercise. She was given increasingly intricate lessons on camouflage and that most vital of all talents: how to appear silently and disappear with the swiftness of a snake bringing its head down to strike. She was taught target practice and given lessons in using explosives. She learned how to make IEDs – Improvised Explosive Devices – that could be set off using basic, easily available and seemingly innocuous things such as catapults made out of twigs and rubber bands, flashbulbs in cameras, hypodermic syringes, water pistols, even battery-operated children's toys.

In that first year of training she went to a school run by Maoists; there were several such schools, mobile or permanent, in the base area. There she was taught English, mathematics, science, geography and Communism. She learned about capitalism, labour, exploitation, about the bourgeois and the petit bourgeois, about false consciousness and the dictatorship of the proletariat.

The recruits got training in how to set up their bunker and, equally important, how to dismantle it quickly and move on without leaving a trace. Bunker meant no more than a plastic sheet or thatch spread over four bamboo posts. Soni's squad had five women and six men. The women got extra rations of food, particularly eggs, and if eggs were not available, groundnuts. Life on the move, in the open air, was tough. Sometimes it felt that they were little more than wild pack-animals, carrying loads on their backs and heads, sacks of rice and grain, heavy kitbags, moving from one village to another through the jungle. The guerrillas' main – often only – source of sustenance was the food levy they imposed on the surrounding villages: they took five kilos of rice and lentils from the thirty kilos that every villager who held a ration card was entitled to, from the public distribution system. Not infrequently they would have to collect the food from villages which had missed the ration day, because they were so far away from the distribution hub, so there was either nothing the guerrillas could be given, in the worst situation, or they had to do with very little, with food that could barely be called food: rice that was more stones than rice, lentils that had gone maggoty. There were days when they subsisted on this stony rice and tamarind paste or a fiery chutney made with ants, salt, tamarind and dried red chillies. On such days they looked upon every animal they glimpsed in the jungle – a bird, a scurrying rodent in the undergrowth, a crashing boar, a snake – with hunger, wanting only to bring it down, roast it over a fire and fall upon it. Weakness and exhaustion slouched and pressed against them.

The guerrillas slept outdoors in the winter months, with nothing but a thin blanket to cover them. They learned how to harness nature for their purposes: which trees were best to hide behind because their trunks could withstand or absorb bullets; how to read the forest so that they knew how to navigate, where to walk, where to go, where to hide, even though there were no visible paths; how to create traps with trees or in the undergrowth without any sign to betray their existence; what kind of formation to follow while spreading out in the forest to surround the paramilitary forces sent to hunt them out, so that the soldiers did not know from which direction they were going to be attacked.

There were speeches on most evenings to remind everyone what and who they were fighting, to keep them fervid, their anger shiny and whetted. Her blood ran swifter, hotter, when she listened to the leaders. Theirs was a different approach – no longer the old lies of 'If you vote for me, I promise to bring about this and that change', but the direct action of taking power in your own hands. 'If you kill, we kill too. If you have guns, we have guns,' as one comrade had put it so simply. Here was a kind of equality, at last.

6: *Jamshedpur*

Milly's mother considered the new position in Jamshedpur a move up because Milly's salary increased. The increment was only by a hundred and fifty rupees, but to her this meant a week's worth of staples. The young Bengali couple at whose home Milly began work – Debdulal, a railway engineer, and Pratima, his wife – did not mistreat her in any egregious way, but worked her hard and grudged her any leisure or resting time. 'Standing at the window again?' Pratima would scold her. 'Don't you have work to do? Is the rice picked? Did you hang out the washing?'

Once Milly made the mistake of responding. 'I've done all that,' she said meekly.

'How dare you answer back?' Pratima shouted. 'Idling away all day! Go soak the bedcover and wash it, then make the bed in our room. Why is this table here? I have told you to move it to that corner so many times that my mouth is foaming. Why are you standing here, staring at the floor?'

Pratima was particularly incensed if she caught Milly napping in the afternoon, even if there was no work to be done. She invented tasks to prevent this – an errand to run in the blood-drying heat of the afternoon, spice pastes to grind, various forms of spring cleaning. She gave Milly two square meals a day, generous portions, heavy on the rice, but Milly felt the food discrimination here more than she had at Dumri. If Pratima's nagging, scolding and surveillance hadn't existed, Milly wouldn't have noticed, but one kind of ungenerosity sensitised her to another.

There was one incident that lodged like an arrowhead inside her. Pratima discovered Milly with a book, one of several of Vinti's from her earlier school years.

Pratima had laughed with open derision and said, 'Turned into quite the educated lady, huh? Shouldn't you be doing something more suitable? Have you kneaded the flour for tonight's rotis?'

Much later it occurred to Milly, as she was picking the scabs of this wound, that she was far better at Hindi than her Bengali employers were: they always got their hota and hoti, karta and karti wrong.

The thing she learned in Jamshedpur, however, was how to cook Bengali food. Like most Bengali people, Debdulal and Pratima wanted to eat their own food all the time and looked upon what they called non-Bengali cuisines with a degree of contempt and suspicion. Milly was taught how to cook egg curry and, when Pratima was in a more economising mood, omelette in a thin gravy with diced potatoes. She learned about the use of the Bengali spice mixture, panchphoron, and various ways of cooking cabbage and cauliflower and peas in the winter months.

Milly had a plate (stainless steel) and bowl (aluminium, enamelled, chipped and dented) for her food, and a small stainless-steel beaker for her water. These were separate from the crockery which Pratima and Debdulal used; she wasn't allowed to eat off those. Her things had to be kept in a different cupboard, the one that held the gas cylinder for their cooker. The rule was set on the very first day she started work. But to Milly, it was the availability of regular food that mattered, not the plates and bowls from which she ate it. She never gave the business of separate plates a thought.

There were other, subtler rules, made known to her by some process that eluded her, leaving only the strictures in her mind. She had to make the bed but she wasn't allowed to sit, let alone lie, on it. On the occasions she could only reach a tricky corner to tuck in a sheet tightly or smooth a crease by lying partially or by supporting a part of her body – say, knees or upper half or haunch – on the surface of the bed, she used the special broom to beat, extra-hard, the areas her body had touched. This rule did not need to be spelled out simply because no servant would ever have thought of the possibility of sleeping on their master's or mistress's bed. And although Milly had never broken this cardinal rule – in fact there was no rule holding her back, since the act was unthinkable and had, therefore, never occurred to her – she was once reprimanded by Pratima after she discovered the imprint of Milly's palm indenting the soft surface of the bed. She had needed to press her hand down in order to shift a corner of the mattress, but from that day she had taken great care to erase all traces of her touch.

She wasn't allowed to sit on the sofas and chairs. She could watch television when Pratima turned it on, but she had to either stand or sit on the floor to watch it. Again, she didn't mind; she knew the rules. But when she was alone in their home, she sometimes sat on all the chairs, armchairs, sofas and divans in turn, just to see what it felt like. She was also very careful to remove any traces of her sitting on sofas and armchairs: she dusted them again, and used the special broom for the bed to beat the seats and fluff them up. After a while, she lost interest in sitting on the forbidden furniture when she was alone.

One evening, hypnotised by *Kyoon Ki Saas Bhi Kabhi Bahu Thi*, Milly was told by Pratima, 'Don't lean back, your spine will become crooked.' Milly, sitting on the floor, was supporting her back against the edge of an empty armchair. She straightened her back but it still touched the chair.

'Move forward a little bit more,' Pratima said.

Milly obeyed. She still didn't get it.

After ten minutes, Milly, lost in the world of television, heard Didi again, her words a little bit more commanding this time, 'How many times have I told you not to lean against that chair? Sit up.'

The following evening, before the television was turned on, Pratima reminded Milly, 'Don't lean back against the furniture.'

Milly nodded. There was no melodrama unfolding in front of her eyes to dilute the message this time.

Watching television was a flexible activity that sometimes depended on Pratima's mood. Generally speaking, it was allowed if Milly had finished all her chores and didn't neglect her duties. She was mostly undiscriminating about programmes – she was so fascinated by audiovisual entertainment at the flick of a switch that she could joyously sit through anything that involved moving, speaking figures far removed from her life. But slowly distinctions began to open up: she preferred serials to the news, films to talk shows, programmes that featured a suite of songs from different films. She quickly picked up the times of the day and the days of the week when her favourite shows went out, but whether she got to watch every one of them was up to Pratima's whim. Pratima strongly believed that servants 'sat on your head' if you indulged them by letting them watch television or allowing them anything they appeared to enjoy. Whenever she got a whiff of any such activity from which Milly derived pleasure – and watching serials was an obviously readable one – she clamped down on it by inventing extra, unnecessary chores. If Milly did them swiftly enough to leave her some time in front of the television, Pratima invoked the mistress's prerogative: a curt 'Don't sit here and watch TV, go to the kitchen.' Milly had never been able to detect any rhyme or reason behind Pratima's conflicting signals on this matter, unlike the clear directive about sitting on the furniture, for example. Still, orders were orders; she couldn't question them. What the fickleness left

Milly with was an escalating tension in the evenings: would she be able to watch *Nukkad*? Or would a mood swing see her banished to the kitchen from where she could hear every line of dialogue, every note of the billowing music, but not see any of the action?

It was in Jamshedpur that the matter of accidentally broken or damaged household items became an unpleasant issue. Pratima used some of the vast reserves of time on her hands to form strong attachments to objects. She had what she called a 'showcase', a wooden cupboard, about six feet high, glass-fronted, with shelves inside. It housed objects precious to her – porcelain plates and cups and saucers, a few framed photographs, glass and terracotta decorative bric-a-brac; in short, things she thought of as suitably indicative of her status as the wife of a man who had a government job. The crockery inside the showcase was never taken out and used, not even for guests Pratima and Debdulal were trying to ingratiate themselves with – it was for display purposes only. The moot question was who the showcasing was for, the couple themselves or for their infrequent visitors. Milly was not allowed to touch the contents of this display cabinet, which was kept locked anyway. This did not hold back Pratima from complaining how dusty and untidy everything inside looked and blaming Milly for it. By this time Milly had learned that she was not to answer back. If that china was ever used, she would have to clean it, handling it with all the care and delicacy extended to a newborn's head; the very prospect filled her with terror.

So when she was asked to clean the interior of the showcase – 'Take out every single thing, I don't want to find dust hiding behind and between things, understood?' – Milly thought she had avoided great danger: it was, after all, the safer job of cleaning the cupboard, not the dangerous task of handling the fragile contents. She took out the china very carefully, set it on newspapers laid down on the floor and did the same again with everything inside. Pratima sat on a stool, watching her and repeating, 'Be careful, very careful.

I don't want a single thing broken.' By the time Milly finished dusting and cleaning the inside, and putting everything back, intact, her hands were shaking and she felt that she hadn't exhaled since the task began. Then she turned and thought she saw something on a piece of newspaper that she had forgotten to put back in – it was nothing, just a large picture on the paper that had caught the corner of her eye – but in her tense state, nervous that she was going to step on something fragile, she overcompensated her correcting movement, lost her balance and hit the showcase with her shoulder and side. A neat crack went through the pane that she collided against. Pratima was speechless for what to Milly felt like aeons, before she exploded. It was a relief to be slapped by her, and shouted at, after the build-up to the inevitable.

'I'll deduct it from your wages, you just wait and see,' she screamed. 'Everything you break, big or small, will come off your wages. That'll teach you to break things you won't be able to afford in your lifetime.'

It was not an empty threat, made in the heat of the moment; Pratima deducted money for every article that Milly broke during her time in Jamshedpur.

7: *A change of place and a meeting*

Just when she had begun to think that the low hum of unhappiness in Jamshedpur would last for ever, Milly went back to her village on her annual leave and was told that she wouldn't be returning to Debdulal and Pratima's, but instead going to Mumbai, for five times the pay. It had come about through Sabina, a Christian woman from the village, who worked as a domestic maid in Mumbai; Milly barely knew her. When Sabina had returned home for a month's holiday after her first year in Mumbai, she had told everyone how there was this endless demand for housemaids in the city. Word reached Joseph, a local clergyman, who was always on the lookout for ways to make the hopeless lives of his poor flock a tiny bit better, whether through using what little influence he had to get them small jobs, 'loose-change work', as they called it, or through acts of charity. What he managed to acquire for them was, in the long run, trivial – a week's work as replacement labour in a bottling factory, slightly higher margins on sales of basketloads of tamarind or mangoes or mahua flower, getting an NGO based in Patna to give some kind of vocational training, such as machine wool-weaving classes,

to women – but this business of going away to big towns and cities, especially Mumbai, to work in people's homes, struck him as
a somewhat bigger opportunity. Besides, there was nothing to do,
especially for girls, in this village; gathering kindling, grazing cows,
helping in the fields ... that was the extent of it. And now some of
them had started joining the guerrilla squads in the surrounding forests, a course of action that could only end in one thing. A Mumbai
salary could mean significant money sent back home to the families; the girls would, after all, be living and eating in the homes they
worked in, therefore saving the larger part of their wages. His head
buzzing with hope and ideas, Joseph went to see Sabina.

It took Sabina a few phone calls to find a home for Milly; what
helped was the fact of Milly's work experience. Sabina, about to
return to her job in Borivili, was taking two girls from the next village for whom she had found jobs as housemaids, also in Mumbai.
Milly's appointment was to the home of a Sindhi family in Lower
Parel, the Vachanis. The biggest city she and people in her village
had ever heard of, unimaginably big with an unimaginably large
number of people living in it, everyone making money, living a
life of ease, of four meals a day, a brick house with two or three
rooms, a world of opportunity and plenty, a world very far from
their own ... the excitement, stoked by stories Sabina had to tell,
was so palpable that even Milly, who was slowly being gripped
by an escalating fear at the prospect of going to such a big place,
occasionally felt its touch. Sabina wore a wristwatch with a golden
metal strap on her right hand. Her sandals, a tiny red flower at the
junction where the two side-straps met the toe-peg, had big city
written all over them. She spoke more Hindi now than Sadri.

Budhuwa's first reaction to Milly's new job was a laconic,
'You'll find it more difficult to come back here on holidays.' Ever
since Milly had returned home from Jamshedpur, she had struggled with watching Budhuwa go about his daily life with his one,
left hand. He was much better, of course. He had learned to do

most things with one hand, even his work unweaving the large plastic sacks, separating out each cord and then tying it on to a spool. He could now do it with a degree of deftness; the money he earned was calculated by the number of spools finished and Budhuwa could often manage to do up to four or five bobbins a day, depending on how many sacks had come his way. In the months after the attack, he had found it impossible even to take apart the sacks, holding them down with his foot and using a pair of pliers to pick out the threads: an entire day would go and he would have disassembled about one-third of a sheet, the frayed, untied ends sticking up like the unruly hay at the extremities of a bundle. Now, however, he had a rhythm, and a fleet one, too, and an ability, his own peculiar, imperfect way of getting things done.

Milly watched him at work and said, 'You've become quick at this.'

Budhuwa looked up at her, turned his head back down to his plastic cords and said nothing. After a while, noting that she hadn't gone, he said, 'Yes. Doing the same thing every day for hours ...'

Pause.

'Not that I'm good at anything else,' he added as an afterthought, or maybe a negation.

Milly gave a wan smile which he didn't see. She could not say why witnessing him in this state, when he had managed to rise above what had been inflicted on him, should overcome her so – this feeling of disintegration was so much more powerful than when she had watched him struggle and lose, struggle and lose, time and time again, to trivial, powerless inanimate objects such as sacks and pliers and cord and wooden spool. It was all he could do; it was everything. The knowledge slayed her.

Nearly nine years had passed since Milly had left her home village for her first job as a live-in domestic servant in Dumri. During this time, Milly visited her home only four times on annual leave from work: three times while she was at Dumri and once after she began working in Jamshedpur. She saw Soni the first couple of times but missed all that befell her family while she was away at Debdulal and Pratima's. Milly's memories of Soni had not exactly faded but had slowly become unvisited, tangential, irrelevant. Childhood friendships were often like that – intense in presence and in the present tense, remote and unreachable in absence. But coming back home again after so long gave sharper outlines and brighter colours to those memories, and Milly found herself curious to know how her childhood friend had turned out. Did Soni get married to a man who had a government job? She was the one who had managed to stay still the longest, despite the annoyances caused by red ants or mosquitoes, to keep the tamarind stones balanced on her forehead and neck. Asking about her now revealed more than Milly had reckoned: the death of Soni's mother, all the business with her sister, came out tersely from Budhuwa and their mother. All Milly could do was ask if Soni was still living here or had she, like Milly, moved far away from home.

'No, she's still here. She is a member of the Party now,' Milly's mother said. Her face was unreadable.

'Party?' asked Milly, shocked. It was the Party that had been responsible for Budhuwa's hand. Milly knew about the death of Soni's mother but not much else besides.

'Yes, she has become a samaj sewi,' Budhuwa said, but Milly couldn't quite judge if he used the term with anger. In these villages people who joined the Party were seen both as extremists and as 'social workers'. Many looked on the guerrillas as 'our boys and girls', as 'one of us'.

'She lives in the forests now,' Milly's mother said. 'They come to the villages in the dead of the night for food, then they go back before sunrise. They carry guns.'

Milly was too stunned to say anything.

Her brother said, 'She's joined the liberators, that's what they call themselves. Two months ago these liberators blew up the school building, the school she and you went to, because the CRPF men were using it as a base.'

Milly, eyes now round as plums, said, 'You saw?'

'No. What's there to see? They went around telling people they did it. Some others saw, they said it was the guerrilla group she had joined.'

The pressure of the unsaid became so intense that Milly couldn't bear it any longer. She began to ask Budhuwa, 'The same group ... the same group that ... that ...' but couldn't proceed any further.

Budhuwa helped her out; it was all one to him now; he wasn't going to get his hand back. 'No, she joined the other group, but there's no difference between them, not really. They are all part of the same Naxalbadi party.'

The bitterness in his voice was now another presence in the small, dark room. Milly looked down at the floor. Their mother was trying to light the LPG gas cooker she had bought with money that Milly sent home.

In the end it was Soni who came to her first. A weak hammering of fists on the door very late at night, around one or two o'clock, sent fear running through the whole family, but it was soon quelled by a young woman's voice, 'Milly, ei Milly, is Milly there? This is Soni.' She was trying to balance waking up Milly with keeping her voice down; it was the rattling of the chain on the door that awakened everyone.

In the moonlight, with the shadows so accentuated, and with the changes wrought on her by time, it could have been someone impersonating Soni. They stood facing each other and they had nothing to say.

'It's very late, no?' were Milly's first words.

Soni had nothing to return to this except an obvious 'yes'. They stood looking away from each other, at the shadows, heard the taut, watchful silence of Milly's family behind her, all of them waiting for something to happen. Milly imagined she heard objects being moved very stealthily, objects that could be used as weapons. The awkwardness between the girls continued to tick; time had made them strangers.

Soni gave a little laugh and said, 'I can't tell in this dark what you look like now.'

That laugh hadn't changed. Milly was, in the blink of an eye, back to the age of six.

'I can't see you properly, either.'

'I have to go soon. You'll come to me tomorrow? On the other side of the river? Not the village side, but across the water. Stand exactly opposite where the gram sabha sits. You'll come?'

Milly hesitated.

'Don't be afraid. Nothing will happen to you, you're with me.'

Much later, Milly thought that it was this reassurance, unprompted by anything she had said or done, as if Soni had read the silence, that made her keep the rendezvous the following day.

At four o'clock on an April afternoon it was impossible to stand anywhere except in full shade. The river, Baniya, was green; one could cross it at its thinnest spot partly by stepping over the stones that had come out of their underwater hiding during the run of dry months and partly by wading across. On the other side lay what looked like the border of a jungle, but there were narrow paths through it and one could walk down them to the edge of another village. Right now, the mahua trees were in bloom, the red soil decorated here and there with small rugs of fallen cream flowers. Milly was surprised that they hadn't already been picked by the villagers to make mahua, or eaten by deer and langurs.

Beyond that was the larger surprise of not being able to fit the seventeen-year-old Soni to the image Milly had of an eight-year-old girl. That old image was not sharp, but she would never have thought the new reality in front of her as a development from that faded memory.

'What are you staring at?' Soni asked, laughing. That sound again, like cool, green water flowing over rocks.

Was there something of the girl she had known in that smile, that laugh? Would Milly have recognised her in a crowded street of a different town? Was Soni thinking the same things about her: that Milly, too, would be unrecognisable to her?

As if she had looked inside Milly's head, Soni said, 'You know, you've changed a lot, I wouldn't have recognised you if I bumped into you somewhere else, somewhere far away from here.'

Yes, that flowing chatter, that complete ease with everything, that's not left her, Milly thought. She said, 'I was thinking the same about you.'

'They tell me you live in big cities now, Ranchi, Jamshedpur. You've moved up in the world. You earn lots of money? Have you married someone from the city?' Her eyes were dancing with excitement.

Milly felt shy and turned her head away. They were still strangers to each other and she didn't know if their shared past was going to be like a change of weather they could easily slip into as they walked the red paths through the trees, shafts of sunlight falling on them wherever there was an opening in the canopy. She noticed that there weren't one or two people from the village in here, collecting firewood or kendu leaves. Budhuwa occasionally picked kendu leaves from the forest floor now, to supplement his income from the plastic-thread-making, but he complained that he was not too good at it, not sufficiently nimble. Besides, Budhuwa had said, the traders, to whom the villagers sold their bundles of leaves, had to pay a tax to the Party people, which they resented, so they were wary of taking on new, unfamiliar collectors, whom they suspected were in cahoots with the Party. Milly looked at the thick, fissured bark of the kendu tree, a regular grid of rectangles, like cracked earth during drought. It didn't seem so benign any more. She had learned in her childhood that spirits lived in some of these large old trees, Burubonga and Ikirbonga and Chandibonga and many others, not all of them benevolent. Lutkum Haram and Lutkum Buria had their very own sal tree. She had always wanted to see the bonga in his or her tree but when she had asked, her mother had waved a hand in the general direction of the forest and said that they could be found there. Father Joseph had tried to discourage them from believing in such things, but Milly had left the village before either system of belief could take hold.

She breathed in that familiar vegetal smell, the smell of sun and the sun-baked bright earth. A dazzling butterfly flitted past. Did she miss this in Dumri and Jamshedpur? Did she prefer to live in a town which had none of these things? Yes, she did. Sabina was going to send her to Mumbai. She wanted to be in Mumbai rather than stuck here with forests and rivers; you can miss something without wanting to be reunited with it, without wanting the other things that necessarily came with the thing you missed.

'Why have you become quiet? There *must* be a man. Tell me quickly,' Soni was laughing again.

Milly laughed, too, and said, 'No, no man anywhere. But I hear you're carrying guns nowadays. You joined the Party? How come?'

The one question that was like a fishbone in her throat was one that she couldn't bring herself to ask.

Soni didn't reply.

Milly asked her again, thinking she hadn't heard.

Soni said, 'You haven't lived here for a long time, you don't know how bad things have become. You can't fight them with votes. How can you fight a lion with toy bows and arrows made for children to play with?' The words seemed dragged out of her.

There were cloud-islands of insects, a dense patch for a few inches, hovering in the middle air, then clear light-and-shade-and-heat again. On a low bush, a spider's web was teeming with scores and scores of tiny baby spiders.

'Do you understand? Elections are not going to improve our lot,' she said. That ease, that familiar laughter, all had disappeared. In their place was a focused avidity in her face. If the red soil of the place, and the April heat, had a face, Soni's, now, would be that.

'But why did you join?' Milly asked. 'I thought you wanted to get married and move away from here.'

'I told you, I started to go to their meetings. Then I thought, we are women, we are killed over dowry, and our parents cry and say, oh we lost a girl, and then they forget about us. We are forgotten. We'll all die, but why not do something in the short time that we have, so that people remember us? If I die tomorrow, my father won't cry and say, oh we lost our girl, he'll cry and say, she fought for the people, she laid down her life for the people, she died fighting for adhikaar, for the rights of our people, and they won't forget me. My comrades will build a monument to my name, keep it alive.'

Milly was silent, absorbing the torrent of feelings that had gushed out of Soni. Eventually, she said, 'You fight too? You know how to fire a gun?'

'Yes, of course I do.' Soni proceeded to explain their training, their life of drills and exercises; of muzzle-loading rifles and country-made revolvers, learning how to shoot, target practice, raiding police armouries, lifting guns off policemen killed in encounters; of the art of hiding and running away, of the greater art of surrounding and disappearing. She left out the recurring bouts of malaria and diarrhoea, the exhaustion like a second skin over them, the slow erosion of the body that was the gift of living in the open, like animals.

It seemed to Milly that they were talking about children's games, hide-and-seek in the forest, jumping around with sticks and leaping on each other in a game of ambush. All this military training, guns and bunkers and guerrilla warfare seemed unreal to her, and to Soni, too – she talked about it so casually, so laughingly, that Milly, hearing her, could not invest it with either seriousness or menace. Yet she wanted to: she had witnessed, as a little girl, that these matters were not play-acting and could blast lives, but what she couldn't do was draw a strong, legible line between that childhood memory and what she heard now from a friend who was still associated with days of play, of innocence and stippled sunshine under tamarind trees, of dolls made with bamboo and leaves. How did guns appear in the picture?

Then all that she had been holding in came hurtling out against her will.

'Your people cut off my brother's hand,' she said.

Soni looked puzzled; she didn't know what Milly was talking about. But when she worked it out, she was stunned, as if Milly had slapped her.

'How can that be? It cannot be,' Soni said, shaking her head.

'Yes, the Party did it. Everyone knows that.'

'But how can it be? There was no squad until four, five years ago. And your brother, that was when? Much before that. We were small then . . .'

It was Milly's turn to fall silent with confusion. She could only repeat stubbornly, 'Haan, it was the Party that did it. Everyone says that.'

They walked on in silence for a long while. The setting sun had turned all the sunlit patches in the forest a glowing golden-red. Occasionally their faces encountered strands of invisible webs. Previously, this would have made Soni laugh and gently curse the spiders but that ease had vanished. Milly couldn't read the darkness that had settled on Soni's face; the light under the areas of dense canopy was fading.

Breaking the crust of uneasy silence that had settled over them, Soni said, 'Let me walk you back to the river. It's getting dark, you should go home.'

'Are you going back to your ... your place in the forest? How will you get there in the dark? How far is it?'

'I will stay in the village with you. We are taking food to the camp with us tomorrow night, so I'll need to be in the village with some comrades tonight.'

The birds were headed homewards. Milly thought she could even discern one or two early bats.

Suddenly Soni said, 'Do you live in a big house in the city? How many rooms?'

'Yes, a big house. Three rooms – two for sleeping, one for sitting. And another room for the kitchen.'

'There are separate rooms for sleeping and sitting?'

It struck Milly that besides wonder, there was something else in Soni's voice, some wistfulness, a longing for what she had never experienced and her friend had, perhaps even the slightest touch of envy. It made it easy for Milly to bridge some of the distance between them.

'And cars? There are many cars in the city? You've been in one?'

'Haan, hundreds and hundreds of cars, but I've never ridden one.'

'They pay you a lot of money? What do you do with it?' The question made Milly coy, but Soni was now saying: 'They are exploiting you. If you are providing labour and those punjipati are paying you wages, they are exploiting labour. This is one of the reasons why we have started our deerghkaleen ladai, our protracted battle. Kranti is the only way forward.'

She continued, driven by some opaque reason to narrate. Her lines of thought became jumpy and disjointed, moving erratically between lifeless political jargon and the animated account of her daily life in all its density and details. Her face had become flushed with the passion of the telling. All those big, new words that Soni brandished – burjawa, punjipati – were incomprehensible to Milly. She found herself deeply uncomfortable with this kind of talk. The long words felt so odd, so *wrong*, coming out of Soni's mouth. Ten years ago Milly had sung the hymns she had been taught in church – 'God's love is so wonderful', 'Praise Him for He comes to save us' – without understanding a single word, learning them instead by memorising and repeating the sounds and the intervals. When she had sung them to Soni, she had asked Milly, 'What does the song say? What do the words mean?' Rather than confess to ignorance, Milly had given her version of what little she had understood of Father Joseph's preaching and stories and added her own colour to them.

Soni now continued, 'You don't feel scattered, a little bit of your life here, a little bit of your life there? A broken life, in bits and pieces.'

Milly tried to change the subject. 'Aren't you afraid? All this kranti, explosives, guns, sentry posts, the police hunting for you … Don't you feel fear?' she asked.

The revolutionary's mask still intact on her face, Soni repeated her earlier words, 'What's to fear? We'll all die, anyway. This death is more honourable. I'll be immortal, written about in the Party's letters and papers for other comrades to read. The lives of people like us are nothing. But you can make something of *your* life, stop being nothing.'

The mosquitoes had come out in force; the girls knew they were nearing the river. Suddenly, Soni's mask slipped and she said, in a completely different tone, 'Yes, this will take my life. If I go outside the jungle, I'll be killed. I can only get out after the revolution.'

Something sounded extinguished inside her. Milly couldn't see her face in the dark.

The brief river-crossing turned them into little girls again: squealing over the possibility of falling into the water, mock-fear about not being able to discern the stepping stones in the dark. But it was only playing at being children; that time was over.

Later that night, Budhuwa said to Milly, 'Careful. They often force people to join them.' For a few moments, Milly had no idea to what he was referring. Before she could react, Budhuwa asked, 'Did she persuade you?'

'No! You must be mad to think that.'

'You shouldn't stay here, in this village, much longer. It's good that you're going away to Mumbai. Now that young people have started moving to the towns and cities for jobs, they are finding it hard to recruit guerrillas. We heard that they are holding some young boy who was visiting his family from his school hostel in Rourkela. They are holding him in the forest and teaching him about revolution and not letting him go, either back to his father's village or to the hostel. Once they get their claws into you . . .'

Milly countered meekly, 'No, it was nothing like that . . . We haven't seen each other for so long, she was asking me about my life, and telling me about hers.'

'Did she say anything about police informers?'

'What?'

'If you were seen chatting to her in the forests today, the police would be after you very soon and they would keep harassing you.'

'How would the police see? Soni said that they are so afraid of the Party that they dare not step out of their new buildings.'

'No, not the police, but someone from the village might have seen the two of you and informed them.'

Milly was confused. 'But . . . but the villagers are on the side of the Party people, I thought. You told me so. So did Soni.'

'It's too complicated. The villagers are caught between the police and the Party. They play both. It's a risky game but they – we – have to survive too, na? If we are seen to be permanently for one side, without any change, then we'll suffer when the other side has all the power. Do you see?'

Milly felt dizzy.

'Don't think about it,' he added, as if in consolation. 'It's good that you're getting out soon. Good for you and good for us. Bad times are coming.'

Something in his voice discouraged Milly from prying. In less than a week's time she left for a new world and a new life in Mumbai.

8: *Imprisoned*

Milly's first train journey. To get to Ranchi, from where she would catch the Hatia Nagpur Special to Mumbai, there was a series of bus journeys: anything between an hour to two hours from her village to Manika, then over an hour's wait for another bus, which took three and a half hours to get to Hatia station in Ranchi. She had a send-off party of one: Budhuwa. They were joined by Sabina and the two girls. They had all set out at five in the morning to join the crowd for the unreserved general compartment early.

It seemed to Milly that uncountable numbers of people were waiting to board. She had a ticket but how was she ever going to find a place? Yet it was not this particular anxiety, or the seethe of people, that was at the forefront of her mind. It was the sight of Budhuwa trying to jostle, and bring tea, holding three hot glasses in one hand, needing to go back for more, that broke her anew. She had to hide her face, but not before Sabina had taken note of the welling eyes and the quivering mouth hastily covered with the dupatta.

'No need to be afraid,' she said. 'You're going to a better life. You'll be able to send money back home regularly, quite a lot of money.'

Budhuwa's face was intense with effort. He sweated easily now, Milly noticed. Was it because small things were more laborious for him to execute? At the same time his face had become more and more impassive, withdrawn, she felt, as if in some kind of protective measure against the contempt or pity instantly visible on the face of the world when it encountered a man with a missing limb.

The face got tighter and tighter as her departure time approached; some mechanism inside him, connected to the skin of his face, was being screwed slowly and surely. The chaos and density of people on the platform and even inside the narrow corridor of the compartment were smothering; and dangerous, she was sure – any minute now someone could be crushed, or trampled underfoot, or dragged by the more able, the stronger, and hurled away and dashed against something like a thin clay pot. But the fears were not for herself, they were for Budhuwa – how would he, with only one hand, be able to secure a firm standing point at her window, watching her as the train pulled out? Would he get pushed on to the tracks? How would he be able to withstand the wave of people and prevent himself from being swept away, pushed under the wheels?

In the end it was she who couldn't get to the window because so many of the passengers were pressed against the metal rods, saying goodbye to the people who had come to see them off, that you could hardly tell they were windows – the blocking out of any chink of outside light was total.

The train started to move with a giant judder and a high-pitched creak; an enormous sleeping beast waking up. Was Budhuwa running on the platform, trying to keep pace with her moving window in the hope of catching a glimpse of her face? Was he going to collide with someone and fall as he ran with dozens, scores of others? She was seized with such a desire to run out and throw herself on to the platform from the slowly inching-forward train that she put her hand to her mouth and bit the fleshy bit at the base on the inside as hard as she could bear, and then a little bit more. A woman sitting opposite her was unknotting a bundle which, it was revealed, contained stacks of rotis. Later, Milly thought it was just as well that she hadn't caught a glimpse of her brother's face on the platform – how would she ever have coped with the sight of that tense impassivity, that skin wet with sweat, that mouth slightly open with a mild breathlessness?

In the foetid general compartment for women, with people packed in like puffed rice in a sack, and some staking out their sliver of sleeping space on the floor – the bunks had long been taken – by stretching themselves out or spreading a bit of cloth, Milly was forced into companionship with the two other girls and with Sabina. After the first six or eight hours, it didn't feel strenuous, instead companionable, even welcome. How would she have survived this long journey, pressed on all sides by strangers, without the help of Sabina? Sabina was doughty, street-smart, a seasoned traveller – she knew at which stations the train stopped for half an hour; she knew to get out of the train and buy tea and poori-aloo and samosa; she led the girls to the ladies' toilet in the station. Without her, Milly would have been lost; or worse, if it was discovered that a young woman was travelling alone.

When she got her turn at the window, she saw, speeding past on the other side of the iron bars, a brick factory with piles of bright red-brown bricks stacked around it like unfinished walls and tall, thin chimneys spewing out blue-white plumes of smoke; scrub; endless stretches of fields and dry earth; a tin shed in the middle of immense empty land; deserted temples, some, it seemed, no bigger than a doll's house; a scarecrow, arms akimbo, its figure tilted to one side, the rags covering it flapping in the hot breeze ... there was too much place in the world and it made her afraid.

At one major station one of the girls asked, 'Where have we stopped?'

Milly looked out of the window, peered a bit and said, 'Bilaspur Junction.'

'How do you know?'

'The name of the station is written on that yellow board.'

The girl turned to her with a changed expression. 'You know how to read?'

Milly looked down and didn't answer.

The girl persisted. 'How come you're coming with us to work as a servant if you can read?'

Within minutes, the other girl knew this amazing piece of information. Milly refrained from telling them that she could read the names of the stations not only in Hindi but also in English.

Huddled on the floor at night, pressed tight between the bodies of two girls, she was lulled into a kind of hypnosis by the regular jhikki-jhikki-jhik-jhikki-jhik racket of the wheels, right under the floor. Right under her! Soon, she thought they were saying something, a mantra, unvaryingly repeated. They caught a half-line from a snatch of song inside her head and fished it out, set it to their relentless music and made it their own. Now the wheels only chanted those truncated song lyrics until she fell asleep. Or maybe it was the gentle rock-and-sway motion of the carriage that brought on sleep, for she kept waking up whenever the train halted at a station for any length of time.

There was the spontaneous camaraderie of their fellow travellers: the Bihari woman sharing her last littis with strangers; the elderly Vaishnav woman who occasionally broke into Krishna-bhajans; a middle-aged woman, on her way to visit her son in Mumbai, chattering away, spouting stories about everything and anything – a big temple, shaped like a chariot, in Puri; the crush at Gangasagar Mela on Sankranti; her little grandson's amusing mangling of words he was beginning to learn; miracles at some shrine in Gaya; people she said she knew who had been affected by consuming adulterated palm oil sold in a ration shop in Rourkela ...

The whole world was fitted by magic into the tiny confinement of the train carriage, so that when they got off at Lokmanya Tilak Terminus in Kurla, Milly could at least give a name to the sensation that swallowed her. It was drowning.

The Vachanis lived on the first floor of a high-rise apartment block on Ganpatrao Kadam Marg in Lower Parel. Milly, who had never seen large, multi-storeyed apartment blocks, not even in Jamshedpur, certainly not in this density, felt awe and fear. The building had a name: 'Sukh Niwas'. It had a cage-like machine that carried you upstairs and downstairs. Milly was to learn later the name of this machine that made the staircase unnecessary – 'lift'.

The flat was laid out in a way not dissimilar to the one in Jamshedpur. There were two bedrooms, each with a bathroom attached to it, a big room which was used as a sitting room at one end and had a dining table and four chairs to the side nearer the kitchen. The kitchen was narrow, a standard size. It doubled as Milly's bedroom at night. For her food, she had the use of two plates, both identical melamine ones, white with a green rim and green circles all over the surface, the white background of which had discoloured with time and the turmeric in the food. She had a plastic beaker for her water and an old, chipped mug for her tea. As in Jamshedpur, she had to keep her things separate from the family's, although here she was allowed to stack her dishes, after washing up, right at the end of the hanging draining rack above the sink, but, crucially, leaving a gap of anything between three to six 'slots' between their plates and hers.

Her toilet and bathroom were on the ground floor, which had no flats but served as a car park for the residents of the building. The guards sat in the pillared open space next to the entrance hallway housing the letter boxes, staircase and lift. The bathroom and toilet cubicles were at the far end of the car park, at the back of the building, away from the entrance and the guards' gathering place.

Milly learned, very early on, on her second or third day, how to avoid the guards' gaze as she went to use the public conveniences meant for the servants, drivers and security guards who worked in the building. The experience of going downstairs to use the facilities was a mixed one for her – on one hand, there was the ever-present anxiety that she would be seen by one of the guards; on the other hand, there was the undiminishing joy of using the lift to go down and come up, even if it was for the elevation of only two flights of stairs.

Jayant and Hemali Vachani appeared elderly to Milly's eyes – she learnt soon that they had two grown-up daughters and a brood of little grandchildren – although she could not have put an approximate age to them. Her division of people's ages was broadly descriptive: very young, young, a middle stage of neither young nor old, then old.

The outlines of Milly's tasks were explained to her over the course of days. Besides the usual duties of cleaning, sweeping, dusting, doing the laundry, the washing-up, it emerged that she was also expected to cook. She would be trained by Hemali Vachani to cook Sindhi food – sai bhaji, elaichi gosht, sata bhaj-yun, toori chanadal.

Although her salary in Mumbai was nearly five times what she got in Jamshedpur, she discovered later that she was being paid only one salary, the live-in housemaid's, when she should have been given twice that sum, since she was saving them the wages they would have had to pay a cook. There was no way she herself could bring up the matter of a double salary. She called Sabina's mobile to see if it couldn't be sorted out.

'They're giving you a place to stay and food to eat, saving you rent and food money,' Sabina said. 'Stop complaining. Who has been putting such ideas in your head? You've been here for three months, four months, and you've already started to get so greedy?'

Milly felt chastised. The Vachanis had set up a bank account for her. They had helped her to negotiate how to send, every month, most of her salary back home. How could she ask them to pay her more money? Where would she go if they took umbrage and fired her? Where would she live?

But over the four months that she had been in 'Sukh Niwas', something more worrying emerged: she wasn't allowed to leave the building. Her only forays outside the flat were to the bathroom downstairs. The stricture hadn't been announced to her from the very outset, but was rather something that she came to understand in slow degrees. It didn't strike her as odd, at first, that rather than sending her out for a small item that had been forgotten, or run out of – say, milk – they would go without milk in their tea. An entire dish at dinner would be foregone if an ingredient, one that required a small walk to a corner shop, was missing; Milly wouldn't be sent out to fetch it.

Without noticing that this was the deliberate order of things, Milly said one day, 'I can go out and get laundry soap. Just tell me where to go and what brand of soap you want.'

Hemali gave her a look and said curtly, 'No need. We'll send the driver out tomorrow morning.'

Milly, who was at once curious about and frightened of the world outside the gated compound of 'Sukh Niwas' but had not seen anything of it, except the large segment of road on which the building stood, felt an increasing impatience to venture out. She lingered over the dusting and cleaning of the windows facing the street and, when she realised that an excuse was no longer necessary, she simply stood gazing out. Two big trees framed the view; she didn't know their names. People passed by, and cars, autos, Tempos, cycles, taxis. A clutch of vendors set up their makeshift stalls on the far side – they sold snacks, cucumber, vada pao and pao bhaji, starfruit, peanuts, and Milly wanted to run out and taste all of them and feel the traffic fumes and the warm, humid outside air on her skin. The whole world was caught up in movement; only she was still and rooted to one spot. She began to identify a few people who regularly, and at more or less set hours, passed up or down the road. There was the woman with stainless-steel utensils balanced in a wide basket on her head who came every Sunday morning. She had a long, thin, unintelligible cry to announce her presence. There was the ironing man, who collected clothes from people in the apartment blocks, and carried off a huge bundle tied in a large bed sheet on the back of his bicycle. He visited the Vacanis to take in their ironing too, four times a week. There were the snack vendors, of course, but they were too far away for her to make out their faces. There was a young man who walked towards the right at five o'clock every afternoon. She knew this because he had looked up at her once and their eyes had met for the briefest of moments before she had looked away. She wouldn't have given it another thought, or even remembered it, had the same thing not happened a week or ten days later, then again on the consecutive day. Three times amounted to meaning. Every time he looked up, Milly turned her gaze away almost instantaneously, although she allowed herself – and perhaps him, too – the luxury of what could only be called waiting, waiting for him to walk past and look up when he was exactly opposite her window.

The first indication Milly had that she was strictly forbidden to step outside the two heavy iron gates of 'Sukh Niwas' was when she decided that she would go for a little walk to see what lay beyond the margins of her view from the window. The Vachanis were away and there was no one to stop her. She walked to the iron gate and started opening it – it was heavy and she first had to slide the bolt out of its socket. Before she had even begun, one of the guards came running.

'What are you doing, what are you doing?' he barked. 'Get away from the gate, you can't go out.'

Already daunted by having a man, and a stranger at that, speak to her in such an aggressive way, Milly was even more cowed by the spectacle of his companions, a loose gaggle of guards and some of the drivers who were on duty, all standing up and watching the spectacle that was unfolding. She felt naked.

She asked weakly, all prepared to flee upstairs, 'But why?'

'Your masters' – he used the words 'malik' and 'malkin' – 'have given us orders: no maidservants can leave the building.'

Disbelief silenced her. A dozen questions struggled to come out, but the weight of the words 'masters' and 'orders' were too power-ful. Besides, the awareness that all these men were gulping her in with their eyes, enjoying watching her get into trouble, was even more powerful. She turned tail and walked up to the lift, feeling the air behind her back turning to something hot and crackling.

Most likely the guards were bullying her, she thought; how could it be possible that she wasn't allowed to go out for even a few minutes?

After the Vachanis returned, she asked Didi, 'The guard down-stairs wouldn't allow me to go out.'

'You wanted to go out?' Hemali asked.

'Yes, just to walk and see what's outside, I haven't been out once since I came here.'

Hemali's face hardened. In a voice that could cut stone she said, 'There's no call for you to go outside. Young girls going outside on their own – it only leads to trouble. And others have to pick up the pieces afterwards. You stay where you are.'

The tone of her voice denied any possibility of a rejoinder from Milly. Besides, she was a servant, she couldn't question or argue or oppose. When she found a sliver of time away from Didi – not an easy thing to do; it took days – she called Sabina to complain, and also to ask for an explanation, a reason for the existence of this strange rule. Sabina could shed no light on the matter but she added, 'They're just being cautious. You've come from a village far away, and Mumbai is a very big city. They're afraid you'll get lost, or ... or something worse. I'm sure they'll let you go out soon.'

Milly wasn't convinced but she tried to draw hope from Sabina's words. But something tenacious and easy-growing had lodged inside her head and it let its presence be known, only occasionally at the beginning, then with such increasing frequency that it became everything.

First, she noticed the collapsible iron gates on all the windows, including the ones at the back of the flat, but this was not unusual in any city – she had seen such security in Jamshedpur, too. What was unusual perhaps was that they were kept locked all the time. She had never seen a key, or seen the gates ever opened, even by Dada or Didi. Then the business of not being sent on errands took on a different meaning. As did several other seemingly innocuous things: the fact that the front door to the flat was padlocked from the inside every night; that the kitchen windows had nets on them (although she knew well that this was to prevent birds and insects from flying in); that she was never told, or never discovered for herself, where the key to the night padlock was ...

Slowly, she became unable to think about anything else. It was not that she needed to go out – where would, could, she go, in this endless city, without knowing anyone? – but something so fundamental denied is that thing made disproportionately enormous, consuming, and she began to think of herself as a caged bird, defined by the fact of nothing except its imprisonment. The Vachanis didn't treat her badly – they didn't hit her, or deny her food and clothing, or shout at her, at least not too much or too regularly (there was, of course, the usual chiding when Milly got something wrong, accidentally broke a glass or a plate, or when Didi, in a magnification of her persistently nagging mode, found fault in everything Milly did, but these instances, while upsetting her temporarily, she had learned to accept as part of her job). But there were times when she thought that she would happily put up with crueller behaviour if this one overarching cruelty could be removed. What was a slap or two, angry shouting, compared with this?

She experienced a new feeling, at night, of the kitchen walls inching forward slowly from all four sides to crush her, lying in the middle. Their hut in the village had been tiny and eight of them had to sleep together, huddled, but she had never thought of that as small. Besides, there was always the great open outside – fields, forests, groves, river bank. The idea of space as something small or big, something that could be reduced, had never occurred to her, not even on the train, in the general compartment so dense with people that the air had sometimes felt too thick to breathe, not even in that battery-cage had the thought ever crossed her mind that 'this is too small'. Now, in a Mumbai flat bigger than any house she had ever known, she felt trapped and squeezed. She called up Sabina again to complain tearfully. And everything that Sabina had to say in response – 'You are getting things wrong, how can they lock you in? You are not telling me something; you don't know the full story yourself; they may have their reasons' – Milly felt was worse than unsupportive: Sabina was defending the Vachanis.

Things continued in this vein for a while. During one of Milly's plaintive phone calls, Sabina said with considerable irritation, 'Whinge, whinge, whinge! Do you know how good you have it out there? Thank Jesus that you weren't the ten-year-old boy working for this Marwari woman in Kolkata. Do you know what happened to him? She picked him up and threw him down the hole through which the lift goes up and down. You know what a lift is? And you know how high up she lived in the building? Eight floors. The boy was thrown down eight storeys. You think not being allowed to go out to walk and look at the people and the shops or whatever is comparable? You should be grateful for what you have – things are far worse out there.'

Milly knew then that she wasn't going to get any help from this particular quarter, but before this understanding had settled inside her head she had blurted out the words, 'What happened to the boy?'

'Oh, he survived. He went to hospital with many broken bones. The woman and her husband are rich and powerful people – the police came but nothing happened. She said he fell down because he was playing with the lift and didn't know how to work it, when he should open the door to get in. It was their word against the boy's. Who would believe an illiterate boy from nowhere over a city-woman dripping with jewels? You think anyone would believe you if you whined about not being let out?'

Milly's blood froze when she heard the story, but later she wondered about how exercised Sabina had got in the telling of it, practically screaming, as if the boy's situation had caused her great anger and pain. So why was she so unsympathetic to her, Milly, and on the side of the Vachanis? A feeling of intense loneliness swept through her – she felt she was going to be blown away by it. She realised that she could not rely on the only person she knew in this city, the only link between her new life here and the old life back in the village. She had been untethered, set free, when all she wanted was the security of being fixed to one place, the safety and comfort of not being alone.

The sense of desolation broke her. It was as if the feeling made the fact of her imprisonment final and irreversible, whereas before her last phone call with Sabina, Milly had hopes that it was a mistake, or temporary, or some simple thing she was failing to understand. Her reaction to this hopelessness spanned a whole spectrum. She cried in private a lot, and sometimes in front of Dada and Didi, unable to escape that weighed-down feeling even for the short duration when it was required of her to put on a public face. The constant crying annoyed Hemali so much that her manner towards Milly changed from one of cool and indifferent lordliness, the hauteur of a mistress towards her maidservant, to one of active, angry dislike. She shouted at her a few times, 'Stop snivelling! Someone's died or what, that you're like Water Supply Corporation all the time, eh? You think I'm the kind who yields to tears?' When this seemed to have no effect, she lost all restraint one evening and slapped Milly across the face. Milly dropped the teapot she was holding. It shattered into fragments of all sizes; the tea splashed all over the floor and caught a large corner of the rug. Hemali lashed out with her fists and hands with abandon. Shocked, and busy with cowering to avoid the blows, Milly forgot to cry.

That night, in the dark kitchen, with the whispery rustle of cockroaches emerging from their daytime hiding places, Milly felt the cold, metallic taste of fear and it froze her tears. From now on, all her thoughts and energies were concentrated on one thing only – an escape plan. But surely they must know that she, or any-one in her position, sooner or later into their stay here, would plot to run away and, consequently, had put in place all kinds of meas-ures to prevent such a thing? Where, where could she find a crack, an opening? How could she slip out? She checked, and checked again, the solidity of the doors and windows of the flat. When no one was watching, she tried to slip an arm or a leg through the col-lapsible iron shutters on the windows to see how much of herself she could get through. She got stuck one day when she managed to get one leg out up to the thigh – there was no way she could fit in both, or her hip – but then couldn't pull it back in. She tore her shalwar to get the few extra millimetres or two of leverage, but her leg was held fast. A pincer movement of panic began to crush her: what if her masters walked in right now, and what if someone outside, a neighbour at a window, someone passing in the car park downstairs or, worse, one of the guards, saw her like this? She peed with fear and anxiety and felt even more ashamed; much better to yank the leg out of its socket than risk being seen like this. She pulled and stretched and twisted; the skin on her thighs broke; the pain was irrelevant, she wanted to make it far worse if it could have been the price for freedom. Her mind whirled – if only she could reach for some soap or oil, if only there was the thigh equivalent for sucking in one's stomach, if only she could summon someone reliable and trustworthy for help, if only she had a knife to slice off bits of her flesh … and, then, suddenly, with another pull, and not a ferocious one, she was free. She toppled over and fell awkwardly on the floor, hitting her head on the corner of the bed.

Desperation gnawed away at her until she felt she was losing her mind. She woke up at two or three in the morning and looked for cracks and fissures in the corners of the kitchen she could use as the point to begin digging a hole secretly. The thought of digging would then send her looking for suitable implements. Would the biggest knife do? What about the smaller ones, with sharper points? She tried one on a small area next to the fridge where there was an indentation on the floor, close to the wall where the electrical switchboard was, and broke the blade in one clean snap. Did Didi count the number of knives she possessed? Would Milly have to pretend to break it while cutting something tomorrow? Would she be slapped for it? She looked at the huge rake of tines the collapsible window had left on her thigh and thought how pain could be ignored. Every time an action defeated her, such as digging a hole through the wall – either through the sheer impossibility of executing it, or being brought up short by the immovable barrier that was the iron gate of 'Sukh Niwas' and its guards – she inflicted some damage on herself out of frustration, knowing that the lash of pain would allow her mind to get away, if only for a moment, from battling the thing that was eating it. She bit her arms, sinking her teeth in; cut her fingers under a cold running tap; tore out clumps of her hair … and had the idea that if she could maim herself, or catch an illness so severe that it would necessitate a visit to the hospital, she could make a run for it. For a while she would soar on the wings of this fantasy, until one question brought her down crashing: where would she go? From that one question a maze in hell emerged: could she go to the railway station and buy a ticket to return to her village? All on her own? She would first need to go to the bank to withdraw money, but her passbook was with Didi. How would she ever retrieve it? Even if she could, how would she negotiate all the bank business? How long would it take between running away from the hospital and getting herself to the railway station? And again: all this on her own? She didn't have any money with her ... She felt she was drowning; the whole world was empty and it was just herself on an endless stretch of water and she knew that it was going to swallow her.

Prodded not so much by guilt as pity, the kind that made people throw one-rupee coins to beggars from the hastily rolled-down windows of their air-conditioned cars, Hemali Vachani had not only allowed Milly to watch whatever television she desired, but had also taught her how to turn it on and operate the remote control. The television was a lifeline, especially when Dada and Didi were away and she could forget the great burden of her imprisonment for a few hours, watching the joys and sorrows of other people's lives; her own felt thin, colourless, flat.

Nearly a year passed until Milly, now resigned and fatalistic, had another idea – what if she performed her duties so badly that they had to let her go? She began subtly, then escalated in gradual steps. First, oversalting the food, burning the rice and rotis, putting salt in tea and heaped tablespoonfuls of sugar in the savoury food at lunch and dinner. Hemali complained about the first couple of instances, then scolded severely, finally resorting to hitting Milly, who seemed to have become inured to corporal punishment. This fanned the flames of Hemali's rage. She forced Milly to eat all the ruined food in one sitting, shoving her fist full of food into Milly's mouth when she could no longer ingest anything.

'I'll punish you so badly that you will be screaming for help,' Hemali shouted, 'and there won't be a soul on earth who will lift a finger to help you. Next time you think of such tricks, remember, I'll brand your face with a hot iron, you'll be marked for life. How would that feel?'

Flat 10, 'Sukh Niwas', Lower Parel, had become a circus.

Then one day, a real possibility of walking out of the building and never returning presented itself. Sabina called to tell Milly that her father had died. Before she felt the loss, she was lifted up with hope and joy – they must let her go to her village now, they must, how could they not?

'Will you call them and ask them to let me go?' she said to Sabina.

'You ask them first, see what they say.'

'She'll say no, I'm sure of that. If you speak to them, they may agree.'

'Ask first, na.'

So Milly did, reluctantly, unhopefully, and it was while uttering the words 'My father has died' that she was overthrown. The tears that welled out were simple tears, uncomplicated, pure in origin, out of an altogether different source from her tears over the last year.

Hemali grimaced and said, 'You're lying. It's a ruse you've cooked up.'

'No, I'm not lying. Ask Sabina. She called me to give the news.'

'Then the two of you are in cahoots.'

Milly fell on her knees and pleaded. Stone idols were more responsive.

For the first time in who knows how long, Milly's mind moved away from its usual obsession. She felt she was being lashed by a different kind of anguish now. Under the greasy mosquito net, a sleepless Milly thought of one of the earliest memories she had of her father: herself trying to run away, giddy with delight, as her father, pretending to be a tiger, chased her, but kept top-pling over every time he stood up, something that sent her into gales of squealing laughter. She had understood years later that the instability on his feet had not been part of his attempt to entertain her but because he was drunk. She felt something being wrung inside her and she howled noiselessly, her fist in her mouth. She would never see his crumpled face again. They were certain to have cremated him by the time Sabina had called. Milly didn't know how long they would keep his bones until they were buried under the sasandiri at the jangtopa. Had she been back home, the church people would probably have forbid-den her from going to the ceremony, but they were not rigid in enforcing their rules and were easily dealt with. She wouldn't even have the luxury of rebelling against Father Joseph because she would be stuck here.

Would she ever be able to leave 'Sukh Niwas' any time before Dada and Didi died? Would she be passed on to one of their daugh-ters after their deaths and continue imprisoned in another house until she herself became old and died? Wasn't that what happened to birds in cages? Did that shambling, drunken man, who beat his wife, and was useless at any job, did that man ever think that his daughter would be in a situation like this? Would he be as helpless at rescuing her as he had been when his son's hand was chopped off? The thought of her father's habitual feebleness rinsed her insides again with pity. She wanted to protect him but he was gone beyond all that now.

In the end, Milly wasn't allowed to go back home, not even for the jangtopa. Hemali Vachani told Sabina on the phone that, if she didn't like the current state of affairs, she was welcome to go to the police. This provoked Sabina to come over to Milly's side; no doubt, Milly reasoned, because Sabina was afraid of the damage it would do to her reputation back home, if people found out what kind of life some of the girls from the villages had entered in the big cities with her help.

Two days after she was rebuffed, Sabina called to say, 'I'm trying to find a place somewhere else in Mumbai where they could take you in.'

The conversation went aimlessly in eddies, and Milly had no energy to sustain chatter that consisted of Sabina's suggestions and ideas for escape, which Milly had already been over hundreds of times. And then, in all that well-ploughed soil, an unexpected gem – Sabina said, 'Be careful not to give them your mobile if they ask for it.'

Milly became alert. 'How come?' she asked. It was a rhetorical question: neither she nor the Vachanis had considered her phone as something that could be used as a tool of escape. She didn't know how yet, but here was something to think about. It was just as well that Sabina had taken care of topping up her pre-paid Air Tel account.

Was it quite by chance that she spotted him again or had he been walking past every day, looking up faithfully, sometimes seeing her, distracted, unhappy, not noticing him, and at other times glancing up but not spotting her at the window at the usual hour? A weak memory of distant familiarity – no, not even that, just a whisper of recognition – stirred in her mind; it was a different life, perhaps one that had still held the promise, or hope, of freedom. She did not remember. This time, however, she fell into the routine of looking out for him, waiting for the moment in the day when their eyes would lock and she would turn her face away in shyness. She began to take longer to avert her eyes, until one day she forgot to do it. He smiled; a shy, tentative smile. And one day she returned his smile.

Shortly after this he was emboldened to ask her to come down. She shook her head and moved back into the darkness of the interior. She watched him from the shadows, unseen herself, as he

waited for a long time for her to re-emerge. This delicate equilib-
rium, of looks exchanged, followed by watching in hiding on her
part and waiting on his, lasted a good while until he took his courage in his hands and mimed the urgency of her necessity to come
down and talk to him. The gestures were all extemporised, so she
took some time to read them correctly, but she signalled back,
with a heightened version of a stricken look on her face, that she
wasn't allowed to go out ever. Again, this short act of the silent
drama was repeated over several days until she showed him her
phone, then provided her number, one numeral at a time, with
the correct number of fingers held up and displayed. He called
her while she was still at the window, holding her phone, but the
moment she answered, she looked out at him, staring at her and
smiling, and disappeared into the inner gloom while continuing
with the call.

Shyness affected both sides. Milly didn't utter a word after her
first 'haan' unless she was asked a direct question.

'What's your name?' he asked. She noted that he had used the
politest form of 'you' to address her.

She could barely bring herself to reply and, when she did, he had
to ask her to repeat the name several times before it was audible. A
long pause descended. She was clearly not going to ask his name.

'Binay,' he said. 'My name is Binay.'

She offered nothing but her silence.

'Did you hear? My name is Binay.'

This time she whispered a 'haan'.

He asked, 'Come outside? Just for a few minutes?'

Long pause.

'Will you come?' he pleaded.

Pause, then a faint, 'They don't let me go outside.'

'Can you not make up an excuse and come out? On an errand?'

Perhaps this was what Milly was waiting for, an expression of
interest from the world outside, a door opening to another, bigger

place, that would allow the echo-chamber in her head to become a story that could be told. That story started spilling out, but halfway through she heard the front door open. She whispered a panicked, 'They've arrived, they've arrived, don't call me', and hung up.

It took her over a week to give him the whole account. At the end of the story, he surprised her by remarking that the problem was not so much her masters as the guards: her masters went out of their home often, leaving Milly on her own, an interim when she could have done anything, including escape, but they relied on the guards to prevent any such mishap. It was the guards that they – no, he – needed to think about.

Ten days after the last instalment of the phone conversation, the doorbell rang. She opened the door and there he was, hardly the distance of two hands from her, standing with two large paper boxes in a plastic bag, his face a picture of sweaty nervousness, one of the 'Sukh Niwas' guards at his side. They had planned this meticulously – when the Vachanis would be away, how he would say to the guards that he was the delivery man from a shop, how she would corroborate when the guard accompanying him to Flat 10 rang the bell – but no amount of rehearsal ever took the dread away from the first night of the performance. As soon as Milly had confirmed that something had been ordered by her malkin, the guard went downstairs to resume his game of cards.

She kept her head down throughout, refusing to make eye-contact or speak to Binay directly, choosing instead to address the doorframe, the threshold, the white-grey-and-black tiled floor of the landing. When she had to look up, her eyes focused on the red swastika on the lintel of the door to Flat 11, behind his head, and on the tiny glass Ganesh perched on top of that, right in the centre. She had never seen it before, never having paid such attention to the front door of the opposite flat.

'Take,' he said, handing her the plastic bag.

She didn't take it, but asked, 'What's in it?'

'Food.'

'What food?'

'I work in a restaurant. It's food from there.'

A pause as she absorbed this.

'I had to have something in my hands to convince the guards that I had come to deliver,' he said, almost injured that she shouldn't accept the food, although it was only a prop in a somewhat elaborate game.

'What food?' she asked again.

'Chow mein and chilli chicken,' he said.

She didn't understand a single word; her mind was elsewhere. 'If they see the food, what am I going to say to them?' she asked. 'I'll get into trouble.'

'You can eat it now.'

She smiled, then said, 'So much?', and went back to looking anxious.

He knew it was dangerous for him to linger, and unwise of him to force the food upon her, but he wanted to eke out the moment – who knew when he would be able to come next? Above all, he wanted to hear her speak the words she had said on the phone, but face-to-face, looking into his eyes: 'You'll rescue me from this place, na?'

They moved with the stealth of stalking predators. Binay knew that making friends with the guards and depending on their connivance, or even sympathy, to smuggle Milly out was not a reasonable option. They planned on the phone, in conversations snatched hastily during the rare moments of privacy that Milly had when the Vachanis were out of their home. She had little to contribute to the plans except to convey her fears – fear of the plan failing, fear of being found out before it was executed, fear of the hundred and one things that could – would – go wrong, fear of repercussions, fear of the guards being sent after her ... The world was one giant pitfall.

The greatest of the insurmountables was the question of the police. 'What if we are found out?' Milly would chant her mantra.

'In that case we can call the police, if they force you to go back,' Binay would reassure her.

'The police won't bother to listen to people like us.'

Binay knew this was true, but he didn't want to be appear to be daunted. He said with bravado, 'The world has changed, the police can't get away with everything. This is a big city, not a village. There are crores of people here. We can make a big havoc with the people in the streets.' He didn't have a clear idea of the hue and cry that he said he was going to raise, but it sounded good and it seemed to calm her temporarily. But at night, when Milly was alone with the indefatigable choir inside her head, the questions would come out of hiding again, like the cockroaches, stealthy but unignorable. What if they sent the police to find her and bring her back after she managed to escape? They were the police, they were in the business of knowing how to find people hiding from them. Binay's words about how in the city the two of them would be like two grain-sized pieces of stone in a granary packed with rice sounded hollow at this hour. Didi could easily bribe the police. And who knew if they didn't already know of this racket? The thought of that Marwari woman in Kolkata resurfaced, as if in illustration of her fears. Milly curled up like a foetus. She didn't think she had it in her to go through with the plan. Then it struck her – what would happen to her bank passbook? Would she be able to get her hands on her money without it? Would they send the police to the bank and wait for her to show up? Even if that were not the case, the bank people could easily inform on her when she went in to take out or deposit money ... Various scenarios played out in her head until, exhausted, she thought: perhaps it was better to stay put and see it to the end of her days in this cage. Some of the possibilities that could follow, if the plan was put into action, could be far worse than what she had in this house. Why not shut up and put up with the present state of affairs? Look at Soni – what was she doing with her freedom? Running around in jungles, wielding guns, living under the sky, barely getting two proper meals a day; she was a marked woman who would have to remain in hiding for the rest of her life – that was a kind of imprisonment too, wasn't it? Especially that life? Wasn't she, Milly, better off? She thought of Soni's words, 'The lives of people like us are nothing.' Yes, her life may be nothing to others, but to her? Wasn't it something to her? Everything?

It had to be on the day the Vachanis went to the Siddhi Vinayak Temple for the big festival of Ganesh Chaturthi. Didi talked about it for days beforehand and Milly remembered that temple visits often took three to four hours; a good, clean window for her and Binay. Their plan seemed more and more absurd, unworkable, as the hour approached. She found herself thinking of ways to sabotage it, just to have the inevitable consequences happen early and put her out of her misery. What if the guards didn't let Binay in? That wouldn't be such a bad thing; to have the plan ruined at such an early stage meant that at least she would not be implicated.

No such mercy. She watched the iron gates downstairs open to let in two cars, then close again. A woman, clearly someone who worked in one of the other flats in the building, clanged on the gate and was let in. Milly's heart was a rattle in the hands of a child. A guard opened one of the two panels that comprised the gate to chat to someone – she couldn't see who it was; she felt faint. He closed the gate again. Was it Binay? Had he not been allowed in? How could that be? There seemed to be a hollow where her chest and stomach used to be. There was another short banging on the gate. A guard walked up and opened it a crack. Brief exchange. Then he lifted up the bolt that fitted into a hole on the ground and opened both doors wide. A huge wooden cupboard was carried in, held aslant by Binay and another man, both of them dwarfed and angled sideways and slightly backwards, by the effort of wielding it. Before she could assimilate this sight, there was a rapping on the front door of the flat.

A guard stood outside. He said, 'Almirah delivery. There are two men downstairs. Shall I send them up?'

'Haan,' she said, but she couldn't hear herself above the roaring of her blood.

The cupboard had to come inside the flat horizontally. The door was shut. As planned, Milly walked into the wooden box – there was room inside for at least two of her. Beyond her own weight, Milly didn't have much to make the cupboard any heavier. She had very little to take with her: two shalwar-kurta sets, her Hindi textbooks, a book of elementary English words, a toothbrush, a comb, a small hand-mirror, her mobile, her little purse, which held next to nothing, and the most important thing, her ration card. This was the card that she had to show to the bank to prove that her account was hers. This was the card that Sabina had said she must hide from Didi, and guard with her life and never, ever give up if Didi asked for it.

Binay and his friend tested the thing on which everything turned – whether the bolt could slip and the doors fling open while carrying her out. They had even come prepared for this eventuality: a lock they could attach on the outside, securing the bolt in its place. It was roomy inside, and the cupboard was made of wood, not cheap plywood boards, so she imagined it must be very heavy. The men lifted. She felt the whole world, or what little there was of it in the confined scrap of pitch-darkness, tilt around her. She gave a little scream. They set down the cupboard gently.

She heard Binay's voice, muffled, 'Everything all right?'

'Haan.'

'What?'

'Haan,' she repeated, louder.

'Listen. We'll lift the almirah and lean it forward, so that you are pressed against the door. Do you understand? Put your entire body on the door, don't resist, don't rest against the back wall. Understood?'

'Haan.' She didn't, not quite, but she wanted to get this over with as quickly as possible.

Again, that lift and cant, that brief feeling of weightlessness followed by the tiny, dark space going topsy-turvy. Then an awkward jerk brought her sharply in collision with the door. It held. They rehearsed this three more times. Milly could hear the exertions of the men, their grunts and huff-puffing, even smell their sweat. She felt like a ball in a game of catch-catch between giants. She summoned all her courage and asked meekly, 'Can I come out for a minute?'

Outside, the world was full of light – blinding – and air. Standing on the tiled floor of the living room felt so solid, so good; she had never thought she would consider any part of this flat, however fleetingly, as offering a feeling of liberation. The smell of the men's sweat was ranker now. Their foreheads were wet.

Binay said, 'We have to be quick. Is it too bad in there? Give us a glass of water and then we'll get out of this place. You're sure you aren't leaving anything important behind?'

Milly said, 'Why don't you put the almirah – with me inside it – in the lift? It'll save you having to take this down the stairs.'

Out on the landing, Milly showed them how to operate the lift. 'Make sure you close both the doors tight shut. Like this. And press this button after that, the one with the zero on it, do you see?'

They went back into the flat and Milly entered the cupboard, which Binay locked from the outside. They were ready at last.

In her dark, moving cabin, Milly heard her own pounding heart, that betraying beast, and was certain that the guards outside could hear it, too: the wooden walls of the almirah were fairly pulsating to the beats. The world outside came to her in the form of muffled sounds – traffic, perhaps the aimless conversation of the guards? – and that needle-thin line of light where the doors joined. Would she be able to see thin segments of the world if she pressed her eye to it? Here she was, in a rocking boat, like the one she had read in her Hindi book: 'The fishermen go out to sea in boats. The sea is full of waves. The waves rock the boats and the boats sway. The fishermen, too, sway in their boats.' Here she was, borne aloft in a locked box from one life to another, swayed not by waves but by the imperfect strength of those delivering her and the cumbersome nature of the delivery. She heard fragments of conversation: ' . . . taking away the old one . . .' in Binay's voice, then something she couldn't make out in another, unfamiliar voice. She held her breath. She had put her trust in one man, a man she didn't know at all, with whom she had only had a number of phone calls, she was putting her whole life in the hands of this man. The air in the cupboard was suddenly not enough. She put her nose to the hairline of light and tried to breathe in. It did not improve matters. Were they out of the building compound? She did not remember hearing the sound of the iron gates opening and closing. If they were outside, why weren't the street noises louder?

Suddenly she felt elevated higher, as if Binay and his friend had lifted the box up above their heads, their arms fully stretched vertically. It was not possible. Just as suddenly, she was lowered with a thud: the cupboard had been put down on some surface but on its side; she was in the sleeping position now. Voices, again, but speaking unintelligible words; sound of slamming vehicle doors, metal on metal, a metal door or gate being bolted. The long, thin crack of light had disappeared. She could not breathe, she was going to be choked to death. The sound of a vehicle starting up. She understood then that her almirah was in the back of a truck or Tempo and that it was moving. She let out a trial scream, but who would be able to hear her above the incarnation of noise that was Mumbai? So she screamed and screamed and pounded on the door with her fists, but in that cramped space she couldn't get enough leverage to strike with full force . . . But who could hear her weak cries, dampened by the coffin enveloping her on all sides, and swallowed by the roar of life's unimpeded flow outside?

She stood on the open deck of the Tempo, clutching one of the metal bars behind the driver-and-passenger capsule. Binay sat on the floor next to her, holding on to the side. The almirah lay open, still on its side; inside, two plastic bags containing Milly's worldly possessions. She breathed in huge lungfuls of the heat and dust and traffic fumes and was silent. Her eyes were wide open to take in everything. She felt small yet infinitely alive, like a tiny baby sparrow in the middle of a huge human palm. When she spoke, it was almost to herself, in just above a whisper.

'So big? We'll get lost here.'

Binay, who couldn't hear her, who didn't even know that she had spoken, said, 'We're coming into Bandra soon.'

She sat down and held the side of the Tempo with both hands. So many cars. So many people.

Binay said, 'Look, the sea. Have you seen the sea before?'

That, the sea? Like a huge pond whose other side you couldn't see?

9: *Home*

It was Sabina who found Milly a new position in under a fortnight of her escaping from the Vachanis. Binay had to keep reassuring Milly that her former employers couldn't come after her, since no one knew who he was, where he lived, what his role in the escapade was. They married the week after she started her job on Mount Mary Road, a ten-minute walk uphill from her new home in the seaside jhopri between a luxurious hotel, Taj Land's End, and Bandra Band Stand. The job, in a seventh-floor apartment in a high-rise called 'Sea Crest', was not a live-in one: she had to turn up early, just after 6 a.m., to make breakfast for the family of four (a couple and their two children). The man left for work around seven-thirty, taking the children with him to drop off at their school on the way to his office. Milly stayed for another hour and did the dusting, cleaning, washing-up, laundry, and even ran a few errands. By eight-thirty she was done. Binay, who worked evenings in a restaurant in Pali Hill nearby, would still be asleep by the time she got back home.

She thought of her village as home, too, but she used the word gaon for it, never ghar; the jhopri in Bandra was home now. Three narrow alleys traversed the slum, each wide enough to fit one person of average height, fully stretched out, with some wiggle room at the extremities. She knew exactly because she saw, on numerous occasions, drunken men lying at full stretch, barring the way.

The homes – a room for each family – were ranged along these lanes, packed tightly and joined. The sizes of the rooms varied, as did the number of people living in them; some of the rooms housed as many as twelve members of a family. The walls were brick, most of them painted, some in eye-piercing blue or pink or green, while others were simply whitewashed. The tight, dense cluster of rooms built alongside and behind each other meant that access to a lot of homes was through the patchwork of even narrower side-alleys, down which it was impossible for two adults to walk abreast, and through back yards or even part of the living quarters of some of the dwellings. These spider-web alleys turned into overflowing drains during the monsoon.

It was a watery world in other ways, too – the western side of the slum, bordered by the sea, was built almost flush along the water's edge and separated from it by a raised-stone, compacted-mud and brick walkway, crooked and cracking in places, of a width that allowed people to walk on it only in single file. Water lapped against one side of this path permanently. On the other side, two feet from the water, were the backs of the rooms that formed the western extremity of the slum. During low tide the walkway stood about four or five feet above the surface of the sea, and at high tide about less than half that height. For the three months of monsoon, this path, which was also a boundary wall, remained submerged under water and those homes backing on to it regularly and continuously flooded. When the rains were extremely heavy, the entire slum got inundated, parts of it swallowed by the rising sea, and the inhabitants had to be evacuated by the police and the fire brigade. Milly and Binay's home was towards the eastern side, nearer the road that connected Band Stand to Land's

End, so they were spared these contingencies, although flooding caused by heavy rains turning the interior alleys and lanes into temporary waterways and overflowing drains was something they still had to contend with.

Each of the alleys had a runnel along one side – in one case, on both sides – which was the drain, a channel for general liquid filth and sometimes solids too. In the monsoon the drains brimmed over, turning the alleyways into tributaries of mud and effluent; veins of liquid the colour of milky tea, with small islands of waste, running through a close huddle of dirty, dark organs in the innards of an unknown animal. These tributaries spilled their borders and the liquid oozed into the homes, even into those that stood on stretches raised a couple of feet above the lanes, not level with them. Still, these minor annoyances brought out the innate resourcefulness of some inhabitants, much as the toasting of spices releases their aromatic essence. Someone had the bright thought of putting several sealed bags of cement – stolen from a building site – just outside the front door of his home, the idea being that the cement, like sponge, would absorb all the water and if not keep the front powder-dry, then at least prevent water from entering the room, especially through the unsealable space under the front door. The bags of cement were not enough for the volume of water that the monsoons unleashed. Absorb water they did, but the sacks got super-saturated quickly and were drowned intermittently for three months, sometimes lying submerged, at other times showing their swollen grey backs like some stranded dolphins. Three or four months after the end of the rainy season, they had hardened into concrete boulders, forming a set of disorderly giant beads in an unfinished amateur-crafted necklace discarded permanently outside the front of the home. Sand would have been better, several residents with the gift of hindsight advised; we told them so many times: get sand instead of cement, they said. No one pointed out that sand was not saturation-proof.

Toilets were communal. A set of nine cubicles – four for women, separated by the width of the slum from the five for men, serving the twelve hundred or so residents – stood on the northern edge, beyond which there was a strip of black rocks giving way to the placid sea. The women's toilets were built of brick, had rusting tin doors, which had to be tied with a piece of coir or plastic rope into a metal hoop hammered to the inside wall in order to be locked, and the most common kind of roof in this slum, not brick or concrete but an improvised thing made of beaten cane boards, bamboo, plastic and wire. Black plastic sheets on top were meant to keep the toilet waterproof. There were no windows or ventilation, save for two postcard-sized squares punched on the top of each back wall. Since there was no electricity connection in the cubicles, these holes served as the only portals for letting in light during the day, although the light was so ineffectual in the enclosed darkness that some women joked they couldn't tell if it was a stationary rat or a pile of shit that hadn't been sluiced out, the latter an all-too-common occurrence since the toilets – or the entire slum, for that matter – did not have a water connection and the small plastic mug, canister or bottle of water that most of the users carried into the toilet all went towards cleaning themselves, leaving nothing for flushing, which, in any case, was not a priority.

There was no running water in the jhopri and the residents said, not entirely unseriously, that they valued water above gold: the neighbour two doors down from Milly and Binay maintained that his son's dowry would be a home with a twenty-four-hour legal water connection. Taps, not jewellery, he said. The wish was not far-fetched. Each home had a small army of containers – cans, buckets, drums, jerrycans, canisters, ewers, empty litre- or two-litre plastic bottles – occupying a significant proportion of the indoor space; indoors because thefts of water were not uncommon. There were fixed hours when the municipal corporation turned on the water supply at designated spigots dotted through the city. The slum-dwellers had to queue at these taps with their empty containers, fill them up and carry them back home. If you didn't make it to the tap on time to join the line, you had no water for the next twenty-four hours. The queues at this spigot were long and intensely competitive and bad-tempered: this was the only tap within convenient distance of the slum. The supply was activated for such a limited time that it was vital to be at a point in the line that would ensure filling up; too far back and the connection was turned off before you got to the front and you were left to return empty-handed. As a result, the number of containers each person brought to the tap was ruthlessly monitored, with the vision of vultures, by fellow residents.

Milly had always been the person responsible for fetching water. She had done it when she was a child, back in her home village, and she did it now in Bandra, not only because it was mostly the work of women and children but also because she was free in the evenings, when the spigot was turned on, while Binay's job in the restaurant meant that he was away during those hours. She now had two jobs, both nearby, the second one from around nine in the morning to noon, which left her free for the rest of the day.

Their water came free of charge but the electricity did not, although this was not because they paid electricity bills sent by a power company. The power in the slum was illegal, siphoned off from the supply by tapping into power lines. A slumlord paid the man who did the technical work, and in return the slum residents paid the slumlord. In the case of Milly's jhopri, the man in charge of providing stolen electricity also owned a number of rooms, which he rented out. Milly and Binay paid three thousand rupees a month in rent, and an additional charge for cable television and electricity connections.

Besides a television mounted on a wooden trunk, their ten-feet-by-fourteen-feet room had a bed, the rank of water containers, a single-burner stove connected to a five-kilo LPG cylinder, and a cheap metal almirah that could be locked. Their two plates, one pot, one pan and one tawaa were kept on the floor, beside the gas stove. There was a chaupai on which Milly sat while she cooked. A rope was suspended in one corner, held in place at either end by two iron nails hammered into the walls; this was used to hang clothes. A naked light bulb was suspended from the ceiling. A laminated picture of Christ, halo behind his head radiating rays in all directions, white robe bared at the chest to show the sacred red heart, auburn locks cascading down to his shoulders, was pinned to the wall beside the television; in fact, he looked a little bit like Salman Khan. Milly had bought it from one of the vendors who sat outside St Mary's Church, selling candles in the shapes of hands, legs, arms, all looking like waxworks of amputated limbs, and other things deemed necessary for devotional purposes – prayer books, posters, pictures, matches, incense, ordinary candles, oil, holy water.

Over time, Milly and Binay acquired other domestic necessities: a table fan; a second bed, made of coir rope and wood, that was left upright, leaning against a wall, with one of its narrow sides on the floor, and only put down at night; two steel bowls; two big tins, one for rice, the other for dal. The battle in this matter was a three-way one, between space, money and need, and need almost always lost.

IO: *Work, money, accounts, the reproduction of everyday life*

Milly held on to the two jobs in Bandra until late into her first pregnancy. They liked her at 'Sea Crest' and 'Baseraa' well enough to have her back when her daughter, Mallika, was three months old; better still, she was allowed to bring her child with her. She had to juggle the hours a bit, and was anxious about the baby crying and annoying her employers. In the event, the people at both places were indifferent to the occasional mewling and squalling. What nearly did for Milly were the sleepless nights, especially when the baby was teething. During this period she often went to her first job at the Chandmals in 'Sea Crest', at seven in the morning, having been awake from three or four. There were days when she knew that if she didn't keep moving – sweeping the floor, cleaning the windows, washing the heavy sheets by hand – she would fall asleep at work, and that would be not only embarrassing but perhaps reasonable grounds for being told off or even dismissed. None of these fears came to fruition. Her employers were not unkind and as long as they felt that their lives and routines were not inconvenienced by their bai's new motherhood, they were mostly helpful, the Didi at 'Sea Crest', who was a mother herself, even going so far as offering Milly advice, giving her a cot and rocking-horse and her two boys' baby clothes, which she hadn't had the heart to throw away.

In gratitude, Milly cooked Sindhi dishes as surprises for the family at 'Sea Crest'. The Chandmals were Gujarati and vegetarian; her sai bhaji, learned in Lower Parel, was a big hit. Her trick was to use the obligatory dill in the dish not as a herb, but as another vegetable, similar to the spinach that was also included. And it required hardly any cooking: she soaked chana dal overnight, chopped generous amounts of spinach and dill, a small handful of sorrel and a bunch of fenugreek leaves, diced a couple of onions, a potato, an aubergine, an okra, half an arbi. In a pressure cooker, she heated oil and sautéed the vegetables and onions for five to seven minutes, added all the greens, the drained chana dal, some slit green chillies, salt, half a teaspoon of turmeric, some ginger paste and a heaped teaspoon of coriander powder, a little bit of water, then gave it a good stir, locked the lid and counted seven to eight 'whistles'. She opened the lid when it was safe to do so, added more dill, and coarsely mashed the contents until it was a thick, jungle-green swamp.

When Mallika grew up a bit, Milly began to leave her at home with Binay. Binay earned seven thousand rupees a month in his job as a cook. He used to send fifteen hundred to his home in Lalthekar – ageing parents, three brothers, two sisters, both of them unmarried, money that disappeared the minute it arrived, like a pot of water on a parched, fissured field – but with Milly earning eight thousand rupees from her two jobs, he decided to increase the amount of money he sent to his village. His parents needed all they could get, particularly now that the expensive business of marrying the sisters was upon them and had to be seen through in the next two to three years. So Binay's entire salary was swallowed up in paying the rent and sending money back home, and Milly's money became the fund for household expenses.

But bringing up a child was an expensive business and the only solution that they could come up with was for Milly to take on another job. Binay could look for a different restaurant kitchen to work in but his salary wouldn't be much higher, nor would he have more flexibility with his hours, since any restaurant would need him for the entire duration of the evening shift. Milly did not find it easy to come by a third job: most people wanted a bai to come in the mornings and Milly was not free until just after noon. Mallika was four and Milly just pregnant with her second child when she got the cleaning job at the Sens' in Band Stand.

On her second week at the new place, she saw a vaguely familiar face leaving the Sens' flat just as she was arriving. She searched her head to pin down where she had seen the woman, but it kept eluding her until the new Didi, making conversation with Milly as she went about her duties, told her that the woman she had seen leaving was Renu, their cook. She came for an hour in the morning, then at around eleven in the morning and left around one, then again in the evening to cook dinner. She lived in the same jhopri as Milly – had she never seen her around?

Yes, of course, Milly thought: that was who she was, the woman she had noticed a few times in the queue for water.

The new Didi, Tulika Sen, was a kind, generous person; also gratuitously helpful and not circumscribed by the unspoken laws that governed the mutual taking and giving in a servant – mistress relationship. She tried to engage Milly in conversation and find out about her life back in her village, her life in the city now, about Binay and his job, about Mallika. Milly, wary from her experiences in Jamshedpur and her first job in Mumbai, gave monosyllabic replies as far as she could; she had no idea that this could be seen as discouraging or insolent. It was not Milly's intention to be cold to the new Didi, only self-protective. But Didi persisted; her warmth and interest were genuine and penetrated through the protective shell to the person beneath. Milly was surprised, because she didn't think her life could be of interest to anyone else; it wasn't to her; she only lived it because that's what one did. She started giving more expansive answers to Didi's questions but some things – Budhuwa, Soni – she felt she couldn't bring herself to speak about. She told Didi about Debdulal and Pratima and the Vachanis and, as an aside to those stories, all her desire to finish Class 12, still burning but now buried under the ash of days, was uncovered.

Tulika Sen looked after Milly. When she found out that Milly was pregnant with her second child, Mrs Sen began to give her a huge lunch every day. There was maximum democracy with food here, the greatest Milly had come across so far. In the beginning, Didi had taken portions of leftovers from the fridge and microwaved them for her around two o'clock. Over time, after Milly had learned how to work the microwave, Didi put out the bowls and Tupperware containing the food that she wanted Milly to have, asking her to help herself; and later still, she pointed them out in the fridge and let Milly do the rest. Milly ate what Didi and her husband ate – dal, rice, roti, sabzi, fish, meat. She was given everything, and not only when they were stale or about to go off.

The Sens ate well, although it was Milly's understanding that their cook, Renu, had been trained by Didi to cook the kind of food they wanted. It appeared that when their son, who lived abroad, came to visit once a year, he gave instructions every morning to Renu on the menu for lunch and dinner and, frequently, the recipes for the different dishes. One day, when Didi was away, he served Milly her meal; in slightly uneasy Hindi he explained what everything was – chana dal with coconut and raisins; chicken in white poppyseed gravy (he used the Hindi word, khus khus, and asked her hesitantly if he wasn't getting it wrong; she looked away and murmured, to the wall, that she knew what he meant); fish-fry; cauliflower with potatoes and peas ... Milly knew that the luxurious food was because his parents wanted to shower their mostly-absent son with love. She knew how affections and feelings spoke through food; and often need, too. Sometimes, when she was given something at Didi's home that she knew her daughter Mallika had never tasted, did not even know the name of, she set aside a little bit and took it away in a plastic bag to bring it to the girl back home. Binay frequently brought back food from the restaurant – chow mein, chilli chicken, fried rice, chop suey, chicken manchuri – new food, new tastes for their tongues, new words for their mouths. Milly ate with gusto, after the first few seconds of hesitation in front of the unfamiliar dissipated into nothing; hunger, or greed, was so much more powerful.

A small corner of Milly's mind was always busy calculating how much household expense was saved when Binay brought home food from his workplace.

'You have to pay for the food you bring home?' she had asked him once. 'Do they take it off your wages?'

'No, nothing like that. There are leftovers of the staples, chow mein, fried rice, almost every day. Sometimes we serve it the next day if we think it's not going to spoil, but some days we just share it out among the staff.'

Silently, she savoured this novelty of excess food, of food being given away for free. A knot deep inside her began its long, slow untwisting, but even then she felt it was never going to go away for good. She felt a sort of mingling of fear and shame and anxiety when she bagged the food given to her by Sen Didi for her children, as if she was stealing. A small question, asking Didi's permission, could easily have sorted it out, but she was too shy, too afraid, to say the words, until one day Didi came into the kitchen and caught her in the middle of spooning crab curry into a plastic bag she had taken out of the cupboard under the worktop, where all the reusable wrapping and containers were stored.

'Aren't you eating that? Don't you eat crab?' Didi asked.

Milly, her back to Didi, let the option of lying flash through her head for the briefest of moments, but the words that came out of her mouth, while she still had her back turned, were, 'No, I'm taking it for my daughter.' Then she stopped, wishing the earth would swallow her.

Didi, however, did not react the way Milly had expected her to. She said, 'Why are you using a plastic bag? All the gravy will leak ... Use one of the tiffin boxes and bring it back tomorrow.' And two days later, 'Milly, if you want to take any food home for your children, just take it. You don't need to divide your own portion and eat less.'

Milly bent her head sideways to acknowledge the permission, but did not turn round from her washing-up to face Didi. It wasn't until much later, after Milly had learned to notice and read the generosity and kindness in this family, things she never looked for or even secretly sought, that she realised what she had been given was a kind of freedom. It took her time to relax into it. Recalling her time in Jamshedpur, Milly thought that the bigger the city, the greater the penal strictures about errors and accidents, so when she broke a teapot at Sen Didi's, she confessed to it right away and asked for her wages to be cut.

Didi laughed. 'It's only a teapot, it doesn't matter,' she said. 'It didn't cost me a lot, don't worry about it.'

Tulika Sen increased Milly's salary but in slow instalments, always adding on some extra tasks or an extra quarter- or half-hour so that Milly wouldn't think it was charity. It was she who told Milly of an adult-education night-school in St Mary's Church, the church Milly attended every Sunday morning, and gently nudged her to attend; you can even take Mallika with you, she said. Shortly after her boy, Amit, was born, Milly's salary at the Sens' went up to five thousand rupees. Following Mumbai custom, she was paid a bonus – one month's salary – every Diwali, at each home she worked for. This money, amounting to twelve thousand rupees and increasing to fourteen thousand by the time Amit turned one, Milly deposited entirely in a savings account.

She had found that the current account she had had, the one in which Hemali Vachani had deposited her salary every month, had not been frozen by the bank, on the instructions of the Vachanis, or its money cleared out by them. When the people at 'Sea Crest' had paid her in cash at the end of her first month there, she had told them about her fears for that account and all that money. Milly had not imagined that it would be so easily sorted out. But Mrs Chandmal at 'Sea Crest' had asked her to bring her ration card with her and had taken her to the Bandra branch of the bank. It was here that Milly learned there was nothing called a 'passbook' any longer; everything was on a machine. They printed out a summary statement for her. She worked out later that day that her money was safe; no one but she could touch it. In a week's time she had what she had presumably been shown as a 'passbook' by Hemali Didi – a new cheque book for deposits.

Over and above her bonus and Binay's, she squirrelled away into the savings account what she could from her net monthly salaries – sometimes a thousand rupees a month, sometimes a little bit more, or less. She sent money home to Budhuwa and her mother every month without fail. After all these outgoings, there was not a great deal left for food, clothes, phone plan, Mallika's school uniform, books, stationery.

Mallika went to the local Catholic school, St Catherine of Siena: a small charitable institution, in terms of resources and achievement, but it had big grounds and took in street-children and children from poor and lower-middle-class families. This last factor, that so many children were from lower backgrounds, was both an advantage and a disadvantage, but people in Milly and Binay's position did not have a wide array of choices: it was either an extremely rudimentary state set-up, teaching only Marathi and Hindi, or no school, which was the commonest state of affairs for children in this jhopri. Who had the vision, will or fearlessness to send children to a private school, even a charitable one? Besides, children were required to bring money in, not be a drain on resources – they had to start work as early as they could, to help out their families. Milly's religion put them in a fortunate position because St Catherine's gave preferential treatment to Catholic children. The school's greatest attraction was the fact that the medium of instruction was English.

Milly's own efforts to attend night-classes for adults at St Mary's were sporadic; the working day, followed by looking after the children, devoured all her time. It was one thing to take a five- or six-year-old girl to a class and make her sit quietly for an hour, perhaps even encouraging her to do her homework, but bringing two children, one of whom was a toddler, was impossible.

As her daughter grew, Milly had to start thinking of a secondary school for Mallika, since the highest level in the current school was only up to Class 4, until the age of ten, although, in reality, the class level was no indication of the ages of the students in it – Mallika was a rare instance of a student in St Catherine's whose age and class-grade coincided. There was no way of sending her to a bigger, better school without having to pay more, much more, and that, in turn, was not a possibility without Milly taking on a fourth job. The school she had in mind was Carmel on Hill Road, a girls' school where the monthly fee would be two thousand rupees. Milly had already found out that the fee was only a rough indication of how much they would have to spend: there would be more expenditure for uniform, books and the huge initial admission cost of nearly ten thousand rupees.

When she broached the subject to Binay, he was sceptical. 'What will she do, studying, going to school? We can't afford it.'

'I can take on work at one more home.'

'But she's a girl, what's the point of educating her to such a high level? There's the boy to think of now.'

'They'll both go to school.'

'But it's beyond our means to send two children to high school,' he repeated. 'She knows how to read and write. By the time she finishes in this one, that'll be enough education.'

'No', Milly was adamant. 'She's going to go to school.'

'But look at you, you didn't go to school, you earn fourteen to fifteen thousand every month ... If you are going to take on another home, save that money for Amit's school.'

Milly had, without knowing it consciously, become resigned to the fact that she herself was never going to go up to Class 12, even through the more informal channel of night-school, and sit board exams. With the necessity of a fourth job looming, she now acknowledged it.

All the enveloping noise of the slum that they always heard but were never disturbed or bothered by – it was the very medium of their lives, like air, and who singles out air for attention? – suddenly took on a singular clarity for Milly, each outlined in its sharp auditory shape. More than one television was blaring out the theme song from the opening credits of *Balika Vadhu*, the little girl's voice clear as a bell, '*Chhoti si umar, par nai re babosa ...*' The woman next door was shrieking at her husband, drunk again, 'Churail! She's a churail! I'll blind her with my own hands, we'll see if I'm the daughter of one father or not.' Then: the sound of a crash and breaking glass, followed by sobbing. A group of boys walked past their door, trailing behind them the song playing on one of their mobiles: '*Why this kolavery kolavery di?*' The song faded slowly as the boys moved further and further away. Mallika's head was bowed over her homework. Milly couldn't see her face, only the head of thick dark hair, which was shining, almost blue in its blackness, in the light from the bulb overhead. How could she see her books if her head was obstructing the light? There seemed to be an invisible wall around the girl, something to hold the world at bay.

Milly said, 'She is going to school to the very end, until she's eighteen and has taken her board exams.'

II: *An epilogue*

It's Budhuwa who calls her. This is surprising because she is the one who always phones him. Her first thought is that there is bad news. The timing is not encouraging: it's seven in the evening on a Wednesday, and she is on her way back home after picking up Mallika from school, because on Wednesdays her daughter does three hours of computer lessons offered by the school to interested students from Class 7 and higher. Milly has to pay an extra five hundred rupees a month for this. Before she can disengage her right hand from her daughter's left and hit the green button, he has rung off; maybe he meant to give her a missed call as a way of signalling to her to call back. The thought of bad news deepens. She phones him immediately.

'What?' she asks.

He plunges in straight away. 'Soni's died.'

It takes her a second or two to work out who he is talking about; the life here is a great distance from the one she has left behind.

'What? How?' she whispers when the meaning hits her.

'No one knows. The paramilitary have started to come again, lots and lots of them. It could have been them, or it could have been her

own people. There are lots of stories buzzing around. Some say she
had become a police informer and her people found out and killed
her. Some are saying she was caught trying to escape her squad –
otherwise why would her body be found just outside the village?'

'Where did they find ... it?' She has to say something; this is
the only thing she can manage. Without looking in her daughter's
direction, she searches for Mallika's hand with her free one and
laces her fingers through hers.

'The big mango tree after the turn-off from the road.'

She cannot bring herself to ask the next question, not in Mallika's
hearing, but Budhuwa seems to have guessed it.

'Bullets, not machete,' he says. Then he adds, 'I didn't see the
body.'

She flinches. She doesn't want Mallika to get wind of what
they're talking about but she doesn't want to let go of her, either.

Budhuwa keeps talking: 'The soldiers' clothes that she had on
her, everyone's saying that it's CRPF uniform. Apparently the guerrillas bought it as a job-lot in some market somewhere.'

She wants to ask so many things but cannot in her daughter's
presence. She says she'll call him later.

All the things that Soni had said to her on that walk in the
forest tumble through her head. So many questions ... Before
she has fully finished thinking one, her mind jumps to another.
Something Soni had said suddenly appears, like a light she didn't
know existed around a corner: 'Your life is in bits and pieces – a
little bit here, a little bit there. One year in Dumri, another year
somewhere else, then another year yet somewhere else again ...'
Milly disagrees silently, vociferously. Her life is not fragmented.
To her, it has unity and coherence. *She* gives it those qualities.
How can movement from one place to another break you? Are
you a terracotta doll, easily broken in transit? But she can no
longer give Soni the answer, which has occurred to her so many
years later.

V

Someone whose name he has now forgotten one of their lot maybe or a foreman from another site tells them a story one night while they are drinking their adhaa or pauwa of Toofan whichever size each can afford someone tells them you see that Taj Mahal the great Mughal emperor Shah Jahan built it for his dead wife hundreds of workers in construction like us lot thousands of us it took years and years to build and when it was done the emperor saw it was so beautiful that he did not want anyone who might want to rival this gem to copy it not even a single part so he cut off the thumb of the right hand of each of those mazdoors just imagine you're building this big hotel and at the end of it you go back home without your right thumb buss khel khatam you'll never work again and you will have to beg and your life will end with dogs eating your flesh

but before the dogs something else is eating his flesh the flesh on the inside of his chest because when the coughing comes it feels like the insides are turning into the kind of cloudy wool-like dust which emerged when he was once asked to remove yards and yards of a corrugated grey roof by breaking it up into manage-able chunks manageable for the women working on the site to carry them away on their heads except the transference of that dust inside him is the human flesh version so he imagines a kind of red foamy wool where his chest is and it was all fine it began slowly just a little cold a cough and when it grew from little he went to a dawakhana and got a red mixture in a bottle marked with white squares standing on their corners in a long strip show-ing how much he should take every day but that didn't cure it so he paid more money in a bigger dawakhana the one with angrezi medicines and got a small bottle of thick green stuff which did nothing either except perhaps send him to sleep until another mazdoor pointed out that the combination of the green medicine and Shokeen or Toofan gave a nice depth to the buzz from the alcohol all he got from it was the feeling of being a stone and a sleep like drowning impossible to rise to the surface in the morning to go wait in the line of mazdoors to be picked for a day's work and sometimes he didn't bother to get up or couldn't bring himself to become human again from stone on time and just let the day's work go laziness and ache like a vast snake that has got him in its coils and will not let go until it has squeezed out the last drop of breath from him and then he will be husk and where would he be then floating away in the breeze

but the green medicine didn't work and someone told him that it only soothed the throat and his coughs were coming from deeper down from his centre and now there is the fever a chhip-chhup bukhar as they used to say never so high as to fell you never so low as to make you feel that nothing's the matter with you it doesn't burn you up but rumbles on a bubbling drain under the surface of your skin and some lafanga mazdoor sleeping alongside him on the pavement near the big chowk so that they can be in the queue the moment they wake up instead of having to walk with a pounding head its shattering weight feeling odd sitting atop the slightly shaking weightlessness of the rest of him this lafanga says with that face of yours when you cough you're like a barking fox this isn't new at least two mistrys have laughed at him asking him if he's come out of a human and one of them refused to take him on because foxes brought bad luck to a building site he said this is a cremation ground or what that foxes should roam around in human form he said

he thought he could escape the shame of his looks by leaving his home far behind but no his face is everywhere he is but no that was not why he left not seriously although when he was a child he had often thought of leaving just because of that and when he grew up more pressing reasons pushed down that child's anger or maybe the rage became something else like a seed becomes a tree bearing fruits that contain the seed from which will grow the same tree but the original parent tree he thinks the one that produced the first seed of rage is always one thing money and lack of work to make any money and how long could he and his brother till a scrap of land the size of a raees admi's garden land that could barely provide one square meal a day throughout the year to two men their wives and children let alone produce any surplus that could be sold to get money for all the things apart from just food one needs money for and sometimes often for food too because that patch produced nothing for three months of winter and money to produce money as their father said when they were little money makes money like cats and dogs have kittens and puppies which grow up and go on to have more kittens and more puppies but you need to start some-where and his father wanted to start with a government job until the fire swallowed him the whole forest in flames and the strange sound of birds in the dead of the night over the hum and crackle of fire and he watching his twin's face aglow as if the fire was light-ing him up from the inside but he wasn't going to go down the road his father had attempted to take he wanted to leave his village because there was nothing there nothing everything was in the cit-ies in construction in building which someone said always needed people endless supply of people like feeding a fire as his father and his forest had fed a fire and he could make so much money that he would be able to send money home and save and then one day he would have enough punji to start a business and punji is what one needed if one wanted money to bear money-children and money-grandchildren like cats and dogs

and look what happened how many years in big cities two three four he has lost count how many years digging breaking rocks stone bricks digging carrying rubble and sand and stones and

cement and sacks on his head on his back digging and lashing two
or three ladders together with rope and tying the tall bamboos for
the scaffolding verticals and horizontals in a giant criss-cross and
the long training to get it right putting together the bamboo the
planks the cloths and securing them to the outside of the building in a way that no one could fall or nothing could dislodge and
land on another mazdoor working below how the bamboo had
a gentle rocking give swaying him ever so slightly when he was
on that skeleton of wood a lulling comforting movement almost
one that could soothe him and make him forget almost forget the
world below it made his head spin to look down better to lean
forward and keep himself connected to the wall inches in front of
him with his fingers and paint or scrape or hammer that almost
imperceptible rocking flipping between comfort and terror the
gingerly sideways movement that hint of elasticity in the bamboo
like sitting on the pliable branch of a tree is this what birds feel like
that temporary bit of solidity between air below and air above or
do they feel like husk too and maybe when he was lucky he could
put brick upon brick upon brick with the slather of wet concrete
between each be indoors to whitewash a wall surface a floor make
it smooth

all of this better no comparison really than days sitting on the
road in a bazaar or a chowk waiting waiting to be picked sometimes you are and sometimes you aren't sometimes there is need
for only so many and he is not among those needed in the end it's
not despair that kills you but hope at other times when he is chosen
the work can be for a day or three days or weeks then there are days
when there is nothing only waiting only time and hunger in the
end it's not despair that kills you but hope in the beginning he was
lured in with the promise of hundred and twenty-five rupees a day
but got only seventy-five and when he asked timidly he was told he
could leave if he didn't like what he was getting there was always
someone else to do it so he settled for seventy-five for ten hours of

hauling twenty-kilo sacks of cement on his back and carrying wet concrete on his head up three four seven floors and breaking stone every day the same repeating the same actions yet every day singular the destination the fellow workers even the work changing ever so slightly while remaining the same and digging in the sun for eight ten hours when stepping out in that heat could evaporate your blood and make you a different kind of husk seventy-five rupees was something

yes something to put away in the triple-inside-pocket that he had had sewn on the inside of his one shirt on the advice of some other mazdoors who were also getting it done because money was safe nowhere someone had his shoes stolen off his feet as he was sleeping the sleep of the dead because that's the sleep you sleep after mazdoori work then the friendly embrace of Toofan and in his case the additional caress of the sickly sweet green medicine you could have your head taken off you and you wouldn't notice but what kind of cast-iron protection was it you could have your shirt torn off you or cut skilfully with a knife and you wouldn't know you would be sleeping the sleep of the dead and he keeps it in the plastic pouch that houses his ration card folded into quarters to keep it from damage from moisture rain and his own sweat the money in that bluish plastic pouch too and in the beginning when he felt the ties of home and the faces of his wife and children and brother floated up in his mind when he was still hopeful about saving for punji and sending money back home simultaneously looks laughable to him now but then he was hopeful and it's hope that kills you in the end he sent back god knows how much how long ago it was three or four times maybe thousand rupees in total nothing really a baby's piss he had to live after all how to live on seventy-five to hundred rupees a day when that income was random and uncertain the thought of saving makes him laugh like he is barking someone will call him a fox again the only thing to save is himself and how is he going to do that

when his earliest dream for himself all he wanted to be was the pampered son of a rich man who rode in cars and looked out at the world from behind a pane of glass which could be lifted up or down depending on how much of the world you wanted it could be turned on or off like a tap he would like that world to be able to turn it on or off whenever he wanted he saw a boy like that in his village they must have been the same age and the boy in the car had looked at him and his twin and a few of their school friends standing by the side of the narrow road doing nothing staring at the car watching it halted and trying to start up again to negotiate a hairpin bend up to the big new house in which the boy and his father came up for the summer months the boy had looked at them and their eyes had locked and he had said something to his father then the window had come down and the boy had stuck out his hand and given them all tangerines from a bag inside the car no words had been exchanged he and his twin and the boys had moved closer to the car and taken the tangerines then the window had gone up again as they sat on a stone peeling the fruit they both discovered that there were little cloves chhora hiding near the bottom in between the bigger ones and someone told him and his twin that they were for motherless boys they had been secretly put into the fruit by their dead mother's soul for her children for them how did he know how did that boy know that they didn't have a mother and now a father swallowed by fire the boy was not from here

he doesn't know whether he dates his obsession with that boy from that day he never saw him again but he wanted to be him to be inside a car with his father on their way to a big new house distributing tangerines to children on the roadside and the boy's face floated up too unbidden at strange times so many years later and even now even now he can picture that face the big eyes looking at him the shape of the tangerines in his hand and their dull yellow-green glow oh to be born in the next life as a boy in a car sitting beside his father

where was all that time if he got it all back and he was that age again would he be here at this point again a mazdoor on the streets or would he could he walk along a different path and end up being that boy then he smiles and thinks he cannot be the boy at the end of that path because the boy has grown up like he has but could he be what the boy is now and what was he not a mazdoor on the streets certainly but he didn't have to try his father had a car in which he rode with the rest of life outside and that was all that mattered you had to be born into the life inside

for without that you are nothing as he is nothing to the great world outside spread out below him the trees so many trees from up here they look like a colony of green animals hulking in the form of huge smudges and sometimes it looks like an inter-rupted green river foaming up here and there among the scatter of buildings like a toy town and the cars like toys moving in a line but more often a narrow snake of dozens of them stuck outside in a jam some waiting to let the ones ahead go into the hotel so that they can move forward to their destinations he has always noticed this sometimes still sometimes sluggishly inching snake of cars outside the big hotel and wondered if one of those cars is carrying a boy and his father to the hotel like a gigantic palace storey above storey above storey what does it look like inside what are the rooms like built by someone like him who'll never get to see what it's really like someone once said to him one hundred times the number of people in his village could fit easily into a single floor of such a building he never gets to see what it's like once it's finished with people living in there people not like him yet it is he or mazdoors like him who built it not they if he turns his head a little he knows it is going to look like a box of stone and glass some giant bird dropped on its flight and he thinks if anyone standing at one of the hundreds of windows can see him what does he look like to them can they even see him an ant on the side of a huge hill

while he can look at the air-lashed world only from the corner of his eye otherwise he feels that strange funnelling feeling that begins in his rectum and moves up how is he ever going to move along the ledge hardly wide enough for a bird to perch on to fix the bamboo and cloth rigging around the corner because it cannot be reached by any other way and then paint the outside of the window frames how is he ever going to do that moving on the pliable bamboo ribs inch by inch on his bare feet the world spread out far below and so much air between him and the world how is he ever going to do that he has heard that in buildings this high it is required by law that the mazdoors work on planks built as wide platforms outside the facade on each level and there are machines to take you up and down and you wear a helmet but where is all this he has never seen any where are the laws and who thinks of laws when the mazdoors are nothing their lives less than nothing

he is not going to look down he is not

he stands there shivering the sun is on the other side he cannot tell if it's the fever again he has to finish it no one else is going to do it and they've promised him two hundred rupees today his fingers against the wall and behind and below him air those cloths flapping what were they doing he inches sideways the bamboo sways the next his fingers can get a grip is a foot away maybe two he cannot tell his head is so close to the wall he has to reach that point is he shivering with fear he cannot think that two hundred rupees if he can do five days of this being a bird then that's a thousand he can send half of it home then that effervescing inside him again no he cannot he cannot not before he reaches that point one or two feet away but there's no stopping maybe if he lets one cough out it'll appease the rising creature inside the one who eats the inside of his chest which has become like keema he can feel it one cough he has to there's no choice he lets out one cough and his chest explodes

in one breath all of his life in one breath because everything is air everything pouring up around the rushing arrow that he cuts through the unimpeded air its short embrace he is husk of course he is at last

Acknowledgements

This book could not have been written without a five-week residency at the MacDowell Colony. To that 'haven-heaven' (Maureen McLane's words), I am profoundly grateful.

Alexander Cappelen and Bertil Tungodden arranged for a three-week stint in beautiful Bergen, where I did the final stretch of writing. I would like to thank them for their generosity and kindness.

Jean Drèze, *sine qua non*.

Devashri Mukherjee.

Poppy Hampson, Penny Hoare.

Clara Farmer, Peter Straus.

Ellen Barry, Rohini Pande.

Kartick Satyanarayan & Geeta Seshamani at Wildlife SOS India, Lis Key at International Animal Rescue.

Jill Bialosky, Meru Gokhale, Mandy Greenfield, Dominic Leggett, Vestal McIntyre, Fran Owen, Mrinal Pande, Aakar Patel, Tushita Patel, Sharmila Sen, Tarini Uppal, Edmund White, Anumeha Yadav, Mari Yamazaki.

For giving me a home-away-from-home, again: Arpita Bhattacharjee & Archishman Chakraborty, Devashri & Udayan Mukherjee, Mrinal & Arvind Pande, Matthew Rabin.

Suzanne Dean.

M. John Harrison and Sjón, for showing how it is done.

Matt Phillips, for his beautiful paintings.

Renu Jena, Mili Kerketta.

Without Matthew Rabin, this book could not have been finished. I am grateful to him for many things, but mostly for cleverly getting me to do all his modelling for the last ten years.